A SUNSET TOUCH

"A blessed companion is a book"—JERROLD

A
SUNSET TOUCH

★

HOWARD SPRING

THE COMPANION BOOK CLUB
LONDON

FOR
DOREEN MARSTON

Made and Printed in Great Britain for the Companion Book Club (Odhams Press Ltd.) by Morrison & Gibb, Ltd., London and Edinburgh 155.VTD

CONTENTS

★

Just when we are safest, there's a sunset-touch,
A fancy from a flower-bell, someone's death,
A chorus-ending from Euripides,—
And that's enough for fifty hopes and fears
As old and new at once as Nature's self
To rap and knock and enter in our soul,
Take hands and dance there.

Bishop Blougram's Confession
ROBERT BROWNING

PART ONE

About Mr. Menheniot

CHAPTER ONE

I

WHEN Mr. Menheniot came in to breakfast, Mrs. Sara was still dusting his room. This annoyed him, but he was a mild fellow, and he rarely allowed annoyance to appear. For one thing, he might have had to put up with someone worse than Mrs. Sara. She did understand the value of his things, and respected them. They were the sort of things she had been accustomed to in her young days. Then, she was a housemaid in a Cornish mansion. It was burned to the ground now, but it had never been burned out of Mrs. Sara's heart. She wouldn't see sixty again, and she had gone to the great house when she was ten. That was in 1890, and in 1890 things had not changed much in houses like that. There was a butler and a housekeeper; there were footmen and ladies' maids; there was a retinue of gardeners and woodmen; there were horses; and on Sundays the Family went to church in a big coach. Some people rode to church, and there was a long rail outside the churchyard wall to which horses were tied up till the service was over. In the winter there were dances for the staff, and the staffs from other great houses would come to join in the fun. If the weather was bitter, deer from the park would be killed and venison given to the poor. But down there in Cornwall the weather was not often bitter.

Mrs. Sara, who had been Peggy Probus, remembered all this, and she remembered the lovely furniture which was like the furniture Mr. Menheniot had, and so she never bashed about in Mr. Menheniot's room as she was inclined to do in other peoples'. Nothing but junk in some of them, and in others all these flash bits of chromium and plastics; and the people were like the things they owned: slovenly people, or come-day-go-day people who had no solidity or substance. She had no feeling for them or for their things, as she had for Mr. Menheniot and his few Georgian pieces; and they were the sort of people she could never have been bothered to talk to. There was no class about them, but anyone could see that there was class about Mr. Menheniot, even though he was only a bank clerk. When she or Sara talked to him, he knew what they were talking about; and so she liked to tell him of how the Boer War came when she was twenty, and Mr. Andrew, who was the heir to the estate, was killed, and his father was never the same again. He was a widower by then, and there were no other children; "and they do say," Mrs. Sara would tell Mr. Menheniot, "that he set fire to the place deliberate." Anyhow, he was seen in a corridor with a lighted lamp, and he and the great house perished together.

"And that's how I married Sara," Mrs. Sara would say. "I suppose I'd have had him anyway, but I had to have him then."

He was an under-gardener, and he came as a head gardener into Surrey. And there he had been till he was sacked five years ago. He was getting old; "and anyway," Mrs. Sara asked, "who can afford to keep gardens up in these days?" They were, indeed, not the days they had been; for it was on a winter morning in January of 1944 that Mr. Menheniot found Mrs. Sara still dusting his room.

II

What a room it was! Mr. Menheniot thought. Even like this, with the curtains pulled back from the window, so that the bleak London morning looked in—even like this it was comforting. In the squalor and misery of wartime London it was an oasis. The white marble fireplace with a little delicate carving upon it, the brocade curtains, the eighteenth-century furniture, the few engravings and mezzotints upon the walls, the books, all leatherbound in the Sheraton book-case, the mirror with just a hint of Chippendale's Chinese flirtings, the pole-screen holding up its panel of charming embroidery, the lustres of the chandelier, which, even on so niggard and grudging a day, achieved a faint gleam and twinkle: what, Mr. Menheniot often wondered, had the world to offer better than such things as these?

Standing in front of that superb fireplace was a cheap electric fire, with one of its three bars faintly glowing. Oh, it was a miserable, misbegotten thing, and he would have liked to throw it through the window. What was it doing in a room like this? But there you are. It is wartime. You must put up with what you can get. You must be thankful that even this faint offering of cheer survives in days like these. He remembered other days. He had been here for five years now, gradually assembling these things about him, and he thought of night, which was his favourite time, with the curtains drawn, the coal fire leaping, the gleam on the furniture, and himself at work on that book of his, which perhaps no one but he would read. He began by calling it *A Cornish Family*, but changed that to *The Menheniots*. He loved the sound of his own name. He loved the look of it as the letters formed under his pen. He liked to turn it over on his tongue in company with other famous names from the county he had never lived in: the Carews, the Elyots, the Killigrews, the Menheniots. He was becoming a crank and a recluse, living with imaginations. He knew it, and he gloried in it. After all, how many men belonged to a family like his?

No; it was not likely that he would ever shake it off now. He had spent too many hours in the Public Record Office and the British Museum, boring like a wood-beetle into the decayed and mouldy fabric of the family that had not for a long time lived on ancestral acres and that now, as far as he knew, had no living member but himself. But never had the Menheniots produced a more fanatical Menheniot, a bank clerk by day, Menheniot of Rosemullion by night

III

He rubbed his skinny hands in the meagre warmth, then went to the window and looked out. Like the Menheniots, this handsome Georgian house had fallen on bad times. It survived amid decrepitude. The Saras, who had bought a lease of it with all their savings to run it as a boarding-house, had never been able to keep it up. Even before the war, the stucco had been unpainted and now was falling away, leaving ugly scabs. The bombs had spared it, but not unscathed. Some windows were gone. Chunks of exploding metal had pitted the front door, hacked pieces out of the four stone steps that led up to it between curved iron rails, broken the glass of the delicate fanlight. Brown paper had been pasted like a plaster over these wounds. But the position of the house was noble. It was on the South bank of the Thames, and looking across the river to the dome of St. Paul's floating above the city, Mr. Menheniot could forget that the other houses in the terrace of which this was part were now storehouses and offices and small shops clothed in that added dinginess that squats upon decayed splendour.

But, to-day, he could not see the dome. It was a miserable morning, and a wind carried slanting across the river a dispirited fall that could have been either rain or sleet. London, which he had always hated, and from which he had shut himself away in his charming shell, looked to-day fouler than Manchester, which he hated even more.

They were all one, Manchester and Salford, Manchester with a Lord Mayor and Salford with a Mayor, but where one town ended and the other began who knew? Certainly not he. There wasn't a no-man's-land, an interregnum; there were just streets and streets and streets, reaching from the Cheshire plain in the south to the Lancashire hills in the north, and it was all one solid block of Manchester-Salford. And up there in the north was Pendlebury, which was theoretically a part of Salford but was in fact a part of the undivided enormity that lay upon Menheniot's childhood and youth.

He would always remember the day when he was fifteen, a day like this upon which he now brooded through the Georgian window. But it was afternoon, not morning, and the air was full of the softest imaginable drift of snow. It was too light to be called snow, really. It was the fog of winter's hoar breathing. Above it was a sky pitch-black, and, coming out from the Manchester Grammar School, a satchel of books swinging in his hand, he was in a busy world of traffic, where the street lights were on and every window, from the pavements up to where the roofs merged with blackness, was a blaze or a glow. Oh, it had enchantment then, the great city, the buzzing hive, vibrant and shining in the dark; but he had always distrusted it, felt a stranger in it; and his one thought was of the small house in Pendlebury where he could shut himself up with his father. His mother he did not remember. There they were, those two, and at night they would shut up together, like the two halves of a bivalve, excluding everything.

He remembered how, that day, he came to the art-dealer's shop in St. Ann's Square, and lingered there a moment, as he always did; and that was the moment when his mania was born. There was a print in the window, and for a time he did not read what was written beneath it, so sharply was he shocked with a sense of looking at a portrait of his father. This man was wearing an odd-looking hat, with a feather drooping from the right side, and the clothes, lightly sketched, were odd, too. But forget all that, and look at this melancholy face, the large brooding eyes, the sad lips, the trim beard and firm nose. . . . It was his father to a T. Then he read what was printed beneath: Holbein—Portrait of a Cornish Gentleman.

In Pendlebury there was not the excitement of the town's buzz and murmur. The air was grey and muffled; only a street lamp here and there burned like a pale unmoving flower; and because this place was higher the snow had body. It fell across the lights and it lay, but not thickly, on the stone setts of the road. Young Menheniot's footsteps made no sound as he climbed the stony brow. The house conformed to the lie of the land. To reach the front door you went up a cobbled ramp that had a handrail, but there was a room down here, too, on the ground level: a half-basement with its window behind a grille at your feet. A light in the window told the boy that his father was still at work, and so, instead of climbing the ramp, he moved to the window and looked down at the cobbler working there. An unshaded gas-jet burned over old Menheniot's head. He was wearing an apron of supple leather, and a boot, sole-up, was clasped between his knees. His lips, which time and use had made as handy as fingers, were fringed with tacks that he took out one by one and hammered into the sole. The awl, the thread, the cobbler's wax, lay handy.

It was to the boy an accustomed sight. He was glad that his father was a shoemaker, that he did not work in a mill. This was a craft, and young Roger Menheniot

14

already had a feeling for crafts, an aversion from mass-things. The boots on his feet, the satchel slung across his back, a trunk they took when they went for a holiday, a screen that kept the winter draught out of the sitting-room: his father had made all these, and Roger would finger them and feel the strength and virtue in them and be glad. But that night he was not looking at the crafts-man. Burning before his eye as if it were still physically there, the Holbein drawing was alongside his father's face. There was no doubt about it. Roger was certain that Holbein's Cornish Gentleman was a Tudor Men-heniot. He turned and ran up the ramp and banged on the front door. They spent their accustomed evening of lamplight and firelight, not saying much but satisfied, happy, with one another's company. Roger spread his books upon the table and gave reluctant attention to Latin. The old man, who had bought a set of Addison's *Spectator* dirt-cheap, went on with his task of ripping off the dilapidated covers and re-binding the books in green leather, tooled with gold.

IV

There they were, still in the Sheraton book-case, those volumes that old Menheniot had re-bound so long ago. There in the room, too, was the leather screen, beautifully embossed, to which time and use had given a glow of light amber. When Mr. Menheniot went on holiday he used the old leather trunk that porters cursed for its weight, accustomed as they now were to the fibre and canvas that Roger despised. The old school satchel, with its shoulder-strap removed and a handle affixed instead, was all the despatch-case he ever wanted to have. He would still be wearing the old boots if his feet had not outgrown them. There was so much in his room that he had bought.

All his savings had gone into these things. At Maggs's book-shop, at Christie's and Sotheby's, he was to be seen, rarely buying, for he could not afford to, but buying now and then with taste, and always buying Georgian stuff. Not that the Menheniots didn't go back beyond Georgian times—oh, they went far, far beyond that; but that was when they burst apart, when Rosemullion ceased to know them, and at that point, it seemed to Mr. Menheniot, he should pick them up again. However, it was not wholly satisfactory, this buying. Even a lovely thing like this Tompion clock on the mantelpiece didn't give him quite the satisfaction he got from the old screen and the other things his father had made. Menheniot to Menheniot, generation to generation. That was the right way. And if he was to be the last of them, as he seemed likely to be—well, let the end at any rate be seemly.

He turned back from the window, from the grey morning weeping over the grey city stricken with the grief of war, as Mrs. Sara came in with his breakfast. And that was something she would do for no one else. The others had to come to their food in the bleak dining-room; but Mr. Menheniot's food came to him. He had demanded it in the first place, made it a condition of his coming there at all. His recluse nature could not bear the thought of "Pass me the cruet, please," or "Will you oblige with the jam, Mr. Menheniot?" It was bad enough to meet people at his work in the bank, where his dully efficient endeavours had made advancement impossible; but, once that was done with for the day, his life must be his own. So it was arranged at the beginning, and now Mrs. Sara herself would not have had it otherwise. She would have been shocked to see Mr. Menheniot sitting down with some of the trash she had to put up with nowadays—fly-by-nights, who lasted for a fortnight or a month, while he and his lovely things were there year after year.

16

Mr. Menheniot knew what they called him at the bank: the last of the Georgians. It didn't either amuse him or offend him: he just looked calmly at it and decided that it was fair enough, and thereafter wore it as unselfconsciously as he wore his clothes, which were a little stiff and old-fashioned. But if he had thought at all about the things Mrs. Sara was now carrying into the room, it would have been with the pleasurable conviction that there was nothing old-fashioned about *them*. No, such loveliness could never be out of fashion. The great tray with its upturned trellised edge; the coffee-pot, milk jug and sugar bowl: all were of silver; and though the crest on the silver was not the Menheniot crest, it was the next best thing: it was the crest of an ancient Cornish family. These things, and the silver dish with the cover that now magnificently entombed Mr. Menheniot's meagre war-time rasher, were the last of his extravagances. The last, he assured himself, not the latest. He must now stop. His floor carried the appropriate furniture, his walls the appropriate prints, and his table the appropriate silver. Though he was single and hadn't a relative in the world, he was poor and there was his future to think of. And what is more, his taste told him that the room was now what it should be. He mustn't clutter it. In this one room, which was all he could afford, he had slowly turned a dream into reality. Now he wanted nothing but to sit down and wait for the beastly intruding war to end. Then the last of the Georgians could live as such a room deserved to be lived in.

Mrs. Sara lifted the silver cover as if she were lifting the dome of St. Paul's to reveal a fried mouse.

"Thank you, Mrs. Sara," Menheniot said gravely, and sat himself at the table.

She was leaving the room when he added: "Will you

please hand me that little silver box from the mantel-piece?"

Mrs. Sara took it up and looked at it curiously. She knew all Mr. Menheniot's things as well as he did himself. "This is something new, isn't it?" she asked.

"Yes," he said, "it's a Georgian snuff-box."

CHAPTER TWO

I

MR. MENHENIOT had not fought in the First World War. He was fit; he was of age; and he himself could hardly have told you how he kept out of it. But he had done so by some odd combination of circumstances, and his mind was never troubled by this fortunate exemption. He would not have said, as someone is reputed to have done, that he was the civilization the war was fought for. He was not given to epigram or to any sort of sparkle. But there was somewhere in the back of his mind a respect for what he would have called, if he had been given to definition, solid worth; and he did not think that this had anything to do with standing up to the knees in mud or slithering on your belly through barbed wire under a shine of star-shells. He had been combed out in the last months of the war, and had even got as far as a drill-square in Aldershot; but then the peace came and he went back to his lodgings, which at that time were in Camberwell. He was glad. He could now forget this furious frantic age and begin to pull layer upon layer out of the past and build it round himself like a shell round a nautilus. Between the wars, the stink of Europe never reached his nostrils. He did not read the daily papers and could not understand why anyone bothered to do so. For current news he consulted *The Connoisseur* and *Apollo,* and for steady reading there were Swift and Steele and Addison, Pope and Dryden.

He was forty-five on the Sunday morning when he sat with the silver snuff-box on the table before him as he ate his breakfast. He picked it up and turned it over curiously. There was nothing about it to warn him. Even the fact that the Menheniot crest was upon it, even the extraordinary circumstances in which it came to him, could not shake the utter complacency into which his life was fallen. It was odd, he thought, deuced odd, that the first piece of silver with the Menheniot crest ever to be in his hands should have come in that mad way. Somewhere in the world there must be a lot of Menheniot silver, unless it had all been melted down; he had always kept his eyes open in the sale-rooms, hoping against hope that a bit of the precious stuff might come his way. And then to get it like that! That wild voice shouting in the darkness, "Menheniot! Menheniot!" and the thing shoved into his hand!

Even so, turning it this way and that, he was not deeply moved. It was odd. That was as far as he got.

II

He had been fire-watching the night before. This second war had caught him up, at any rate, to that extent. There he was, for a few nights every week, with the other members of his team, and not even the hot events amid which their proximity existed could fuse him into association with them. They were a lucky team. They put out a few fire-bombs before much damage was done; but nothing serious ever came their way. Still, plenty that was serious was going on around them. Some nights they stood in their oasis amid an inferno. From their roof they watched great buildings founder in flames. Steam rose to them from the ground; flakes of fire fell from the air; craning over their parapet, they saw the snakes of the hoses run out and listened to the hiss as water struggled with fire. And they had their good times. They became a club. There was chess and draughts and bridge and the thermos flask and the sandwiches of odious *ersatz* meat. They could be merry, while waiting for what might

20

be the end of them all. But Mr. Menheniot could not share their merriment. He could not join in their games. He was not of the club. He would sit apart, with some leather-bound eighteenth-century book, wondering what they found in the torn litter of Cheyneys and Runyons on the table. When there was action, he was there, he was one of them; but when it was over he withdrew. They gave him up. They left him alone.

Last night his spell of duty ended at eleven o'clock. It had been a quiet stretch, and he had sat on his mattress in a corner of the room, his back in the angle of the wall, studying the notebook stuffed with Menheniot facts. His writing of the family history was making headway. Thank God, he thought, he had laid in a stock of beautiful paper before the war began. It was almost like vellum; his formal handwriting ran on the page with hardly a correction in a thousand words. But now he was held up. There was a knot to be untied before he could go on. He called himself in his musing mind Menheniot of Rosemullion, but he knew he was nothing of the sort. In the eighteenth century there were three Menheniot brothers. Lieutenant George Menheniot died on Minden field, leaving a childless widow who did not marry again. That was the end of that branch. Roger, the youngest of the three, fancied himself as a playwright. He made his way to London, had small success, and joined William Siddons's company as an actor. He married a young woman of the company whose beauty was great and talent small. As his fortunes declined she tired of him, and preceded Mrs. Jordan as a mistress of the Duke of Clarence, George III's son. The liaison did not last long, but long enough for her to produce a son. Menheniot took her back, and the child with her. He opened an inn on the Bath road, and there the half-royal brat died and another son was born. This son survived his parents, married the chambermaid of the inn, and became a mason in the Bath stone-quarries. Mr. Menheniot's researches had permitted him to trace from these two the direct descent of the Pendlebury shoemaker who was his father. He had a naïve pride in the knowledge that his stonemason ancestor had possessed a royal half-brother.

Menheniot of Rosemullion, the eldest of the three brothers, remained a bachelor, as far as our Mr. Menheniot knew. He had established his coming to London and the furious quarrels that broke out there from time to time between him and the poverty-stricken actor who was his brother. There was a well-authenticated story of this Menheniot riding his horse through St. James's Street, splashing his brother with the mud of the gutter, and leaning from the saddle to taunt him publicly with being cuckolded by the Duke of Clarence. Roger challenged him to a duel, and in reply he sent a footman to say that gentlemen did not fight with rogues and vagabonds: they merely spat upon them or stole their wives. He was in the set that surrounded the Prince of Wales, and there beggared himself. He fled to France to escape his creditors, and that was as far as Mr. Menheniot had been able to trace him. There was a story that he had made his way to America and fought on the American side in the War of Independence, but it had been impossible to confirm this.

III

Mr. Menheniot, then, his mind occupied with such matters, was not notably present in this sombre twentieth century when he ended his spell of fire-watching and began to walk home. It was a glum clouded night. You could hardly see where the roofs met the sky, but down in the dark valleys of the streets there were still plenty of people. Here and there the prostitutes were practising

the trick that war conditions had added to their reper-
toire: flashing electric torches upon their silken legs, with
skirts lifted to the knees. Mr. Menheniot had seen plenty
of that since he became a fire-watcher, but he never got
used to it. They always terrified him, these women whom
he could not consider as women to be walked past as he
would walk past anyone else: they were symbols of a
great unexplored tract of experience that his heart shook
to contemplate, a tract that seemed to him as vile as it
was oddly alluring. Every time one of these unseen faces
spoke to him out of the darkness in which it was poised
over the slim, or not so slim, columns of the shining legs,
these conflicting emotions met like a strong wind meeting a flowing tide, and produced a dithering confusion
which caused him to swerve away as though the devil's
own hand might reach out and be hotly laid upon him.
But all that reached out and followed him was a laugh,
tinkling and amused, or a voice coarse and abusive, but,
whether the one or the other, likely to remain in his
mind, even when he had crossed the river and reached
his sanctuary—the cold war-starved sanctuary—in the
Georgian house.

It was one of these women who precipitated him into
his adventure. When the adventure had drawn him into
its maelstrom he never again thought of her, never
reflected upon the tiny push that sent him hurtling so far.
But there she was, that night when he was wandering
home with his thoughts even more than usually bemused,
noticing even less than was his custom the here-and-now-
ness of experience, and then coming sharply to the realiza-
tion that this cursed *ignis fatuus* had appeared, lighting
the pavement not a yard in front of him, and out of the
trembling pool of light rose, from a pair of stilt-heeled
red shoes, the slender stalks of golden legs, bearing who
knew what flower of evil?

Mr. Menheniot would have been full-tilt upon her if he had not swerved like a horse stung by a gadfly: swerved with so impetuous a revulsion that he crashed his head upon a lamp-post. The impact was on his right temple. He heard bells ring and slid to the ground.

It was but a momentary unconsciousness. When he came to, the woman's torch was extinguished. Darkness surrounded them, and she was crouching over him, his head cradled in her arm. As soon as he was aware of this —that for the first time in his life, if we forget the mother he never knew, a woman's arms were about his neck—he lurched to his feet, feeling sick and revolted. The woman got up, too, and he moved away from her in disgust. Was she young or old, beautiful or a hag? He never knew; he never saw her face; he only knew that she was a limb of Satan and that from her there came wafting upon him a nauseous smell compounded of scent and liquor. He said never a word to her, and her words to him were few.

"Sorry, ducks," she said. "I didn't mean to startle you. You all right now?"

He moved away from her, feeling far from all right. He was dizzy, and, seeing his plight, she put an arm through his and led him to an alleyway that opened here between the great buildings of this main street. He strove to push her off, but she held on to him, took him a little way down the alley, and propped him against a wall. "There," she said. "Stay where you are till you pull round. You're only a bit dazed."

Then, herself still in darkness, she flashed her torch upon his face as if to reassure herself. "Yes," she said, snapping off the light, "you'll be all right, ducks. Well, so long." And she clicked away from him on her red stilts.

Easy enough to say that he'd be all right: he felt far from all right. His head ached and there was sickness in his stomach, caused as much by the psychological crash of

24

finding a woman cradling him as by the physical crash of his head against the lamp-post. He understood that brandy-and-water was the stuff to pull a man round. So he had read. He had never tasted it. Before the war, when such things were reasonably cheap, he would buy a bottle of good wine and drink a little now and then from one of his beautiful glasses. It was an aesthetic rather than a physical pleasure. But the rough and ready problem of getting himself a drink seemed to him stupendous. He had never in his life entered a public house. The scenes in them, he imagined, must be such as he was acquainted with through Hogarth and Rowlandson prints. Nevertheless, now that the idea of a restorative had entered his mind it was attractive.

This short passage, at the end away from the main street, seemed to open into a courtyard. He could make out very dimly the shapes of buildings there, and now as he looked that way he saw a door burst open and slam quickly shut again. A man came out and staggered past him none too steady on his feet. He brushed roughly into Mr. Menheniot, muttered "Sorry" in a thick voice, and then went on to the main road.

The brief glimpse had shown Mr. Menheniot a room as thick with smoke as the river could be with fog, and men milling about in it, and this, no doubt, he thought, was a public house, too uninformed to know that public houses had closed long ago. But now he did not want to go into this public house. All that smoke, all those men, would make him feel worse, not better. He must pull himself together and get home as well as he could.

He had no sooner reached that decision than the door was again flung open—only seconds had passed since the first man had gone—and there, startling him out of his wits, was the great voice bellowing like a bull: "Menheniot! Menheniot!"

25

Coming upon what had already happened—though that would have been nothing to most men—it was terrifying. His contact with the woman had left him feeling defiled; and now this archangel trump, blaring his name through the darkness, was like something calling him to account. But there was only one Menheniot in the world. He stiffened, pulled himself upright, and shouted loudly: "Yes. What is it?"

The door had swung to and again the night was pitch; but he could hear the man coming towards him. "Here!" he shouted again. "What is it?"

The man was upon him, reeking of liquor. "This," he said. "Take it. You'll be forgetting your God-damned head next, you drunken old hawg."

He thrust something into Mr. Menheniot's hand, smacked him affectionately on the shoulder, and stumbled off into the street.

Too flabbergasted by the encounter to move for a moment, Mr. Menheniot stood there, fingering in the darkness what was evidently a small metal object. When he recovered his senses, he followed the man out into the street, but that was as dark as the alleyway. Impossible to say whether he had turned right or left. The blackened war-time streets had swallowed him. Mr. Menheniot flashed his pocket-torch upon the object in his hand. He saw at once that it was a snuff-box. Then his connoisseur's eye told him that it belonged to the eighteenth century. Finally, he saw the Menheniot crest engraved upon it.

He felt as though he were about to faint. Again he sought the refuge of a wall and leaned against it. He said, half-aloud: "What in God's name is happening to-night?"

A rare taxi-cab cruised by. He hailed it and was driven home. He could not have walked. His knees were water.

MR. MENHENIOT was not feeling too bad on the Sunday morning. He woke with a clear head and noticed in the mirror that his collision with the lamp-post had left nothing but a small bruise upon his temple. Almost all that had happened last night was now as though it had not been. Almost. . . . There was still the snuff-box.

When Mrs. Sara had gone out of the room he opened it again. It was half-full of snuff. That is to say, it was not a curio, a collector's treasure: it was a thing in use. It was a bit of the furnishing of someone's daily life.

He trembled a little at the next implication: the someone was named Menheniot! The drunken man who had pushed this into his hand had not thought he was giving it to *him*, but he *had* thought he was giving it to a Menheniot.

Mr. Menheniot had for so many years considered himself the last of the Menheniots that he felt a sense of personal affront at the thought that he was not. And another thing. Here in his hand at last was something that he had long wanted to possess: a piece of the crested family silver. But he could not keep it. It was his manifest duty to find the owner and hand it back. He knew that the longer he kept it the more difficult it would be to return it. It could become an idol, an icon, the one tangible and certain thing that linked him with the moment of his family's fall from grandeur. There was nothing he wanted more on earth than to keep that piece of silver.

He sat down and wrote a note. He said that a silver

snuff-box had accidentally come into his possession. If the receiver of this note were the owner, would he call at the above address? He signed his name.

He had thought at first of wrapping up the box and leaving it at this place, whatever it might be, from which the two men had come last night. He decided against that. Perhaps the men—the man—Menheniot—might not return and find the note. Then the box would be his.

He set out immediately after breakfast, a rather drab middle-aged man wearing a mackintosh and galoshes— he had a great fear of colds—shoes nowadays were not such as his father had made—an umbrella over his head. A dreary, hopeless, Sunday morning of London's war time: few people about, ruins and rain and a disagreeable job to be done.

He found the place easily enough. Here was the lamp into which he had smacked, here the passage in which he had loitered. There was now nothing of the sinister feeling about the place that had shattered him last night. It was dreary: it merely depressed him.

A man in shirt-sleeves was sweeping out the room into which he had had a glimpse. It was a big room with lots of seats and tables, a bar and a piano. It was one of those odd places that the war caused to spring up. They were comprehensively called clubs, but were, in fact, out-of-hours drinking-places.

There was a slight tightening of Mr. Menheniot's voice as he asked: "Does a Mr. Menheniot come here?"

The sweeping man, with a glowing crumb of cigarette stuck to his underlip, shot him a suspicious glance. Mr. Menheniot could easily have been a plain-clothes dick.

"Gawd knows 'oo comes 'ere," the man said. "I don't."

The place smelt foul and seedy. The bar had not yet been washed. It was a gluey mess. Mr. Menheniot wanted to be away quickly. He took from his pocket the note

28

addressed simply to "Mr. Menheniot," and handed it to the sweeper. "Would you mind," he asked, "putting this where he will see it if he should call?" Feeling a man of the world who knew how these things were done, he fished a half-crown from his pocket and dropped it on to one of the little tables.

"Aw right, guv'nor."

And that was all that was needed to bring Phil Menheniot to Mr. Roger Menheniot's Georgian room. He turned up that evening just as Mrs. Sara was bringing in the tea-tray. He was tall and athletic, young and good-looking, and he was wearing the uniform of the United States Army, with the badges of a captain's rank. He smiled: "You're not *really* named Menheniot?"

"Yes, I am."

"Well, I'll be damned!"

II

Mr. Menheniot felt that this was an occasion. How he loathed that feeble coil of wire faintly glowing in the electric contraption that defiled his grate! He had managed to hoard a small reserve of coal in boxes under the stairs, and now and then, when something happened that called for it, he celebrated with a real fire. This was surely an "occasion."

He said: "Sit down, Captain Menheniot." And Phil said: "Thank you. I will, Mr. Menheniot." And they both laughed to find their odd name passing to and fro like that.

"I'll bring in some coal," Roger said; and presently you might have been, he reflected, back in the eighteenth century. From the middle of the ceiling hung a chandelier of those times, and, mounting a chair, he furnished it with a dozen candles and lit them, and that was another

29

thing he did when he celebrated. His celebrations were always denials: denials of here and now, recoils upon antiquity.

The rich brocade curtains were drawn; the tranquil candle-shine was mellow; the fireplace was properly alive. Mrs. Sara had brought in more tea-things; and there were the two Menheniots sitting in embroidered wing-chairs on either side of the hearth, with the tea spread out on a round pie-frill table whose legs ended in greyhound's feet clutched round balls of mahogany.

Phil looked about him appreciatively. "I guess you've got something pretty old fashioned here," he said, and Roger was able to tell him with pride: "There's not a thing here that isn't eighteenth century. Including this," he said, and reached for the snuff-box. He told Phil how it came to him.

"That crazy Crowther," Phil said. "I'm not a drinking man, but Crowther can swim in it and come out dry. Up to a point," he added. "He took me to that dump last night, and I guess even he ended up a bit cross-eyed."

He put the box into his pocket, and Mr. Menheniot watched it disappear with regret. "I missed it as soon as I got up this morning," Phil said, "so back I went to see if it had been found, and there was your note. Thanks a lot. I wouldn't have lost that for a month's pay."

He sipped his tea, crunched his toast buttered with margarine, and Mr. Menheniot scrutinized his features but could find nothing that would have marked this young man out as a Menheniot. Come to that, he thought, there was nothing of the family features about himself either. Since that day long ago when he had seen the print in the Manchester shop he had run down a fair number of Menheniot pictures. There was a lovely miniature by Nicholas Hilliard that he would dearly have

30

loved to buy. He had gone to bid for it at Christie's in the days before the war, but it was the old trouble—"Too dear for my possessing," he ruefully punned. Anyway, the last appearance of the Menheniot features had been in his father. The very last, for he himself would certainly never marry.

But there was this young man. . . . The thought of the young man was disturbing. Perhaps he was married already. Perhaps there were already Menheniot sons. He might even have a father living, who himself had brothers, who themselves had sons. The Last of the Menheniots began to see a whole clan, a numerous progeny, Menheniot upon Menheniot, plentifully peopling the United States of America. He disliked the idea.

"Captain Menheniot," he began; and Phil said: "Look. I'm Phil. What are you?"

"Roger." But no one called him Roger. It was years since he had had a Christian name. He confessed to Roger with a blush, as though it were a guilty secret.

"Well, Roger, what were you going to say?"

Mrs. Sara took away the tea-things. Phil lit a cigarette.

"I was going to say, Phil, that, if you cared to tell me, I'd like to know something about your family. With a name like ours, we probably belong to the same bunch. After all," he added with modest pride, "our name isn't Smith or Robinson."

"No," Phil said. "I guess it isn't. It's surely one hell of a name. When they've handed me Eisenhower's job and I've won this war, they'll want to buy this Rosemullion place for pilgrims to visit, just as they go to Sulgrave to worship Washington."

"So you know about Rosemullion?"

"Why, yes, in a sort of a way. What's it like?"

That was a question to set Mr. Menheniot off. It was

31

the match to the firework. He took down the portfolio of Rosemullion pictures and spread them on the big table under the chandelier. This is Rosemullion in the fifteenth century. A castle still, you see. First of all there was the fortified mound. Then the keep was built on that, and all round it grew these curtain walls. Well, you didn't want that sort of stuff for ever, of course, and some Menheniot in late Tudor times pulled it all down, except the keep, and built this house here—you see?—half-way down the hill, on this terrace.

"It's still the original place, in a way," Mr. Menheniot explained enthusiastically, "for he used all the old stone from the building up here on the top. Look! This engraving shows how it was in Stuart times. There's the keep, pretty good still, though it's crumbled down to a stump now. And there's the house as it was."

Phil took up the engraving and looked long at it. "Quite a place," he said. "I guess I'll have to find time to get down there and have a look at it before I get back to the Victory Parade."

"Well, you won't see *that*!" Roger explained. "The Menheniot who owned that unfortunately decided to defend it for Charles the First against Cromwell. He defended it long enough to have a lot of it blown to bits, and a fire broke out and all this wing—all this lot, here—fell in. He was taken prisoner, and his wife and children went to live with her parents, and Menheniots didn't come back here till Roger—the chap who had held this—came back with Charles the Second from Holland. He had escaped from prison and crossed the sea."

Mr. Menheniot took up another portfolio. The first one had been labelled in his careful hand "Menheniot buildings." This one was "Menheniot people."

"There," he said, "that's Roger. A reproduction of a Lely portrait."

32

Phil took up this picture with great excitement. "Well, what do you know," he said. "If it isn't the old man!"

Roger smiled with satisfaction. "It happens. The likeness persists. Here's another of 'em. This one is my father to a T."

Young Phil—well, he seemed young compared with Mr. Menheniot who was older than his years—he was just turned thirty—was now deeply excited. "Go on," he said. "What's the next chapter?"

The next chapter was yet another contraction of the house called Rosemullion. In the absence of the Menheniots, the weather had got into the fabric. The burned wing was pulled down; the rest was patched up; and so it remained till the beginning of the eighteenth century, when there arose a Menheniot who didn't like the look of the place at all. He wanted an entirely new house, and that is what he had—a square block of a house, but again built of the stone that already for centuries had sheltered Menheniots. But by the end of that century it had ceased to shelter them; "and now," said Roger, "this is what you'll find if you go down there."

This time it wasn't an engraving: it was a small photograph. "I took it myself," Roger explained. "I still have the negative. I can do you a print, if you'd like it."

"I would very much," Phil said. "It looks like a homy little place."

Roger looked long at the photograph. "Yes," he said. "It does. I think it's lovely. It's my dream to live there some day."

Now his secret was out, and he blushed, embarrassed; for he had never before confided this to anyone—this passion which, beneath his dull exterior, consumed him. He had not mentioned it even to Mrs. Sara, his only confidante; for he knew it was madness. The Menheniots had done with Rosemullion. Nothing but the excitement of this meeting could have jerked the confession from him.

He handed the photograph to Phil. "Keep it," he said. "I'll do another for myself."

Phil thanked him and put the picture in his wallet. He looked at his wrist-watch. "Say," he said. "It's time we went somewhere to eat."

It turned then into a confused night for Roger Menheniot. He did not often eat out, and when he did it was in some simple inexpensive place where he could hide himself in a corner. In this crowded restaurant of a famous hotel he could not have believed, had it not been for the many uniforms—English and American, French and Polish, and others that he didn't know—that he was in war-time London. He who had so confidently been leading Phil through the centuries resigned himself to Phil to be led through the next hour or so. Never had he eaten such a meal—and this was war time! Never had he sat in the same room with such women; and his nervousness of them was so apparent that Phil twitted him: "Come on, Roger, take an eyeful while you've got a chance. When you go to live at Rosemullion, you'll want to marry, and a Menheniot will want a very special kind of woman. You'd better start studying form." But Mr. Menheniot kept his head, with its thinning hair, bowed over his plate. He gave the sense of carrying his monastery about with him. He drank a glass of wine, but refused a second. They took coffee in a lounge, and he allowed Phil to give him brandy in a warm balloon glass. There were a few women in the lounge, some with partners, some alone. The fumes of the brandy, so unaccustomed a drink to him, magnified them into apparitions of loveliness and evil. He would have liked to take his attention away from them, to be discussing Menheniots with Phil, learning all that till now had been hidden from him about the American branch. But Phil had a store of amusing small-talk, and so unskilled a talker as Mr. Menheniot could not switch it into the paths where he wanted to walk. Moreover, he was becoming uneasy at the frequency with which Phil's eye met the eye of a girl drinking alone.

Presently Roger got up. "I must be on my way," he said. "Work to-morrow. Thank you. You've given me a most enjoyable evening."

"Thank *you*, Roger. I'm very glad to have that snuff-box back. It goes with me everywhere."

On their way out, they passed the girl, who was sitting near the door. Phil said to her: "I'll be right back." Then he became a most attentive host, seeing Mr. Menheniot into his overcoat in the cloak-room, conducting him to the swing doors, telling the commissionaire to call a taxi, and shaking hands when Roger was in it. "Well—be seeing you," he said, and strode back eagerly into the hotel.

But Mr. Menheniot did not believe it. That, he thought, is the last of the snuff-box and of Phil Menheniot. The idea of Phil occupied his mind during the drive home. Courteous to the last, then straight back to that woman! In his room, with one poor light burning, he took off his spectacles and wiped the thick pebble lenses. The Chippendale mirror gave him a shadowy picture of himself, standing there with his face thus unguarded, the round face unmarked by any notable experience, the round head with thin hair. The disturbing thought came to him that never had he seen a man who looked less like a Menheniot. He put on his spectacles and sat down by the cold hearth. This Phil, come to that, didn't *look* a Menheniot, "but he's more Menheniot than you," he said to himself accusingly. "That's how they were—soldiers, wandering actors, arrogant aristocrats." They

35

were all men of their moment. Not a man-jack of them, he'd be bound, had ever given a tinker's cuss for the past or for Menheniot tradition. They had mixed with their kind—with women as well as with men—and they had been, like this Phil, doers, not moles rooting among the records of doings.

He went to bed feeling unhappy. For the first time in his life he was not sure what he had to be so proud of. He put it down to the brandy. He shouldn't have drunk that on top of the wine.

CHAPTER FOUR

I

"IT LOOKS like a homy little place," Phil had said when
Mr. Menheniot showed him the photograph of Rosemullion as it is to-day. The last Menheniot to live there
had lived in a Georgian house, and after that there had
been no family continuity. The place had changed hands
often, and at the turn of the century it was derelict. A
London merchant whose fortune had been enormously
increased by the Boer War saw it while enjoying a Cornish holiday, fell in love with the situation and detested
the house. He bought the property and called in Sir
Edwin Lutyens, who created the "homy little place" that
Rosemullion now was. The Georgian mansion was swept
away. It had never had the stucco facing so common to
Georgian architecture. It was always a granite house, and
a granite house it remained. Here, in this Lutyens building, was still the stone that had sheltered Tudor Menheniots and stood against Commonwealth artillery.
Granite is not a pleasing material for domestic architecture until it has endured for centuries in the wind and
rain and sunshine. Then its intractable surface mellows.
Lichens of willow-green and red and lemon-yellow give
a tenderness to its strength. When Rosemullion was re-
built for the last time the lichens were treated as time-
honoured tenants who must not be disturbed. The stone
was gently handled, and when the Lutyens house had
stood there for ten years it looked as though it, and no
other building, had stood there for ever.

Engravings and paintings had made Mr. Menheniot
acquainted with every phase of Rosemullion's existence,

37

but this Lutyens house was the only one his eye had seen. He saw it for the first time in 1919. He was twenty years old. The Great War was ended, and it was May month. He was an earnest solitary youth. He wanted no company during this holiday that was due, especially as he had come to a resolution that greatly excited him: he would go into Cornwall and look at Rosemullion. He had not been in the county before.

At Exeter he took his bicycle out of the guard's van and found lodgings for the night in a temperance hotel. In his room he gave himself to the joys of map-reading, and early the next morning he was off. He was already spectacled, but didn't yet need pebble lenses. He had loaded the bicycle as though it were a furniture remover's van. A tent to sleep in, pots and pans for cooking, books to read: oh, he was an adventurous youth, and when occasionally, in these present days, he looked back on that holiday, he could hardly believe that he had ever had such verve and daring. Had the old owl once so giddily played the maverick? Was he the boy who had worn the Norfolk jacket and the knee-tight breeches (already old-fashioned) and the cycling shoes and stockings? He had gone so far as to ride bare-headed. Certainly it was his wildest adventure.

He slept in the tent only once—at the end of that first day's ride. It was a day of pushing the bike uphill and free-wheeling down; of birdsong and blazing gorse and blue sea. A tender evening came. He had crossed into Cornwall on the Saltash ferry, and then, miles from any habitation, he wheeled the bicycle into the heart of a little wood and set up the tent in a clearing. He was far from being a handy man and did not find it easy to do. He stumbled over guy-ropes and pulled out the pegs he had already driven in. But it was up at last, and he got out his virgin frying-pan and a few rashers of bacon.

And then he quailed. He would make a mess of the job, or his fire would set the wood alight, or someone would see the smoke and come and tell him to clear out. He was an easily discouraged youth. So he took a loaf and sat on the edge of the wood, munching dry bread. A red moon came up, and the scent of hawthorn from the trees behind him filled the air. He was well content to sit there, relaxing the muscles of his legs that ached from the day's hard exercise. "I am in Cornwall," he said to himself. He went back to the clearing, got into his sleeping-bag, and with difficulty fitted himself into the little tent.

The next day he came to Rosemullion.

II

The Menheniots might be mad in their various ways, but they had one fixed principle: they would not sell land—not a yard of it. They were the owners of thousands of acres. At first the land was added to; then for a long time it was constant. It was often mortgaged, but it was never sold. It held together till the final crash. Then all went in one piece. New owners, lacking a sense of inheritance, began to sell, and it was a reduced estate that was bought at last by the Boer War beneficiary. He took over a few hundred acres, and even that was too much. Land was a nuisance to him, not the blood of his life. He had no interest in corn or byres or roots or woods. He wanted a comfortable place to live in, and that is what Rosemullion became. He sold outlying fields and kept only ten acres.

To this shrunken Rosemullion Mr. Menheniot came on the afternoon that he would never forget. He had made a dallying day of it, and it was late afternoon when he stopped at the granite milestone leaning askew under a hedge on a bye-road. It was triangular, and on the western face of it, he read: Rosemullion IV.

There it was. For the first time, the name that had for years drifted like a perfume in his consciousness was concrete, having a local significance. It was a place you could walk to in an hour. His heart fluttered. He shifted the bicycle and sat down with his back to the warm stone: Menheniot of Rosemullion, in old-fashioned knicker bockers and cyling shoes.

Now that he was so near, he was in no hurry to go on. He ate his sandwiches and then closed his eyes, surrender ing himself to one of his labyrinthine day-dreams. How long this stone had stood here! It was all aslant. The granite had lost its surface planing: it was rough and grey, but sulphur-coloured lichens were on it. Its edge were crumbled down. It must be older—much, much older—than the house that called itself Rosemullion now. The sun warmed him; a stream straying along the opposite hedge-bottom chuckled at his youth and inno cence; blackbirds and thrushes, reassured by his im mobility, went about their springtime business, and chaffinches alighted at his very feet to eat his crumbs. Mr Menheniot was asleep.

The sun was dropping to the west and its light was in his eyes when he continued the journey. On his right hand the land began to slope upwards, and he could se that ahead it was fleeced with woods. The milestone went past him: Rosemullion III, II, I. The woods now were thick on his right. They came down to the road which had twisted so that the sun was gone, hidden by the trees. He was riding in shadow, with open fields on his left, and when he had but half a mile to go he suddenly did not want to reach Rosemullion on a bicycle. He would walk the last stretch.

The woods were not fenced. He found a gap, pushed h

machine through, and left it there, hidden in a rusty pile of last year's bracken. It was a wood of scrub and small trees. Overhead, the green had its May-month tenderness; at his feet, blue-bells grew, seeping into the wood, whichever way he looked, with a misty tide. The smell was earthy in a way it never is in a place new-planted. Centuries of life and death were under his feet.

It was a long time since he had seen a living soul, and he saw no one as he walked the last half-mile. When he reached the entrance he had no doubt that this was the place he had come so far to see. He was at the end of the woods, and on his right the road widened into a sweeping half-circle with a low stone coping topped by iron railings. The gates were gone: the lovely gates of intricate wrought-iron that he had expected to find. They had been there, he knew, long before Lutyens had designed the present Rosemullion. There was a picture of them in his Menheniot collection at home, with the family crest in the sweeping arch that topped the two wings of the gates. Now there was only the coping and the rails upon it and a gap through which he looked into pasture dotted with a few fine oaks.

Behind the coping was a lodge that had belonged to the Georgian house. Architecturally, there was nothing wrong with it. It was built of sound material and was pleasant to the eye. But in capacity it was a kennel, big enough for the watch-dog at the gate to gnaw his bone in and to stretch in at night. The usual lodge, in fact. No smoke was coming from the chimney. The little house looked dead, and, venturing through the gap, Mr. Menheniot saw that there were no curtains at the windows, small affairs with diamond-leaded panes. He peeped through at front and back. The place was empty.

He began to feel small and intrusive and lonely. The quietness was frightening. He had seen no men for a long time. There were no animals in the pasture. The only living creatures were the birds whose careless songs made his loneliness greater. They were wild things; and he had a sense of their having taken over a place from which men had departed.

But he had come to see Rosemullion, and see it he would. A carriage-track ran through the pasture, and he followed this, pausing now and then to look at the great oaks and to remember how these had been here in the time of the Civil War. There was a story of how the Menheniot who had held Rosemullion against the Parliament had seen Cromwell's men hacking at the oaks for firewood and had come down in person, full of indignation, to say: "Sirs, those trees have seen the coming and going of kings. You may rebel against my king. You may kill him if you like, but those trees will see many kings when you and I are dust and Cromwell is called a traitor." They had been so taken aback that they let him return to the house, and they did not cut the trees.

Thinking about such things, Roger Menheniot was hardly aware that the carriage-track had swerved to the right till he saw the house. It was not any one of the Rosemullions of his dreams: not the Norman fortress, nor the Tudor house, nor the Georgian mansion. It was Sir Edwin Lutyen's cosy bit of architecture, but it was Rosemullion, and Roger stopped dead in his tracks with his heart beating fiercely.

The house looked west, lying on a terrace within a sickle of woodland. It stood above him, and the sun, which had now sunk low, set its windows flashing and lit up the lively green of the trees that half-encircled it. But there was more than this. Higher than the house, rising out of the wood behind it, was a sombre circle of stone. The setting sun lit its topmost crumbling edge from which shrubs and grasses sprouted. And Roger knew that

42

this was the thing that had seen it all. This was the rotting remains of the tooth that the Normans had first fastened in the land. This was the keep. It was round that stump that all had grown, and from it all had fallen away. The romantic youth in the Norfolk jacket and knicker-bockers sat down on the turf, overwhelmed. The men who had piled those stones one on top of another eight hundred years ago were Menheniots.

III

That was a long time ago, that first glimpse of the keep: it was more than half his lifetime ago. "I guess it was quite a moment for you, Roger," Phil Menheniot said. They were sitting at the window, looking across the Thames at the invincible dome of St. Paul's. It was a pleasanter prospect now, for this was April. A brisk wind stirred the surface of the water; sunlight glinted on the ripples. He had not thought that he would see Phil again, but here he was, stretching out his long legs and looking, as he had done last time, full of lazy energy. He said nothing about his three months' absence, his long silence: he just walked in, bringing food and a bottle of wine. It was again a Sunday. They ate and they talked Menheniots.

Yes, Roger recalled, it had been quite a moment. He remembered how he stirred himself at last and walked towards the house. The terrace on which he stood was retained by a long stone wall, and a noble sweep of steps led up to it from the pasture. With his heart in his mouth, Roger went up the steps, through the blue and white cascades of aubrietia and snow-on-the-mountain, expect-ing at any moment to hear a voice shouting to him, demanding his business; and yet, with another part of his mind, knowing that there would be no voice, that the very stones of the house looked quietly watchful and expectant, as indeed they might, he said to himself, for now, following the intrusion of so many interloping families, here was a Menheniot coming back after a hundred and fifty years.

At the top of the steps were stone urns on low plinths, and others crowned the wall, spilling out their colours to right and left. An immense unattended lawn stretched before him. He swished through it, and in the quietness the sound of his shoes was loud in the grasses. There was a square pond in the middle, with a cypress dark at each corner. Goldfish moved among the lily-stems. The fountain was not working. Nothing was working, he began to understand, except unceasing nature, which would soon make this lawn one with the pasture. The yew hedges that walled the lawn at either end were shooting up uncontrolled, and on the face of the house everything was rioting—wistaria, roses and jasmine.

He was near the house now. It stood on a second terrace, and he climbed to it up another flight of steps. This was a terrace paved with large square stones. The iron-studded oak door was before him, and the windows on either side of it were uncurtained. Another transition family was gone. Rosemullion was empty again. "Mr. Mellows," as Roger in due course recorded in his Rosemullion Journal, "Mr. Mellows, who bought the place and had the Lutyens house built out of a fortune made in the Boer War, had only one child, a son. He was killed on the Somme in 1916. Mrs. Mellows had already died, and Mr. Mellows put the place into the market. It seems," he added, "as though no family can thrive at Rosemullion since the Menheniots left it."

On this upper terrace, under a window almost hidden by honeysuckle, there was an oak bench, and Menheniot sat down there, looking back over the way he had

44

come. The west was red and the east quickly darkening and all the country sloping away beneath his view was putting on the mystery of evening. Rooks were making to the woods, and singing-birds were filling the air with their last songs. It was beautiful, and he felt a weight of sorrow that he could not bear, and he began to cry. Twenty-five years later he said to Phil: "I almost wished I had never come. Someone would buy the place soon, and I shouldn't be able to come again. It might have been better not to have seen it at all than to remember it with such—such anguish." He chose the word shyly.

"I don't agree with you," Phil said. "In the long run, what do we have but our memories? You have that."

Mr. Menheniot smiled at him. He looked so young. "What can you know about memories?" he asked.

"Perhaps more than you," Phil said. "Your memories are hundreds of years old. Mine are more recent and perhaps that makes them sharper. Let it go. But I've got plenty."

Well, there was the memory of prowling round the house that evening and finding all bolted and barred, and coming at last to the back parts. You remembered the ivy growing on the wall, and the sparrow, a silly half-fledged thing, fluttering on the path there, and the sparrows at the nest in the ivy making as much fuss as if the falling to the ground of this third of a farthing's worth of life meant the end of the world. So you picked up the gardener's ladder and laid it against the ivy, and you took the fledgling in one hand and climbed up and put it back in the nest. And then you saw that the casement window on a level with your hand was an inch a-gape, and you pulled it and it swung outwards. And then you were inside Rose-mullion. You opened doors and searched this way and that, and came at last to a fine stairway. You stole down it, your footsteps loud in the dusk, and reached a room at the front—a room looking out over that vast darkening sweep of country, and there you sat down on the bare boards and listened to your heart beating. You were Roger Menheniot, *inside* Rosemullion.

He had read that in the Midlands there are descendants of the Plantagenets working as farm labourers; and there was Tess the milkmaid, whose forebears were the D'Urbervilles. There was nothing strange about a Menheniot being a bank clerk. Menheniots had been everything in their time: crusaders, farmers, courtiers, soldiers, inn-keepers, parsons, wastrels and scholars. They had been some of the blood in every vein of English life. Roger did not feel alien in this house. He had come with a shy intention of peeping at it from afar, but now, unexpectedly, he was within it, and he decided, as though it were in the nature of things, that he would stay within it.

Presently the moon would be up, but now it was dark. He struck matches and groped his way about. He came to the kitchens, the sculleries, the back door. There was a large iron key on the inside of this door. He went out, locking the door behind him. He was soon back with his bicycle. Again he locked the door behind him, but this time he was on the inside. He found a room that could have been the maids' sitting-room. There were shutters to the windows, and, having closed these, he could give himself a light without fear of discovery. He found a lamp that had a little oil in it. An old wicker-chair had been left behind, and there was a crate that would do for a table. Kindling-wood and logs were in the scullery. He was by now very hungry, and soon had his frying-pan over the fire. When he had eaten, he piled the logs high, put out the lamp, and got into his sleeping-bag. He had had enough for one day. Huddled in the old chair, he slept the night through.

He had not expected his holiday to be like this: the oddest holiday he would ever enjoy. Occasionally he would set off on his bicycle to find a village where he would buy food and lamp-oil. There was not much else that he needed. As soon as darkness came, he would light the lamp and the fire in the little back room. By dawn the fire would be out: there would be no tell-tale smoke. He would have liked to spend his evenings in one of the handsome rooms at the front of the house, but there was no means of cloaking the windows. But in the sunny day-time—and it was sunny right through the holiday —he strolled through them all, dallying to admire the views, passing his hands over the mahogany of doors and the stone of fireplaces, deciding how he would furnish them, which bedroom he would sleep in, which room should be the study. He would be one of the scholar-Menheniots. Here he would compile the history, from the first warrior-cry to the last squeak within himself. For, of course, he would be the last. He would never marry. It would be fitting that Menheniots should end here where they had begun.

His head crazed by such romantic notions, he wandered out of doors in the warm spring weather, admired the camellias and rhododendrons that were blooming everywhere in unending variety; strolled through orchard and kitchen-garden and flower-garden, explored the woods, and came to the keep.

This was on the third day, and he knew that he had consciously avoided the keep till now and that fascination had pulled him there against his will. Trees grew right up to those grey rugged walls, that broken cylinder of menacing stone. Through the gap that had once contained a door, he saw that even within small trees were

47

growing, and as he stepped over the threshold—this timid, spectacled Menheniot—there was a rush and whirr of wings, an indignant chatter, and jackdaws flew upwards, drawing his eyes to the blue circle of sky overhead, against which danced the intrusive saplings of buddleia and sycamore.

He paced from one side to the other, stumbling over the great stones that the centuries had dislodged and that were hidden by tangles of bramble and stunted elderberry. Thirty paces he counted—ninety feet in diameter the floor was; and the walls stood six feet thick. Perhaps for a midday moment or two in high summer the sun would look down into this stony tube; but, even on a cheerful morning such as it now was, there was no sense that such a thing could happen. The air was prison air, chill and damp.

A stone stairway, each step a prone granite monolith, spiralled up inside the tower, and as Menheniot climbed he passed here and there a slit that gave a glimpse into the radiant day. The stairway ended sharply among the foliage that waved green banners above the ruin. Roger lay face-down and peered over the edge at the stones that time had thrown to lie at the foot of the tower like a reef below a cliff. His head was not good even for so moderate a height. He quickly drew back, frightened by the thought of the mangling that would follow a fall into that granite chaos.

He stood on the last step with the sun and air about him and looked forth upon the prospect that so many Menheniots had known: the woods round him, the undulating fields, the stream flowing south towards the sea, which from this height he could glimpse as a distant line of blue. How much of it was still his—for that was how in this holiday mood he foolishly allowed himself to think of it—he did not know; but he did know that it was as lovely as it had been in his dreams, and that, now that he had seen it, he would find it harder than ever to come to terms with the world that he feared and the age that he hated.

It was time to eat. He went back down the stairway and through the deep gape of doorway; and the jackdaws came back, shaking their grey-blue heads, nattering querulously about the intrusion.

There is not much else to be said about that holiday except that, next day, he began to carve his name on the stone lintel of the great fireplace in the dining-room.

"It's still there, you know," Phil Menheniot said, when Roger told him of it during that second Sunday morning call.

"Of course it is. I made a job of it, I can tell you. But how on earth do you know whether it's there or not?"

"I got a letter from that crazy loon Crowther. He asks: 'What's your goddam name doing on the fireplace down here?'"

"What's *he* doing there, come to that?" Roger asked, surprised.

"Say, do you live in this world at all?" Phil demanded. "Have you ever heard of the liberation of Europe? We've come to do it—to give you a hand with it, anyway. Am I giving away state secrets when I tell you Cornwall's full of Americans? The boys have to live somewhere, and our outfit is at Rosemullion. I'm travelling down there myself to-morrow."

Menheniot looked at him with round owlish eyes. "You take it casually," he said. There was amazement in his voice.

"Well, what the hell. You've been blotting-paper for these Menheniots for years. You've soaked 'em up till you'll never get the stains out. I'm not like that. I guess I'm not a Menheniot in the way you are."

49

"But look: there's something extraordinary about all this. First of all there's the woman I told you about. . . ."

"Oh, hooey!" Phil interrupted. "Don't start looking for ghosts." He looked at this grave companion and laughed outright. "I guess, Roger, if you'd just gone home with that floozie, the course of history would have been altered."

Menheniot was shocked. "Phil! I couldn't have done that!"

"All right. Forget it."

Roger padded the room in his heavy bear-like fashion. "No!" he burst out. "I can't forget it, and I don't want to forget it. First there was that; and now there's this."

"Now there's what?"

"Oh, you pretend to be dense, but inside you must be as excited as I am myself. You come back here—the first Menheniot, so far as I know, ever to cross the Atlantic from west to east, and fate sends you to the place you sprang from."

"Forget it," Phil repeated, now with some annoyance in his tone. He too got up and began fiddling with the silver trifles on the mantelpiece. "Look," he said, turning round. "I don't want this. I don't want any part of the Menheniots. I'm an American. We've been Americans for a long time. If it's any good for the Menheniot records, you can put this in. We fought against the English. We fought against the Spaniards in Cuba. We fought against the Germans in the First World War, and one of us died in it. And we didn't fight anywhere as Menheniots for England. We fought as American citizens for America. And that's what I'm doing now. When I go down to this Rosemullion, I'm not going all agape to see where you carved your name when you were a kid. I'm going because I want to be with Crowther, and Rusty Burgess, and Bud Santorelli, and all the other boys. That's all the fate there is in it for me. To hell with the Menheniots, so far as they're knights in armour and ghosts down the corridor. I want no part in 'em."

Roger was hurt. It was impossible for him to understand such a state of mind, but he was too shy, too nervous, to make anything of a protest. "When do you go to Cornwall?" he asked.

"To-morrow. I guess this is farewell. Once I'm landed down there, London won't be accessible. We'll have to find what we can in Plymouth."

Roger looked at him earnestly. "That's where the *May-flower* sailed from. You'll be able to see the very spot."

"O.K. Perhaps we'll even get round to that, if we have time. But it won't be high up on the programme. Not if I know the boys."

"That's where it all began," Roger explained patiently.

"All right. That's where it all began, in a manner of speaking. But don't get it into your head that that's where it all ended. The Pilgrim Fathers have been pretty well diluted, you know. That strain is a bit under proof in the States right now."

They talked for a long time that night, and when it was time for Phil to go, Roger walked over the bridge with him as far as the north bank. There they paused and looked at one another for a while, and Phil said: "Well, I guess there's no *au revoir* about this. Good-bye Roger."

He held out his hand, and Roger took it, and Phil said: "I'd like you to have this. It seems to belong to you more than to me." He took the snuff-box from his pocket.

"But Phil, it's the only thing you've got that reminds you——"

"I know. The only thing that reminds me of the wonderful Menheniot story. Come on. Take it." Roger did so. "You go on pretending you're the last of the Menheniots. Perhaps you will be soon."

"Oh, Phil——"

Phil said brusquely: "Skip it," and strode off swiftly into the darkness. He shouted back: "Try to forget me."

Roger would never forget him; but he never saw him again.

CHAPTER FIVE

I

THERE was peace, but there wasn't peace. There was peace on paper, but in peoples' hearts there was no peace at all. There was anxiety and foreboding, and over the future there was a question mark, immense and menacing. Going about the streets, Mr. Menheniot was aware of faces that were strained and unhappy, of the town in ruins, of a nerve in the national life that was like a nerve exposed in a rotten tooth. He didn't want to do anything about it. He wanted, more than ever, to escape from it, to settle down into some happy vacuum, some island of Avilion. With the whole world testy, uncertain, and on edge, he was grunting about the broken fanlight over the door of the Georgian house he lived in. It had symbolic importance. Rarely a day went by without his asking: "When is something going to be done about that fanlight, Mrs. Sara?" And Mrs. Sara, who had plenty to worry her without fanlights, was at last driven to answer impatiently: "You look about you, Mr. Menheniot. You'll find thousands without roofs over their heads. They'd gladly pay me more for these rooms than you're doing, fanlight or no fanlight."

It was the first time she had ever spoken a rough word to him, and he was not the man to answer back. He said no more about the fanlight, and for that reason the obsession became deeper. What a world that couldn't provide a few shillings' worth of glass, an hour of labour, to make good a thing of beauty!

Unsatisfactory indeed the world seemed to Mr. Menheniot. He was pushed about in bus queues; he was snapped at by café waitresses. In the Underground unpleasant voices shouted "Hurry along! Hurry along!" and the sight of all these people hurrying along—Why? Where to?—amid clanging gates and roaring wheels, out from and into holes bored in the earth, left him sick for another way of living. If he caught a glimpse of newspaper headlines over someone's shoulder he shuddered at what he saw. Thank God, he never bought the things! He stuck to *Country Life*. The advertisements of houses for sale especially allured him: Tudor houses, Jacobean, Queen Anne, Georgian, Regency. There were scores of them, and one day there was Rosemullion.

It was a warm September evening in 1945. He sat in his room, looking at the house-agent's advertisement. The ache in his heart was intolerable. Never, never, he thought, could he be happy in the world about him: the world that the war had knocked sideways and that seemed to his frightened imagination as though it would not be straight again but must topple right over. And there under his eyes was the picture of the beautiful house that Lutyens had designed and that had been built out of the stones of his dreams. "On a historic Cornish site. Just de-requisitioned. The property includes the Norman keep, built *circa* 1100."

His old-maidish precision, his infallible memory, at once supplied the exact date. No *circa* for Mr. Menheniot!

He put on his light overcoat. It was warm enough, but you never knew in September, near the river. He was taking no risks. Not he.

He crossed to the north bank and walked in the thickening dusk as far as Westminster: past Cleopatra's needle, still bearing the pock-marks of the First World War, past the temporary bridges of the war just ended.

He was oppressed and unhappy, feeling that life was cheating him of what he had a right to ask of it.

II

The next evening when Menheniot returned from work the letter from New York was waiting for him. It was an airmail letter—something he had never received before. That in itself excited him: these oblique strokes of red and blue around the edges of the envelope. And he knew, too, at once, that this was a letter from Phil Menheniot. He had often wondered about Phil; he had been hurt at his silence. Not a word had reached him since that almost casual parting on the north bank. He waited till Mrs. Sara had brought in his evening meal; then he opened the envelope to read as he ate. There was a brief letter, and with it a sealed envelope addressed to himself. He read the letter first. It was headed with the address of a New York firm of lawyers

DEAR SIR,

We have the duty to inform you that we have completed our investigations into the estate of the late Mr. Philip Menheniot, who in his will named you, his sole surviving relative, as the only beneficiary. The value of the estate amounts to approximately 500,000 dollars.

This is a first intimation. We shall almost immediately be communicating further with you; and in the meantime we send you the enclosed sealed envelope which Mr. Philip Menheniot forwarded to us in June, 1944, with instructions that it be returned to him should he survive the war, and that, in the event of his death, it should be posted to you.

With condolences, we are, dear sir,

Yours, etc.

Menheniot, with a shaky hand, put the letter down on the table at his side, stood up, and quickly sat down again, for his knees trembled like his hand. Too many emotions assailed him in too close formation. Sometimes he had tried to measure realistically the extent to which the dream-world he inhabited could come true. It was impossible for him to save much money, and money was the root of it. Perhaps, some day, he would be able to scrape together enough to live in the lodge at the Rosemullion gates. That was as far as he dared to hope when he tried to pin himself down to reality. The way things were going, people, even rich people, would not want lodge-keepers. He might be able to rent, possibly even to buy, that humble cottage. He had examined it thoroughly. Small though it was, it was sound. He could fit into it the Georgian stuff he had here. He could live in it with some dignity. He chose that world consciously. And if he was not in Rosemullion, he would be on Menheniot land. "For a day in thy courts," he would murmur, "is better than a thousand. I had rather be a door-keeper in the house of my God than to dwell in the tents of wickedness." This reflection had never seemed to him incongruous.

And now, suddenly exploding in his head, was the consciousness that there was no question of scraping, no question of a lodge. He could buy Rosemullion! And side by side with this was the thought of what had made it possible. Young Phil—that engaging, life-accepting boy, more Menheniot than he—young Phil was dead. He had heard of ghouls on the battlefield who searched the pockets of their dead comrades. He felt one himself. He felt quite sick.

His meal had gone cold before he found the strength to open the second envelope. It was thin. Whatever Phil had to say from the grave had been said briefly. He opened it at last.

DEAR ROGER,

If you receive this at all, you may be sure that you are, then, the last of the Menheniots. Springing from the old scoundrel who dodged his creditors in the eighteenth century, there were a fair number of them. I am the last of that bunch. They became rich, but in recent decades the money has worn a bit thin—1929 and all that. However, it wasn't so bad that any of them jumped out of skyscrapers or became washers-up in drugstores. I've made a bit of it fly since it all became mine at the irresponsible age of twenty, but I think you'll find there's still a useful sum. Why should I give it all to you? Because you're the only person I can think of to give it to. That's the sort of life I've led—plenty of acquaintances, no friends. I had my hopes at one time, but this isn't the time for going into that. And so it leaves just you—Menheniot to Menheniot, as I remember you once said. That's how you like it to be, isn't it? Well then, let it be like that. So far as I shall be concerned, as well that way as any other. If you think you can smell out an undertone of bitterness, let me add that I liked what little I saw of you, and if you care to think of me occasionally—why, so much the better.

Ever yours—though how silly that will sound if you receive this!   PHIL MENHENIOT

PART TWO

By Mr. Menheniot

CHAPTER SIX

I

AFTER my first visit to Rosemullion, that one so long ago when I arrived there on a bicycle, I spent most of my holidays in the district, but they always came in full summer weather. The first visit, the one in 1919, was in May; and all these others missed something of the enchantment of that time. For it is in spring that the place is at its best. Nowhere else that I know do you find shrubs like the Cornish shrubs of spring-time. After I had gone there to live I learned that even May is late for them. Through March and April Rosemullion is glorious with camellias and forsythia, pyrus and rhododendrons, to say nothing of innumerable shrubs that you don't meet elsewhere and that I needn't bother to put down here. All this lighting up the air, and on the ground the daffodils and snowdrops, the small blue anemones and the crocus. It was to this—to the earlier-than-May Rosemullion—that I came when the place was mine. I had never seen it before; I had not imagined anything so beautiful. I had thought of March as a savage month, and here I was in a March of blue sky and soft air.

The Saras had agreed to come and look after the house for me, but I didn't want them there till it was in order. They had had a hard life during the war, and I sent them off for a long holiday. I put my furniture into store until I should need it. It had seemed a lot as it stood around me in that London house, but it wouldn't make much impression on Rosemullion. There would be much to buy, and now I wouldn't have to be for ever "besting," as Mrs. Sara would say, about how I spent a pound or two.

I was so happy at this time that I hardly knew what to do with myself. All over England were people with houses and land who were struggling to make ends meet, to keep roofs over their heads, and as often as not failing, selling up, and going off to face a very different sort of life from what they had been used to. With me, it was the other way about. Life, indeed, would be different for me, as for them. But I was going back to Rosemullion, the house that for centuries had not known a Menheniot, and I had the means to make it what I wanted it to be.

If I say I was exalted, I shall not be putting it too high. I was in a state of such foolish happiness that I went down to Cornwall without bothering so much as to arrange where I was to stay. I spent a night in Plymouth, and the next day hired a car that took me to Rosemullion. Then I sent the car back and left all to luck.

I spent a happy hour wandering about the gardens. They had been neglected for years, and this delighted me. There would be so much to do, so many plans to make. That *my* thoughts and *my* hands would be the ones to bring beloved Rosemullion back to beauty: this seemed good and right.

I had the keys of the house in my pocket, and went inside to make notes about what must be done. For the time of year, it was remarkably warm, and I came out on to the terrace to eat a few sandwiches I had brought with me. They were in a small bag with my night things. I had nothing else.

Henry Savage was sitting on an old oak seat on the terrace. Behind him, against the wall of the house, a fountain of forsythia sprayed up. They made an odd contrast: this springing gold with the sunshine upon it and this thin rusty-black man. A black wide-awake hat had been put down on the stone by his feet, so I saw his face in that first glance. His untidy beard and his hair were iron-grey. He was looking over the countryside with hooded eyes, set deep on either side of a massive eagle-beak of a nose. His clothes were black and careless, and he wore a parson's collar. He was leaning forward with both hands clasped on the knob of a blackthorn stick. I felt annoyed at sight of him looking so much at home there. He rose as I approached, and he was immensely tall and thin. I should have liked to ask him what he was up to, trespassing on my terrace, but his appearance daunted me. He came forward and held out his hand. "Mr. Menheniot?" he asked.

I said that I was Mr. Menheniot, surprised that he should know me. We sat down side by side on the seat.

"I had heard," he said, "that a Mr. Menheniot had bought the place. I have been expecting you for some time. I was taking my walk, and from down in the pasture I saw you go into the house, so I thought you might be the new owner. I often walk this way," he added. "My favourite route comes through your grounds. I hope I shall have your permission to continue to use it?"

I forgot my annoyance. There was a courtesy about him that I could not resist. I invited him to walk through the place as often as he wanted to. Then we were sharing my sandwiches; and after that he lit a clay pipe, first cutting a plug of thick black tobacco into the palm of his hand with a penknife. He said nothing as he smoked. We sat there looking out over the country, and I was happy in his presence.

"You won't find a welcome down here," he said at last. "The tombs of some of your people are in my church, and that's all that anyone round here knows of them They see the tombs Sunday after Sunday—that is, those who come to church—precious few—but who the Menheniots were or what they did I don't suppose a man-jack of 'em either knows or cares. Still, that's only to be

63

expected. There've been a good many generations since the last Menheniot disappeared, and plenty of changes of family at the house to confuse memory."

I was sorry to hear that my very name was now unknown at Rosemullion. I had hardly expected a committee of welcome, but it would have been pleasant to learn that some memory of us lingered in the place which we had made so long ago and lived in through centuries.

Henry Savage got up and knocked out his pipe. "Well," he said, "I don't envy you. Places like this are doomed. Of course, this isn't as bad as some. Lutyens turned the house into a pretty toy. Still, you'll have your work cut out. It's a contracting age. Everything is diminishing: men's houses, men's hearts and men's souls. Well, thank God he'll soon be taking me out of it all. I shall be ninety next month."

I was amazed. I should have given him no more than seventy years. He looked and spoke like a man in lean vigour of body and mind. I think his few remarks had left me looking crestfallen, for he laid a bony hand on my shoulder and said: "I trust I haven't discouraged you. When are you moving in?"

I said that I didn't know, and confessed that I had been so foolish as to make no arrangement about a lodging. I asked him if there was a cottage where I might take a room.

"There's the vicarage," he said. "Yes. You'd better stay with me. I shall be having my son Will back soon, but in the meantime you can have his bed."

I thanked him. He stirred feelings of awe in me, even of fear; but I did not wish to offend him by a refusal.

"Come along then," he said. "There are two miles to walk."

We set off southward, in the direction of the sea. Mr. Savage was a cross-country walker. Here and there we were in a lane, but most of the time we were walking through pastures and spinneys, and if a gate barred the way he was over it with an agility I could not equal. "I like to do my five or six miles a day, rain or shine," he said. "I've been doing it now for sixty-five years and established a sort of momentum. Yes. It was in this month—in March—that I came to the vicarage sixty-five years ago. I was an aspiring young man—Rugby—Balliol. I'd just married. Winchester was my lowest ambition. Canterbury did not seem remote. Well, glory be to God—I've been spared that. It's a bit late now even for Truro."

He laughed and smacked the crest off a ripple of furrow with his blackthorn. We were edging round a ploughed field. "Soon be there," he said. And then, a moment later, "Yes, soon be there now, in every sense of the word."

In the hedge that we were passing the hazel catkins were dangling their myriad tails of dusty pollen. The sun shone on them, and across the earthy ripples of the field, elms, flushed with copper, stood up against the blue sky, and the rooks were wrangling over them. Mr. Savage did not seem to notice any of these things that stirred me so deeply, but I had a sense of his belonging to this scene as I did not. He struck at a hazel with his stick, and a luminous pollen-halo exploded into the air.

We came at last to a narrow valley. The land at its head was flattened out and thickly wooded, and here, seeming in danger of being grown-in and smothered, were the church and vicarage. A stream went in singing cascades down the valley, and in the distance, near the sea, the prospect opened a little, to show a hamlet, and beyond it a beach, and beyond that the sea, quiet now, but sending to us the noise of its heave and rise and fall. Here by the church, it was cold. "The sun misses us for most of the year," Mr. Savage said. Ferns and moss abounded, underfoot and even in the trees. These were mostly

Cornish elms, aged and tattered. Winter heliotrope rioted among the grave-stones. The scent of its flowers drenched the air.

We walked through the churchyard, and a gap in the farther wall led to the vicarage lawn, which was mostly moss and helxine. Under the walls of the house daffodils were blooming. They grew up through a strangle of garlic that was not yet in flower.

The wind that day was off the sea. It blew upon us up the valley, and, though it was light and southerly, it was enough, now that the sun was gone, to make me feel cold. Mr. Savage took from my hand the bag that contained my few things. "Let's go in," he said.

From outside, it was an ungracious house, a big rectangular box of granite that had been put up, I guessed, in mid-Victorian times. Inside, it was cold, of a coldness that seemed to strike at you palpably as you entered. We walked straight in through the open door. I was to discover that Mr. Savage never locked his door. Sometimes he would remember to bang it shut before going to bed, but as often as not it would remain open all night. During my stay with him I once rose early and came down the stairs to be arrested, fascinated, half-way by sight of a badger grunting and shuffling about in the hall, sticking its snout into the row of dirty boots that were always ranged there along the wall.

This hall, which was the first thing I saw of the vicarage, was paved with stone, and so was every room on the ground floor. The hall was more cloakroom than anything else. I never knew Mr. Savage wear any suit other than the one he wore when first I met him, but he had innumerable hats, boots and walking-sticks. The hats, old and rusty, were on nails driven into the wall; the boots, that were never cleaned, were ranged along the skirting-board, and the sticks stood wherever there was a

66

corner to lean them into. He would come down from his study, kick off his carpet slippers, shove his feet into the first pair of boots he came to, grab a hat and stick, and be off. Amid this paraphernalia in the hall a surplice fluttered.

Into this hall we came, then, that first day. Mr. Savage changed into his carpet slippers, then went before me up echoing uncarpeted stairs. At all events, my heavy country shoes raised echoes; but his carpeted feet whispered like the voice of a ghost.

He was beginning to oppress me. His great age, his few words, something dark and mysterious that flowed out of him, weighed upon my spirit. Oh, I hated this world and all its ways none the less for being now, as I thought, securely out of it; but there was something about Mr. Savage that, I felt, didn't hate the world, didn't hate anything, but held everything in such light regard, myself included, that my hate seemed as meaningless as, to me, any enthusiasm for the age we lived in would have done. The sense that he had passed beyond both love and hate to understanding made him oppressive. To be understood makes us feel small. It inscribes our limits.

But there it was. I had accepted his invitation, and his courtesy was perfect. He was going before me now like a porter, carrying my bag.

The house was dark as well as cold, for all the walls were painted in a green that was almost black. And then my spirits rose quickly, for on the landing Mr. Savage opened a door and stood aside for me to enter, and I walked into an airy lightness. He said: "This is my son Will's room. I haven't seen him for five years. He's been in the army. But we're expecting him any day, and Mrs. Hocking has aired the sheets and blankets. You'll be all right here. If Will comes back before Rosemullion's ready perhaps we'll be able to fix up another room for you."

67

I thanked him, and he said: "The room opposite is my study. Come across when you're ready. Then I'll make some tea."

He shut the door, and I stood there idly for a moment, wondering why a soldier should not in five years have seen his father. Men *did* have leave. And I wondered, too, as I began to look about the room, how it came that a man of ninety should have a soldier son. He would be at least, I thought, a veteran, a weathered colonel, or some such, but this was a boy's room. The walls were whitewashed and light apple-green curtains rippled at the open window. There were many photographs hanging on the walls, standing on the chest of drawers and on the mantelpiece. They were of cricket teams and football teams, and there were dates written beneath them, so that I felt as though this were a biography under my eyes and I could walk with young Will Savage, whose recurring image identified him among many changing faces, through prep school and public school up to this last of the photographs: "Exeter College Eight, 1939." He was twenty-five, his father had said, so no doubt that would be his first year at the university. The story ended there. There was no picture of the soldier who hadn't seen his father for five years. With all that schooling, he couldn't have seen much of his father before joining the army. I began to wonder whether Will Savage was not as much a stranger to his father as he was to me. But this prodigal seemed to be lovingly awaited. The room was in perfect order. There was even a fire laid in the grate.

I opened a long drawer to put away my few things. It was full of stuff: wickets and bats, wicket-keeping gloves, a few old Hornby engines and trucks. On top of his chest of drawers was a pair of book-ends: rabbits with their scuts holding the books tight: *Kim, Winnie the Pooh, The Wind in the Willows, Black Beauty, Peter the*

Vhaler, and so forth. I opened one of the books and on
he fly-leaf read, written in a childish hand:

WILLIAM SAVAGE

Penmaen Vicarage, Cornwall, England,
Europe, the World, the Universe.

Steal not this book for fear of shame,
For in it is the owner's name,
And when you die the Lord will say
Where is the book you stole that day?
And if you say you do not know
The Lord will say Go down below.

I slipped the book into place between the others, took
look at the young smiling face of the Oxford rowing-
1an, and, somehow deeply disturbed, walked across the
1nding and knocked at Mr. Savage's door. He bade me
ome in.

There was only one thing in common between this
)om and the boy's room I had just left: photographs
ood on the mantelpiece, on the cluttered writing-table,
n the tops of low book-cases. They were so many that you
)uld not help looking at them wherever your eye turned,
nd they were all of the same woman. I fought down my
uriosity, but as soon as Mr. Savage left the room, saying,
Excuse me. I'll go down for the tray," I got up to look
t them.

Two things at once struck me. First, the woman was
)ung and of rare beauty. I should say there were fifteen
r twenty photographs there, and they showed no progres-
on in years. She might be twenty or twenty-five. Her
1ce had a Pre-Raphaelite gravity. Her beauty was not of
re or any sort of visible animation. She might, in all
1ese photographs, have been a painting by Rossetti of his

blessed Damozel. The beauty was withdrawn and interior
It was a very quiet face.

The second thing was that all the pictures were posed
They had nothing to do with the modern snapshot school
They belonged to the early days when the photographer
arranged a picture, and the sitter held the pose, with the
camera shutter off. This helped the Pre-Raphaelite
illusion. She was reading a book; brushing her hair that
fell below her waist; looking through a window, with one
long arm upraised, holding back the curtain; leaning
down from the chair she sat in to tie her shoe-string
Evidently these pictures had been posed by someone who
knew and loved the various motions and graces of her
body.

"I took them all myself," Henry Savage said. "But
gave up photography long ago."

I turned, confused to have my curiosity discovered. His
carpet slippers had permitted him to come in unheard
carrying the tea-tray. He put it down on a corner of the
writing-table, and then came to me. He rested a hand on
my shoulder in a way he had, and we stood side by side for
a moment looking at one of the pictures. It was an outdoor
one. She stood beneath an apple-tree in blossom, one lifted
arm resting on the trunk, the other drooping at her side
holding a large hat.

"She was my wife," he said. "We married when I came
here sixty-five years ago. She died three years later."

He turned brusquely to the tea-table. Thinking of that
boy's room across the passage, I said: "Your *first* wife."

He answered: "My wife," in a tone that warned me to
say nothing more.

There was no fire in the room, and it was getting colder
He had boiled the kettle, a flimsy tin affair, on a Primus
stove that stood in the fireplace. The nauseating smell of
methylated spirit filled the room, and Mr. Savage got up

70

nd opened the window. The sound of the sea's surge ame in. The tide was rising.

"I apologise," he said, passing a plate of biscuits. "I hould have liked to do something better for you."

We drank the tea and ate the biscuits. "I don't trouble Irs. Hocking more than I can help," he said. "If I'm in t midday, she cooks a meal. But usually I'm tramping, nd I look after myself."

"Not self-indulgently," I could not help saying.

"There's not much left to indulge at ninety," he said.

Certainly this was not a self-indulgent room, if one verlooked the photographs, which seemed to be the ndulgence of a memory that could not die. The floor was overed with brown worn linoleum. The brown velvet urtains at the window might have been there to welcome he new vicar and his bride sixty-five years ago. The book-helves were stuffed with dark volumes, and the two arm-hairs had burst their upholstery and released their prings. Looking through the window, I saw the evening rawing in darkly. The valley was obscure, but a fretted noving whiteness beyond it was the rising tide.

"I think, you know," Mr. Savage said, as though a really lorious idea had suddenly struck him, "we'd better have fire."

It seemed to me that for a man of his years he had had heavy day. How far he had walked before I met him I id not know, but since then he had been in incessant novement. Not that he looked tired: far from it. But I aid: "If you will tell me where to find things, I'll see to he fire. And while I'm at it, I'll wash the cups."

"Oh, it won't be so easy as that," he said airily. "It's nore than a matter of finding things. There's wood to be ut. Come along."

We went down through the dark house, left the tea-tray n an enormous gloomy kitchen, and passed thence

through a door that led into a walled yard. A sawing-hors
stood in the middle and the branches of trees wer
higgledy-piggledy round the walls. Mr. Savage brought
two-handed saw out of a shed, took off his coat and hun
it on a nail driven into the wall, and said: "I haven't bee
bothering with fires. I just wrap up in an old blanke
That does well enough. But with Will due home, I'
better start a log-pile. Well, come on."

We heaved a branch on to the horse and began to sav
I was in poor condition for this unaccustomed exercis
and was glad when he said: "That'll do. Enough to se
us through the evening is all we need now." He wa
undistressed by his efforts. We carried the logs up to th
study and piled them inside the fender. "Now," he sai
"if you want to wash up, you can. I'll get the fi
started."

When I went back to the kitchen, the great room w
quite dark. I struck a match and found a candle by tl
sink. There was only cold water. It didn't take me lor
to wash those few things, but I didn't hurry back.
lingered there, bemused by what I had seen and what
had divined: this bare, bleakly furnished barrack, the
two oddly assorted lives: the boy with his room full
playthings, looking forward to such future as there cou]
be in this world for anyone, the man adrift in dreams of
past that even to me, so much nearer to him in age tha
his son was, seemed immeasurably remote.

There were no curtains to the kitchen window, and tl
light of the candle, little though it was, sufficed to deepe
the darkness out there, so that suddenly I had a sense
being watched, and something amounting almost to frig]
took hold of me as I listened to the rising wind, to the no
heavier thud of the waves upon the land, to the sound
the trees beginning to move uneasily through all the
battalions in seige about the house. A word that M

72

Savage had spoken to me on the terrace at Rosemullion came back to my mind: "I have been expecting you for some time." I hadn't paid much attention when he said it, but now it rushed upon me, and what on earth, I asked myself, had he meant by that? How could he have been expecting me, knowing nothing of me? An impulse to go out of that house was strong. But now it was dark, and the weather was becoming wild, and I had no sense of where I was. I could not easily have found my way to Rosemullion. I took up the candle and used it to light me back to Mr. Savage's study.

As soon as I had opened the door my apprehensions seemed foolish. The brown velvet curtain was drawn across the window; a paraffin lamp was lit, hanging from the ceiling; and in the fireplace the logs were burning well. Mr. Savage stood upright on the hearth, cutting plug tobacco into his left palm. He looked gentle, grave and benevolent. We sat down in the broken chairs on either side of the fire.

"So that American boy got killed," he said without preamble.

The words startled me as much as I had been startled in the kitchen by my recollection of what he had said on the terrace. My surprise must have been evident, for he went on: "Well, if he hadn't, you wouldn't have been here, would you? You hadn't a penny to bless yourself."

This was too much. I sprang up in agitation, but he only laughed gently and said: "Sit down, Mr. Menheniot. There's nothing to be alarmed about. I'm no wizard or soothsayer. You haven't already forgotten that young Phil was quartered for a time at Rosemullion?"

"Oh . . ." I said, my wits at last waking up.

"I saw a good deal of him. The horrible modern vocabulary includes the word hard-boiled. Young Menheniot thought himself hard-boiled. Indeed, he said to me one day: 'Don't get me wrong, Mr. Savage, I'm a hard-boiled guy.' "

He was smoking a churchwarden pipe, and as he pulled on it he chuckled. "Hard-boiled! I've rarely met a more sentimental young man. From what he told me, you're another, but you're old enough to know better."

I suppose I looked contrite. He reached for a log and threw it on the fire, and I noticed the grey woollen mittens on his thin hands and long wrists. "Well, never mind all that," he said cheerfully. "Now that I've brought you here, let's make ourselves comfortable. Hark at that!"

The trees had gone beyond shuddering and whimpering. Suddenly they shrieked and a spatter of rain rattled like shot on the window. And I saw the room then not as it was now, with me in it keeping him company and with fire leaping, but, as I had gathered was usually the case, with himself alone, with the hearth dead; and, but for that chance meeting with me at Rosemullion, he would have been like that now, with the tide's dirge beating on the beach, and the wind and the rain. There he would have been, wrapped, as he had said, in an old blanket. . . . It would have driven me mad. My eyes sought his, full of apprehension.

He said placidly: "It was no chance meeting with you at Rosemullion," and this echo of my thought set my fears leaping anew.

"I knew you would be here sooner or later, for when I said I brought you here I wasn't speaking merely of bringing you to this house to-day. I mean I brought you to Cornwall."

There was nothing I could say to that. Let him go on. Let him tell me in his own way.

"Phil told me that you had spent a good many holidays in these parts. But you never got down to my church. Not so far as I know. I never saw you there."

74

"No," I said. "I never did. Seeing that it's only a few miles from Rosemullion, it's extraordinarily hidden and hard to stumble on."

"A few miles—yes. But all the Menheniots—all of 'em who died at Rosemullion—made the journey. It's out there now," he said, waving his long arm, holding the pipe; "half a minute's walk from you, all the dust of your people and the rigmaroles that were written about 'em."

He got up and took a cool pipe from a rack containing half a dozen. "They get wet on a night like this," he said, standing tall in front of the fire. "The roof leaks." He filled his pipe, and added: "Well, let the Ecclesiastical Commissioners worry about that. I shan't, at my age, and I doubt whether the ghosts do, poor chaps."

When the pipe was going and he had replenished the fire, he said: "Well, young Phil Menheniot had more curiosity than you. It was among the tombs that I first met him. There is one of them so high-flown that it has inscriptions in Latin, Greek and Hebrew. He asked me to translate, and I was able to oblige him. That's how it started."

Of course it was. Being so near to the Menheniot church, Phil had naturally come to look at it. I had been building a mystery in a mind bemused by my strange companion, by his lonely house, and by the boisterous, but still quite normal, sounds of a late winter night in the country. But there was no mystery. I took hold of that fact, and my mood lightened.

"If you'll permit me, sir, I shall drink," Mr. Savage said politely. "Join me if you like, but you don't look a drinking man."

I asked to be excused. He unlocked an oaken corner-cupboard and took out a bottle of brandy and a glass. "I like it neat," he said; and when he had poured and sipped he went on: "I didn't know who the boy was that first time, but he was back again a few days later, and then he

75

told me he was an American Menheniot. We had a high old time."

He was sitting back in his chair now, the glass in his hand, his slippered feet resting on a great iron-studded oak chest that stood alongside the fireplace. "This thing," he said, smacking a foot down on it, "is stuffed with all sorts of parish records. Plenty in there about the Menheniots, believe me. To read what's in here and then to read some of the epitaphs—well, that's an amusing study. You're no mystery to me, you Menheniots. I know you inside out. I've been through all this—intended to write a book on the history of the parish—but bless my soul, there are books enough without my adding to it all. Still, it was in my head, and I could answer Phil's questions."

I said it surprised me that he had asked questions: he had seemed, during his visits to me in London, unimpressed by the Menheniot story.

Mr. Savage tipped some more brandy into his glass. "I told you," he said, "that he was a sentimentalist. Those meetings with you were manna to him. You don't seem to have looked an inch below the surface of him, if you'll excuse my saying so, Mr. Menheniot. He remembered every word you told him. Did you ever drink with him?"

There had been no more than a sip, I assured him.

"Ah, well," he said, "it's a good lubricant if you want to unlock a mind. He was so full of the Menheniots that it was easy to convince him that he should leave all his money to you."

This shocked me. "Mr. Savage . . . !" I began, but he waved me down with a flourish of his churchwarden. "No need to get excited," he said. "Put on some wood, there's a good fellow."

I did so. Sparks flew up the chimney, rain hissed down; and all round the house now there was a roar and rumble.

"He had to leave it to somebody," Mr. Savage said

reasonably, "so why not you? He was going to die anyway. I knew that. I always know when a man's going to die. When you're my age, there seems nothing remarkable about that. You become easy and familiar with Brother Death. He's not a bad chap. Why not have just a tot, my dear boy?"

I felt that I really should. There was no second glass in the corner cupboard, so I lit the candle I had brought from the kitchen and made my way down through the shadowy house. Once I had left the warmth of the study, the damp cold struck at me like the breath of a tomb. I was feeling miserable to my heart's core. I had arrived at Rosemullion that morning—and how far away already this morning seemed!—full of a happiness, an expectancy, that permitted me utterly to forget Phil Menheniot, the dead man to whom I owed everything; and now here he was, suddenly wrenched back into the front of my consciousness with a brutality that included what seemed to me this shocking circumstance of him and Mr. Savage discussing me as his heir. I shivered, as if I had suddenly realized myself to have been his executioner; and then I noticed a line of yellow light pencilled on the darkness ahead. The kitchen door was ajar, and the room was not in darkness as I had left it.

My first impulse was to go back and tell Mr. Savage, but I knew him well enough already to feel that an unexpected light in the kitchen was hardly a thing to interest him; so I went forward and pushed open the door. A shapeless woman with bulging ungainly legs looked up from the table on which a candle burned. "Who are you? What are you up to?" she asked sharply.

It was what I wanted to ask her; but I am never good at a first encounter with a stranger, so I said: "Mr. Savage kindly asked me to stay the night. I just looked down to pick up a glass."

77

"Oh," she said, "he's at that again, is he? Well, don't encourage him. Anyway, I'm off." She began to pull on an oilskin coat. "You needn't say I was here. Or, if you must, say that Miss Hocking, his sister-in-law, looked in to straighten up a bit."

She put on a sou'wester hat, took up a basket from the table, and went off through the door into the yard. I stood for a moment peering out into the slashing rain and the howling wind; then I shut and bolted the door, took a glass, and went upstairs. Mr. Savage was still comfortably relaxed, his feet on the oak chest, his pipe drawing well. "I hope you didn't disturb Miss Hocking," he said.

"Well, there was a woman—a big shapeless woman ——"

He chuckled. "My sister-in-law, Annie Hocking. She looks in now and then to steal my food. Did she have a basket?"

"Yes."

"A pity you didn't peep inside. You'd have been surprised."

I had put water into the glass which I now held out to Mr. Savage. He poured in brandy, and said: "Well, now that Annie Hocking is gone I don't suppose anyone else will disturb us. I wanted to go on telling you about young Phil, but we shall have time enough for that. Let me tell you about Annie—my relative by marriage, but a blood relative of you and Phil."

That is how it was. Every time I thought this conversation was settling down into a normal course out would come a remark like that to shoot me off the rails again.

"But now that Phil's dead, I haven't a relative in the world!" I cried.

"Folk memory is an odd thing," he said, looking contemplatively into his glass. "I'm usually inclined to trust it. In a place like this you'll find all sorts of stories going

78

round. The people who tell them haven't a leg to stand on if you question them. They couldn't give you one thing that you could call a fact of history, but they're right, all the same, more often than not. One of these days, if you get to know Annie Hocking a little better, she'll say to you: 'It's up to Rosemullion we Hockings ought to be.' She won't be able to tell you why she thinks so, but I can tell you."

His foot thumped the chest. "It's in there," he said.

It was, in fact, a laconic entry in the diary of an eighteenth-century predecessor of Mr. Savage in the vicarage. "Alice Phillpotts, an impudent baggage, has been bed-warmer once too often at Rosemullion. Now Sir Roger has given her a fat belly."

That was the clue, and Mr. Savage had followed it up, with the help of the parish documents, from the christening of young Jacky Phillpotts, the fruit of Alice's fat belly, through his marriage and many other births and marriages, to the two Miss Hockings, one of whom Mr. Savage himself had married. "It was not till after she was dead," he told me, "that I discovered her illustrious ancestry. Rather diluted, of course, by then. Like your own. But still, you and Annie Hocking conceivably have a corpuscle or two of Menheniot blood in you."

It was not a flattering thought. I recalled the woman in the kitchen, coarse of body, limbs and face, and I hoped Mr. Savage would keep his knowledge to himself.

He got up, stretched himself to his great height, and laughed down at me. "It just occurs to me," he said, "that, through his mother, my son Will has about as much Menheniot blood as you have."

He drained his glass, put it down on the mantelpiece, and said: "But still—Menheniots! What do *they* come to?"

Now, I am a quiet and modest person; but that galled

79

me. A protest rose to my lips, but before I could utter it he interrupted.

"Mr. Menheniot, I am forgetting my manners. Night after night I sit here alone, and food means nothing to me, but it should mean something to my guest. There's nothing in the house fit to eat, unless you have a fancy for bread and salt—a classic but insufficient repast. We shall dine out."

It sounded as grandiloquent as if he were about to take me forth to a famous West End eating-place, but the sounds of the night, undiminished in their ferocity, made the thought of going out unwelcome, even to assuage the hunger which had been gnawing me for some time. I had eaten an early breakfast in Plymouth, and since then nothing but a sandwich at Rosemullion and a biscuit here. Even so, I was ready to stay where I was. But Mr. Savage had blown out the lamp, put a screen in front of the fire, and was at the door with a lighted candle in his hand. "Come, my dear fellow," he said.

We went down into the cold hall, and among the things hanging from nails there I found oilskins and sou'wester hats. Wellington boots stood by the wall. We arrayed ourselves, and Mr. Savage took an old-fashioned bull's-eye lantern and lit it. He pulled open the door and we stepped out into the scream of the night. "I thought it appropriate," he shouted, as the rain lashed and pattered on our oilskins, "that we should dine at the Menheniot Arms."

It is about three-quarters of a mile from the church and vicarage to the cluster of cottages called Penmaen. The pathway is barbarous, nothing but a stony track, dropping steeply. Trees on either hand reach to an attenuated height, seeking the air and light above this gulch. Beyond them on one side are fields in the midst of which vast stones, smoothed and polished by the centuries, lie like the backs of whales half out of water. On the other a stream leaps towards the sea, sucking and gurgling and slapping its way over and between impeding rocks.

That is how I was eventually to see it; but that night I saw little save the white tossing manes of the water on my left and the scud of overhead cloud through which a full moon occasionally could be seen leaping the chasm from one darkness to another. It was a matter of feeling and hearing rather than seeing. Mr. Savage had taken my arm and was swinging the lantern low so as to reveal the stony impediments that went by the name of path. Even so, I found it difficult enough to stand upright, for though down here in the glen the wind was not troublesome, the water flowed underfoot as though, soon, path and stream would be one downward swirl. The stream was raving with the tons of water that had drained into it, and the wind overhead was shaking the trees and sending down drenching showers. Again I thought I would rather have starved than chase my dinner through such confusion; but Mr. Savage was unperturbed. Indeed, he seemed to be enjoying himself. "Quite a night, Mr. Menheniot!" he shouted. "Dinner or no dinner, I think it does a man good to be out occasionally in such weather. I rarely miss getting out when it's like this. It opens your eyes to a thing or two!"

My own eyes were almost useless. My spectacles were streaming. I felt as if I were swimming under water, and a trickle from the edge of my sou'wester began to invade my spine. With his uncanny way of seeming to divine my thoughts, Mr. Savage bellowed: "Wonderful invention, these sou'westers. You can understand on a night like this where they get their name from. This wind is sou'west. Well, not far to go now."

I was glad to hear that, for a turn of the path now took us into the open. The wind had its way with us, stopping us for a moment dead in our tracks, and before us was the chaos of the sea. Its thunder prevailed over every other sound: a furious bellow followed by the back-flow of the shingle that was like a harsh rasping breath in-drawn to furnish the power for the next bellow. The waves came in, rank upon rank, and as each lifted up its crest the wind seized it and ripped it off and flung it shoreward in a smoky drench.

Mr. Savage stood there looking out upon this primeval welter as though in a communion he was disinclined to break. To our right I could see a dark sickle of cliff, and within the hollow of it, and thus to some extent sheltered from the insanity of the night, a few lights were burning. These, I supposed, belonged to the houses that made the village of Penmaen. Mr. Savage took my arm again and began to lead me in that direction. "Let us reluctantly seek the companionship of our fellow-sinners," he said.

We crossed the shingle, heeling over, till our feet found a road of sorts, and suddenly the wind let us go and I was able to stand upright and breathe. I stood still for a moment, recovering myself. It was this moment that Mr. Savage chose to say: "Young Phil told me you're crazy about the eighteenth century and want to re-create it. Well, you know, the weather could do this then, as now. It wasn't all Adam fireplaces and Chippendale chinoiserie. That's the Menheniot Arms over there. Come."

It was easy to see why men had chosen to build their homes within the crook of this protective elbow of land. The houses were few, but they were snug. Boats were pulled up high and dry. Through an uncurtained window here and there I had domestic glimpses, and we passed an open-fronted shed lighted by a lantern beneath whose beams a man was sorting out withies for the making of lobster-pots. We had stepped into tranquillity on the edge of chaos. Even the rain, or most of it, was sweeping inland above our heads.

Well, that is what Penmaen came to: a cove rather than a bay, a harsh shingle bar rather than a sandy beach, and off shore were rocky fangs that only the experienced would venture through in boats. Thus it remained what it had always been: a place where a few people worked hard for a hard living. Men, women and children, they didn't number more than a hundred. Summer visitors avoided the place.

Menheniots! What do they come to? All very well for Mr. Savage to say that. His derogation did not by a whit diminish the exultation with which I saw for the first time the sign-board of the inn with the name upon it. The inn itself was nothing much: a flat utilitarian building of cob, which is to say mud, hardened and whitewashed. It was fitted into the joint of the cliff's elbow, and the back of it was, as they say, built into the land: that is, the cliff itself was its wall on that side. Here in front were two windows, one on either side of a glass-panelled door. The name was on a board over the door, and beneath the name was written: J. Brokenshire, Free House. Altogether, it was as humble a pub as you would find anywhere, and I wondered how J. Brokenshire managed to make a living out of it.

Mr. Savage pushed open the door and we entered a passage paved with stone. The bar was in a room to the right. A fire burned there; a couple of men were playing darts and two others sat in a settle near the fire with drinks on a wooden table before them. Mr. Savage bent to pass through the doorway, and I followed him. The men greeted him casually and went on with what they were doing. His appearing in the village pub seemed to surprise no one. He pulled off his sou'wester, shed his crackling rain-shiny oilskin, and asked, "Jim about?"

One of the dart players, poised for a throw, shouted, "Jim!" and the landlord came through a door leading into the back of the house. He was a robust middle-aged man, wearing no coat and with his shirt-sleeves rolled back to reveal tattooed forearms: a retired sailor, I correctly guessed.

Mr. Savage explained his needs, and then we moved across the passage to the room on the other side. Here, too, a fire was burning and a lamp was lit, but there was no one to share the room's respectability with us. And it was terrifyingly respectable. It was the "best"—the used-only-on-Sundays—room of any cottage. Enlarged photographs of ancestors hung on the walls. Ships in bottles and pearly nautilus shells were on the mantelpiece. A godly text or two was framed here and there, and the polished gimcrack furniture, the upright piano with a baritone solo open on the stand, had a forbidding *noli me tangere* air. Somehow I could not imagine any baritone being so impious as to make those rafters ring. Nor could I imagine that, after so much stress and tribulation, I would be rewarded with something worth eating in the Menheniot Arms.

On either side of the fireplace was an easy chair of foully-patterned imitation velvet and yellow-varnished wood. Mr. Savage sank into one of them, pulled off his wellingtons, and stretched out his socked feet on the black curly rug. Twiddling his toes luxuriously in the warmth, he asked: "What did you expect to find here, my dear Menheniot? The eighteenth century? Believe me, Jim Brokenshire is not like you. He moves with the times. Look at these chairs." He gripped the arms of his chair with fingers that, though thin, looked like steel. "I could pull 'em apart with my hands. I remember the time when Jim's father had this place, and this room would have made a Bond Street dealer's mouth water. But Jim believes in progress. He sold the lot for a few pounds to some rogue from upalong, raised the balance somehow, and created the gem that, I see, entrances you. Do you still want to go back to the eighteenth century? You'll be lonely in it nowadays. Why not accept the world you live in?"

"Do you?"

"Me? Do you think I live in this world, or the eighteenth-century world, or any other world you could imagine? My dear fellow! These few bones, these shreds of flesh—why, I forgot 'em long ago. As near as dammit, I'm a disembodied spirit. You should see me in my surplice. No wonder the church is empty. They take me for a ghost, and no one nowadays really believes in ghostly comfort."

I had nothing to say to that; and he added: "However, I can promise you more than ghostly comfort in a moment or two. Between them, Jim and his wife can produce a meal. Better a stalled ox where varnish is than a dinner of herbs with Hepplewhite."

It was more than a moment or two before our dinner appeared, but when it came it was good. What it was I do not remember, but I remember that Mr. Savage ate remarkably for a disembodied spirit and that his drink was a tumbler of brandy and water.

Jim Brokenshire hovered around as we ate, and asked at one point: "I suppose we'll soon be seeing Mr. Will home again, Mr. Savage?"

"Yes, Jim. I'm looking forward to my congregation being increased by one. That will give me five I can count on. If Mr. Menheniot here is a churchman, that will be six."

"Mr. Menheniot?"

"Ah, I thought that would surprise you, Jim. Menheniots to you are nothing but a name on your pub and a few old gentlemen with broken noses in my church. But they've been hanging round, it seems, all these years, and here's one of them back where they came from. Mr. Menheniot is going to live at Rosemullion."

"Rosemullion! That belong to Annie Hocking by all good rights, they do say."

"So I've heard, Jim. What those good rights are I've no idea, but I fancy Mr. Menheniot will get round them and live quietly in his own house."

Brokenshire had brought us what I never expected in a Cornish pub, and that was good coffee. He now left us and shut the door. "Well, there you are, my dear fellow," Mr. Savage said. "Your arrival is now announced as if by heralds. The four people you saw in the bar are the doctor, the schoolmaster, the keeper of the village shop and an inshore fisherman. Add Jim to these, and the B.B.C. itself couldn't do a better job. Still, as I've told you, the name Menheniot means nothing here now. It will go round as a bit of gossip, not as anything significant."

"I shan't mind that," I said. "There'll be no more of them, anyway, after me. I just want to bring the story to its end in peace."

He looked at me mockingly. "That's a poor view to take," he said. "Don't you feel laid upon you the duty to continue your illustrious line, to marry, and bless the world with young Menheniots? You disappoint me. I had been looking forward to a christening or two. And who are you to expect peace?"

I was nettled by all this, and answered rather sharply: "I have told you, and I expect Phil told you, too, that I loathe this world and all that it stands for. If I choose to step out of it and seek peace, who is to stop me?"

He finished his coffee and stood up. "Seek it by all means," he said. "Peace! What is peace but the kingdom of God? And the kingdom of God cometh not with observation. Let us go. The rain has stopped."

He was abrupt, as if talking a mystery to a fool whom

he did not expect to understand. "We make our lives, Mr. Menheniot," he said, "whether of peace or confusion, out of the given material. What will be given, we can neither know nor arrange."

The people in the bar shouted good night as we went through the passage. The clouds were breaking up, and overhead the moon and the stars shone amid a scurrying wrack. The wind was undiminished, but it was at our backs as we mounted the lane to the vicarage. The talkativeness had gone out of Mr. Savage and his considerate courtesy came back, somehow making a wall between us, as though denying a free and easy association. In the hall he helped me off with my mackintosh, even made me sit down while he knelt and pulled off my cumbrous wellington boots. Then he lighted me upstairs with his lantern, lit the candle in my bedroom, and put a match to the fire that had been laid ready for Will's return. "I hope you'll be comfortable here," he said. "My bedroom is next door to the study. Don't hesitate to call me if there's anything you need. I don't sleep much."

CHAPTER SEVEN

I

I DIDN'T sleep much, either. Young Will's bed was comfortable, the fire warmed the room, and I was dog-tired in body and mind. But I had been thrown too suddenly into too much. My beloved Cornwall had taken on aspects of threat and savagery, and, padding about in the room across the passage, was as disturbing a creature as I had ever come upon. I lay for a long time fretting and tossing, thinking of Phil Menheniot's visits to this place, of the illegitimate line of Menheniots now represented by Annie Hocking and Will Savage, and of many other things that kept me awake as effectively as if a pile-driver were pounding outside my window. The fire had burned out and the wind had dropped before I fell into fitful sleep.

I woke to find the morning come, and, having dressed, I went in search of my host. He was nowhere to be seen, upstairs or down. I wandered into the garden, and my spirit was soothed by the peace that had followed the night's chaos. The sky was misty but cloudless, the wind was utterly gone. The daffodils shone under the house wall, blackbirds and thrushes were running upon the drenched lawn, and here was Mr. Savage coming from the church, pushing through the gap that led from garden to graveyard. He was bareheaded, a surplice flapped loosely about him, and beneath its hem incongruous wellingtons swished through the wetness. He was carrying a Prayer Book, and I guessed that he had been conducting the eight o'clock service.

"Not a soul," he shouted cheerily. "As usual, not a soul.

Occasionally there's a pious visitor at Penmaen who honours me, but, apart from that, God and I have the place to ourselves. I always go through the service, ringing out my part and mumbling the responses. Really, it's much more comfortable to be alone—much more. Old Edwards has forgotten to stoke the boiler. It's as cold as death in there. Still, he can't do everything. He's supposed to keep down the grass in the graveyard, and he's the grave-digger, and very dignified at the graveside he is, I must say. But I wish he'd think of our bodies before they're ready for the mould. My wrists are blue, mittens or no mittens. Annie Hocking knits them for me, now that her sister's dead. A remarkable thought, Mr. Menheniot—don't you agree?—that to knit mittens may be considered a sufficient discharge of religious duty. I now have seventeen pairs."

He seemed in good fettle, and I asked if I could help him in preparing breakfast.

"Leave it to me, my dear boy," he said. "Have a look at your ancestors, and be back in a quarter of an hour. The rain got at Sir Roger pretty bad last night. Soaked, the poor chap is. He'll be glad to see a friendly face, especially one of the family."

However, I didn't want to go into the church at that moment. The mist overhead was thinning, the sun was coming through, and I was content to be out of doors. I strolled to the path that led beside the stream down to Penmaen and stood there watching the turbulent water frothing over the rocks. A man was coming up from Penmaen, and I saw that he was one of the two who had been sipping pints in the Menheniot Arms. He recognized me, shouted a good morning, and came up to shake hands. "So you're a Menheniot," he said. "Jim Brokenshire says you're opening up Rosemullion again."

So the news was spreading. "My name's Littledale,"

he said, "Doctor Littledale. Are you staying long with Mr. Savage?"

I explained how I had met the vicar, and said I should stay till his son Will came home unless I found myself intrusive.

"A rum set-up," Dr. Littledale said. "I don't think the old man wants to see Will at all. He's perfectly happy on his own. I brought Will into the world. One of my first jobs when I came down here about twenty-five years ago. He's more Hocking than Savage."

Littledale looked a man of about fifty. He would have been a youngster then. He went on to tell me that M . Savage's marriage after so many years of widowhood had still been, when he came, the village sensation. "Well," he said, "I've got one or two patients to have a look at. But I hope we'll find time for a talk now and then, Mr. Menheniot. Come and drink a cup of tea with me this afternoon. Could you?"

I thanked him and said I would; then went back to the vicarage. Mr. Savage and I ate breakfast in the kitchen. There was neither gas nor electricity in the house, and no fire had yet been lit. For his cooking, Mr. Savage made use of primus stoves. Two were roaring like plumber's blow-lamps when I came into the kitchen, and their nauseous smell filled the cold room. On one was a double saucepan in which porridge was heating. I guessed that a large quantity was made to begin with, and warmed up day after day. A kettle was boiling on the other. Mr. Savage poured a spoonful or two of a black viscous liquid from a bottle into each cup, filled up with boiling water, and announced that coffee was served. He ladled dollops of porridge on to two plates, pushed the milk-jug across to me, and we began our breakfast. After the porridge we ate bread and marmalade. It was horrible marmalade, and Mr. Savage apologized for it. "I have tried and tried," he said, "to get Annie Hocking to make jam and marmalade. But she's a lazy slut. She'd rather spend good money on this filth and save the trouble. I've given up bothering. When I contemplate the quantities of fish, flesh, fowl and what not that have passed through my old guts in the course of ninety years, I am horrified by what is necessary to keep a man alive. However, the fact remains that Sylvia made excellent marmalade."

I did not ask him who Sylvia was. I felt there was no need to do so. It was the first time he had used her name.

"Well," he said, "how were your illustrious ancestors? Reading their epitaphs, you would at least have no cause to blush—except for the hardihood of the liars who wrote them."

I said that I had not been into the church, but had talked with Doctor Littledale.

"I have never had a doctor in my life," he said. "Not even when I was born. My mother was a remarkable woman. She had nine children and dropped them all like pups. The day I was born she breakfasted with my father as usual and then said: 'I think I'll go back to bed, William.' An hour later, she rang the bell and said to her maid: 'Send to Dr. Williamson to say that his presence will not be necessary.' The next morning she breakfasted with my father as usual, and a week later was in the hunting-field. So, you see, I have escaped doctors from the beginning. However, I understand Littledale is a good man, though he hasn't been here long enough, really, for us to form an opinion."

He filled his clay pipe, and said: "Do you think you could look after yourself to-day? This is the morning when I write my two weekly sermons. I keep them to ten minutes each. Perhaps Annie Hocking will be along to knock up a midday meal. Join me if you feel like it. This afternoon I shall take my usual walk, and I like to walk alone."

I was glad to have the chance to look around that part of the country undisturbed, but said that at least I'd wash the breakfast things. "Don't bother," he shouted, half-way up the stairs. "I expect the slut will give them a lick."

However, there was a lot of hot water in the kettle and in the pot under the porridge, so I washed up and then went upstairs to make my bed and re-lay the fire and leave my room in order. I had finished by about ten o'clock, and at once walked out into what had become a warm and cheerful morning. I went through the gap and into the churchyard and through the low Norman arch of the west door.

That morning, more than ever, it seemed odd to me that I was a Menheniot. Here, on tombs and on marble plaques, their lives and deaths were recorded, and I could not figure myself living such a life as any one of them had lived, or dying such a death. They had gone down with ships in battles at sea and they had died in battles on land. They had been friends of kings, in England and in exile. Some had been statesman, and one had been a bloody-minded judge; and over them all was an aura of raffish efficiency, of knowing how to shoulder their way through the world and how to shoulder other people out of their way. Look where I would the name recurred: Menheniot, Menheniot, Menheniot. Ralph and Roger and Richard. And suddenly they were all strangers to me; their world had nothing to do with my world or their spirit with mine. Phil, I recalled, had always seemed more Menheniot than I; and I remember now that Dr. Little-dale had said that young Will was more Hocking than Savage. And that could mean more Menheniot. I recalled the face in all those photographs that stood about the room I had slept in, and it seemed to me a confident face.

92

even an aggressive one. Wandering forlornly about the empty earthy church, I felt the sort of person that a Menheniot would push ruthlessly aside. I wondered what fearful combination would result from a drop of Menheniot blood on one side and Mr. Savage's on the other.

And then I came on the plaque recording the death of Sylvia, who had made excellent marmalade, Sylvia of the upraised arms and the bending knees, Sylvia of all the bodily graces. She had died at twenty-three: "Sylvia Brookhill, fourth and youngest daughter of the Seventh Earl of Powerfleet, wife of Henry Savage, Vicar of this Parish, and himself the fifth son of the Fourth Viscount Fallbridge. In her Beauty, she was called to Heaven, to illustrate there the Perfection of her Creator's handiwork on Earth."

I sat in a pew and considered this epitaph, doubtless composed by Mr. Savage, and its hyperbole did not offend me. I knew that that was how Mr. Savage had felt about his young dead wife. Whatever other people had seen in her, that was what *he* had seen. And these titles of nobility: he was not a man who would put them down without meaning. No doubt, to him, they were valid in the eyes of God; that Sylvia was a daughter of the Seventh Earl of Powerfleet would be one ingredient of the perfection that she had been called to Heaven to illustrate.

And I was not surprised now by what he had said to me last night: "Menheniots! What do *they* come to?" For either of these great families mentioned on the plaque was of a lustre that extinguished my own.

What on earth, then, I asked myself, had Mr. Savage been doing for sixty-five years in this parish that might as well have been at the back of the moon? And I saw the answer to that, too. It was yesterday, while we were walking from Rosemullion, that he had said: "I was an aspiring young man—Rugby—Balliol—I'd just married.

93

Winchester was my lowest ambition. Canterbury did not seem remote."

That, too, no doubt, was a literal statement. This had been his induction, his springboard. There would be plenty of family influence to shift him out of it when the moment came. But Sylvia died. And, with that, so much in love was he that everything died with her: ambition and the very common sense of the universe. So here he stayed, near the beloved dust, till it was too late and the springs were dry in him. So, at any rate, I saw it; and I was sure that I was not far wrong.

II

I worked for a while that morning in the yard that the kitchen windows gave on to. I had been the cause of Mr Savage's burning logs last night instead of wrapping his old bones in a blanket, and I thought that at least I should replenish his supply. The two-handed saw we had used was the only one I could find, and an awkward thing it was. By the time I had assembled a small pile I was exhausted. Sweat dripped from my eyebrows on to the insides of my spectacles, and thus I gained of Annie Hocking the sort of view that a fish might have, looking out from an aquarium. She was working at a table in the kitchen window, a blurred, distorted, ungainly creature. I felt unhappy, aware of her scrutiny. My coat was off, my shirt sleeves were rolled back, and I was sure that she would condemn both the pallor and the skinniness of my arms. I wiped the lenses and took up the saw again. She came out and stood before me, immense. She was cut in a straight line from wide shoulders to wide hips. Her legs were grotesquely fat, with ankles obliterated. I thought of the beauty called to Heaven to illustrate perfection on earth, and wondered what Annie Hocking's sister had

94

been like. I had found no memorial to her in the church.

Annie asked truculently: "You spyin' on me?"

"Good heavens, no," I said, surprised and rather alarmed.

"'Cos if you are, you'll need to be a lot smarter than you look," she said.

She was a grey-haired untidy baggage with coarse red hands. "I reckon I got some rights here," she said. "And not only here, come to that. We'll see, some day."

We all have our dreams, and I was to discover that this was Annie Hocking's: that, some day, a swift turn of the wheel would restore to her what was hers "by all good rights," and that, somewhere, she would reign in splendour, divested, presumably, of the indignities that for so long her flesh had laid upon her. Not so different, when you come to think of it, from the dream I had myself nursed and coddled for so long. But, that morning, I was able to pull myself together with the reflection that *my* dream had already come gloriously true, that Mr. Savage and the absent Will and Annie Hocking were nothing but an odd, even amusing, digression from a course of felicity now established beyond question.

"Give us an end," she said, and took hold of one handle of the saw. I had heaved a log on to the horse, and we began to swing in unison. "You don't 'ave to push. Just pull," she commanded.

She had the advantage of me in knowing how to do this small practical thing. She made it all easier, and I didn't sweat so much. She worked like a man. We sawed for half an hour, and then she said: "That'll do," and added, "An' don't you take any notice of what 'e says about me." So I understood her gesture in helping me had been an effort towards enlisting me on her side in whatever warfare was being waged. "You'll see," she said. "When Will comes back, you'll see."

She said then that she was going to knock up a bit of lunch. When I had stacked the logs on the pile and swept up the yard, I followed her into the kitchen. Seen in daylight, it was depressing. It was a big stone-floored room, white-washed, and with a row of antique bells on springs strung along one wall. Dining-room, drawing-room, first bedroom, second bedroom, and so forth, it said on indicators over them, but many a year had passed, I guessed, since one of them had sounded its alarm. Under the chimney-piece was that mass of ironmongery known as a Cornish range, but it was dirty and uncared for. In front of it was a table on which two primus stoves stood. The kitchen sink was in a dark corner. Only a cold-water tap stood over it, supplied from a rain-tank on the roof. Drinking water came from a well whose head was in the yard.

Annie Hocking was knocking up the lunch. She had opened a tin of sardines, and these were sizzling in a frying-pan on one of the primus stoves. She was toasting bread at the roaring flame of the other. I could have done with something more than sardines on toast, but that was what we were to have. As she fussed at her task and talked, I sat on a wooden chair near the sink, idly scanning the odd assortment of tins and bottles on a shelf over it: liquid dog soap, ammonia, weed killer, various insecticides and sprays for the garden, liniment and cough cure. Saucepans and frying-pans hung on nails driven into the walls round the sink. It all looked an unsavoury mess.

"Not that I take a penny for all I do for him," Annie was saying when I started out of a reverie of how the Rose-mullion kitchen would look when I had done with it. "I wouldn't demean myself that far. My own flesh and blood I call him, seein' 'e married my sister, and 'e can treat me like a servant as much as 'e likes, but to take money would be neither right nor proper. I reckon I got some rights in his 'ouse, an' you'll see that when Will gets back."

So here it was again: rights, rights: some worm gnawing the woman, filling her with envy and covetousness. She evidently conceived Mr. Savage as being bitterly at war with her, but all I had seen in him was an amused contempt.

She ripped the opener round a tin of fruit, slopped it into a dish, put the sardines and toast on the table, and said: "Well, there it is. You can call 'im."

I went up to tell Mr. Savage that luncheon was served, and when we got down to the kitchen Annie was gone.

III

As soon as our rough meal was ended Mr. Savage snatched a stick from the assortment in the hall and set off on his walk. The day had become very lovely, and I decided to loiter to Penmaen and have a look at things there before calling on Dr. Littledale. The stream was singing down the little stony valley; the blackthorn was everywhere in bud and here and there in bloom. Occasional primroses shone in the verdant moss that filled the banks of the hedges. It could never be parched here, even in the hottest summer. The trees, bare now, would make a canopy. This would be a green and watered tunnel. Wagtails were hopping on the stones of the stream. Overhead, rooks were making a great to-do about putting a few sticks into their jerry-built nests.

I came out to the sleeping blue of the sea, and the curve of the cliff, and the minute village nestling within the comfort of that crooked arm. The rock rose sharply behind it, veiled here and there with a gossamer of blue chimney-smoke. The summit lay hard on the sky, where gulls sustained themselves effortlessly, gliding in beautiful wide curves. Suddenly I thought of my room in London, and my drear daily work among the mechanical hateful millions, and then I could have wept, so full my heart was of gratitude for deliverance. I sat upon a boulder, glad to be quiet, quit of everybody, even of Mr Savage—perhaps especially of Mr. Savage. Some way off a man in a blue jersey was fixing a new strake to a dinghy The sound of his hammer was the only sound except the mewing of the gulls, his activity the only activity in all the prospect. And it was not excessive. He seemed glad to stop now and then: to light a pipe, to straighten his back, to look about him, or simply in order to stop. I reckoned the strake would be on by this day week.

The village street was a curve of cottages—stucco over stone. The best had been done to make them hideous. The stucco was painted a dark depressing grey and the woodwork a muddy brown. Their situation defied the worst that could be done to them, but I wondered, as I sat there, why the worst had been attempted. I supposed it to be a Methodist legacy, a puritan fear of colour and gaiety, the quality of thinking that had led my man Sara—yes, he was my man now—to say to me more than once: "The uglier the better, Mr. Menheniot." Well, we'd see about that, once we got going at Rosemullion.

I could see from a distance that the middle house of this row was more pleasing than the others. It stood alone, with a lane running down each side. It was of the grey local stone, and had not been stuccoed. The woodwork was white. A few railed steps led up to a front door surmounted by a decent fanlight, and there were windows on either side of the door. "That," I thought, "is Doctor Littledale's," and so it was.

He was glad to see me, and took me into his drawing room, on the right of the small square hall. It was a charming room, with comfortable chairs covered in faded rose chintz, a fire, and a lot of water-colours on the white walls. "I'll go and call Kitty," he said; and as soon as he had left me I went to look at these pictures, my heart beating excitedly. Yes, indeed! They were what I had thought at the first glance: excellent examples of the English water-colour artists. Cozens, Sandby, Girtin, Cotman, de Wint, David Cox—even a small good Turner! Over the mantelpiece was a lovely tender thing of sheep in a fold by Samuel Palmer, and I could not help taking from my pocket the small magnifying-glass which was always with me. I was on tiptoe, scrutinizing this picture, when Littledale came back. "Ha, Kitty," he cried, "here's someone unlike your barbarous brother! Here's someone who'll worship at your own shrine!"

I turned, blushing, and Kitty Littledale came towards me, her hands outstretched to take mine, and she asked: "Do you like these things, Mr. Menheniot? Do you—really?"

There was a pleading note in her voice, as of a mother whose child had been long disparaged and who turns now to a stranger reported to have seen something in the brat.

"Indeed I like them, Miss Littledale," I said. "You must be careful to lock your doors at night, or, when I start to furnish Rosemullion, some of these will be missing."

I can now look back to this moment calmly enough, and even analyse it; and what comes out of it, with great surprise to me, is that I could ever have said a light, bantering thing like that to a woman I was meeting unexpectedly and for the first time. Usually, I was tongue-tied with women, even when they were well known to me, but I was not like that, from the first, with Kitty Littledale. Perhaps her voice had something to do with it. There was no lightness or laughter in it, but it had a quietness and gravity. Her question: "Do you—really?"

was put with such an evident deep desire that the things she loved should be understood that I was moved by her sincerity. I thought at once that she was like a water-colour herself, if a rather faded one. I don't write that in disloyalty or criticism. She pleased me wholly: her lack of flamboyance, the pale gold of her hair, the pale blue of her eyes, the gentle rustle of her clothes, which seemed to me old fashioned, though I know nothing of such matters. Her dress was of silk that had been printed in many tender colours, and these were now blurred as though they had been for a long time in hot sunlight. She was tall and thin.

Littledale said: "Show him your things, Kitty. I'll go and get the tea," and he went out, leaving us together. We didn't talk much. She said: "If you know these things, Mr. Menheniot, there's no need for me to prattle," and we moved about the room side by side. In just this way, I had often moved about salerooms and through galleries, looking at such lovely things, too poor to buy, save once or twice after a severe bout of economy or a stroke of luck. One such stroke came back to my mind now, and, standing with my back to the fire as she sat on a chair before me, I told her of it.

"I should love to have a collection like this," I said, "but I have only one or two. There's a Cotman that I got in an extraordinary fashion. I worked in a bank, you know, and I often spent my lunch-time prowling round the print-shops and galleries. That's how I first saw my Cotman. It was agony to leave it. I've never wanted a picture more. There was a lively chap among the bank clerks who was for ever offering to put me on to what he called a good thing in the racing line, and when I got back that day he had the usual certain winner. 'Come on, now, Menheniot,' he said. 'Just for once, be a sport. I'm telling you—you can't lose.' I was tempted, and I fell

The horse was what this man Richards called a rank outsider, running at a hundred to one. He explained it all to me most patiently. 'None of your backing each way,' he said. 'Put a pound on the nose, and you'll clear a hundred.' I had no idea what all this meant, but when he said the horse was named Postern Gate I remembered that there was a postern gate in the picture. This seemed to me what the betting men called a hunch, and I said recklessly: 'All right, Richards. Put two pounds on the nose for me.' That's how I got my Cotman, with a bit to spare. I think it's the only chance I ever took in my life. So as to remind myself of the occasion, I wrote Postern Gate on a piece of paper and stuck it on the back of the frame."

Miss Littledale smiled at this reminiscence, and got up and took down some of the drawings from the walls. "Look," she said, "I, too, like to have a record of my winnings."

I turned the pictures over, and there were names on the backs. "Maypole Medley." "Lone Sheiling." "Lucky Lucas."

"Good gracious!" I cried. "Don't tell me you buy your pictures out of racing winnings!"

Doctor Littledale was coming through the door, pushing a tea-trolley. My last words reached him, and he kicked the door shut behind him, stopped in his tracks and burst into laughter. "What on earth are you talking about, Menheniot?" he demanded. "Kitty . . . horse-racing? Are you trying to reach the ultimate in improbability?"

We settled in chairs round the trolley, and I repeated to him the story of Cotman and Postern Gate. He looked fondly at his sister. I had sensed the strong link of affection between them. "Kitty'd get more than a few pictures and odds and ends of furniture out of it," he said vehemently, "if people weren't mostly bloody fools

Kitty poured out the tea. "Now, now, Tom," she sai
"I do well enough."

"Well enough!" he snapped. "You're so discourage
you haven't put pen to paper for two years."

"All right now," she soothed him. "I'll put pen
paper again when I've got something to say. I neve
could write just for the sake of writing."

"You ought to get out of this. You've rotted here lor
enough."

She leaned across and laid a hand on his. "Tom—
please," she said.

He subsided at that, but I had a feeling that somethin
had almost blown up between them, and not for the fir
time.

When tea was over, he said: "You go and take you
walk now, Kit. You're looking pale." And she said
"Yes, I think I will. Leave the things. I'll wash up when
get back."

She said good-bye to me, and that she hoped we woul
meet often now that I was coming to live in the distric
and I answered sincerely that I hoped so, too. I had foun
her comforting, a woman who did not scare me, one
whom I could talk about my own things.

When she was gone, Littledale lit a pipe, and said
"Come and have a look round the place." I soon divine
that it was his sister he wanted to talk about, her roo
he wanted to show me.

It was a pleasant room on the first floor, small an
sparsely furnished. There were a writing-desk and chai
a couple of easy chairs in front of the Adam fireplac
breast-high book-cases with more water-colours on th
pale pink wall above them. The curtains were of son
modern peasant-weave stuff, buff and brown in colou
Through the window one looked on to the rise of the cli

hat embraced and protected the hamlet. It was a peaceful, unexciting room, tranquil—like Kitty Littledale, I thought. Dr. Littledale went to a book-case and began pulling out books. "Look, Menheniot," he said. "These are Kitty's. D'you know how you could have given her the greatest pleasure in the world? Simply by saying, when you read those names on the back of her pictures 'But these are the titles of your novels!'"

I was covered with confusion. I had made a fool of myself again, supposing them to be the names of horses. And I had missed the chance of giving pleasure to a woman who, I now clearly knew, I wished to please. It threw me back into my most awkward mood of embarrassment. I stammered apologies. "I'm not much of a reader. Really, I read hardly any modern stuff. But, of course, I ought to have known. . . ."

"Why ought you?" he asked morosely. "Why should I expect you to be different from all the others? She had a nice little run to begin with, and then gradually faded out. The stuff's too—well, it's like these water-colours, too delicate for the barbarians. They want it all laid on with a trowel. Either that, or painted cock-eyed. Ah, well. . . ." He put the books back into the case and began to talk about himself and his sister.

From that talk and others I had with him, I learned that he and Kitty had been left orphans when young. There was enough money for him to take his medical training, and for her, five years his junior, to go to a boarding-school. He had just qualified and had become engaged to be married, when the war of 1914 broke out.

I gathered that it was a head-strong passionate affair between him and his girl, and those were not days that counselled prudence. They married, and both went to France: he as a doctor, she as a nurse. She was killed early in the war, and he told me later, when our intimacy

was deeper, what that had meant to him. "You can'
imagine, Menheniot, the blazing hatred I felt for every
thing wearing a German uniform. I vowed that I'd ki
the first of 'em to come under my hand. I did, too. Ther
was a night raid, and our boys came back with a Germa
prisoner and with one of themselves shot through th
arm. It wasn't a serious case. I saw that at a glance.
meant nipping out a bullet and setting a broken bone.
could wait. But that German couldn't wait. He had bee
bayonetted in the bowels. But I let him wait. I dealt wit
our boy's arm first, and I tell you I took my time about i
That German was lying there groaning. I could at leas
have given him a shot of dope. I didn't. I let him groan:
big, fat chap, with eyes like a spaniel's. When I was read
for him, he was dead. I went up then out of the dugou
and sat down in the trench, smoking a shaded pipe, wit
my back to the parapet. The dawn was breaking; thing
were pretty tranquil just for the moment. I remembe
noticing the white chalk that the trench was dug throug
and the blue of some chicory flowers growing in a tuf
against the pale sky. I felt good. I had fulfilled a vow
When I went back into the dugout, no one was there bu
the dead German and our wounded chap. I had left hir
comfortable on a stretcher, but he had got up and wa
standing by the German. He had pulled away a blanke
that had been thrown over the man, and was lookin
down into his face. Hearing me come, he dropped th
blanket and looked at me steadily for a moment. He wa
no more than a boy, a private soldier. He said: 'You soc
You dirty murdering sod.' There was nothing I could d
I knew, suddenly, what I had done. I—a doctor.

"Believe me, Menheniot, there was nothing I wante
after that more than to atone for that poor devil's deatl
and I think I did. I had almost forgotten the whol
matter. There was plenty to help you to forget in thos

lays. Then came 1917, and Arras. You can take it that we were busy. I had been working for twelve hours without a break. I felt like death, and I suppose I looked it, ed to the elbows. They brought a young captain and laid him on my table, and I saw that it was the boy whose arm had set. He was half-mad with pain, and as soon as he aw me he began to bellow: 'Not him! Not that murdering sod. Someone else! Someone else!' Everyone thought t was delirium, and I gave him a shot and examined him, and saw that it was hopeless, that it would be time wasted where time was so much needed; and I made a silent sign and he was taken away. I was not going to be a murdering od again. When I had time to inquire, he was dead."

What can you say when you hear a tale like that? I, t any rate, could say nothing. I sat and looked at him with wonder and pity.

"I'm glad I told you that, Menheniot," he said. "I shall feel the better for it. All these years it's gnawed occasionally at my guts. I never told even Kitty, and there's not much I don't tell her."

They had been very close from the moment that war ended, when he returned. She had then for some time left school, and, saying nothing to him, had been trained as a dispenser. "To help you," she explained. "You will want someone now that Eve is dead." She had taken it for granted that he would not re-marry, nor did he. Eve's death and the physical shocks of the war had driven him into this solitude. Here he and Kitty had been ever since.

CHAPTER EIGHT

I

I WALKED back to the vicarage with a copy of *Lucky Luca*
in my pocket. It was not the one from Kitty's bookshelves
Dr. Littledale would not allow anything in that room to
be touched. He seemed to consider the place a shrine
rather than a workshop. He took me to his own den, as he
called it, for this house was big enough to allow them to
spread themselves, with rooms of their own. The den was
a rough and ready place of rude comfort and no distinction, reeking of tobacco. Littledale had his own copies of
Kitty's books, and it was one of these that he lent me
"You won't be able to buy a copy," he said. "Out of print.

On the path leading beside the stream uphill to the
vicarage I passed Kitty returning from her walk. She gave
me a smile and a good evening, but did not stop; and a
moment later Annie Hocking came down the same way
and said as she went by: "I've put his supper ready. Jus
warm it up."

However fine a March day may be—and that one had
been delightful—you can't expect much warmth after
nightfall, and the dusk was upon us when I reached the
vicarage. The sky was still luminous, but the earth was
dark and damp, with the trees pressing too close to the
square, ugly house. I lingered for a moment on the mossy
lawn, glad that, at any rate, it was not raining and blowing up for a gale, as it had been doing last night.

Suddenly and silently, Mr. Savage was standing at my
side, leaning on his stick and following the direction of
my glance down the valley. He said that he had had
good walk. "Never undervalue your physical apprehen-

106

sions, Menheniot. The longer I live the more I glory in my flesh—such of it as remains. What I share with the animals—seeing and hearing and smelling and feeling—becomes dearer to me. I regret the decay of my senses more than I should regret the decline of my spiritual perceptions—if I were aware of such a decline, which, thank God, I am not. It is a great mistake to suppose that a man's spirit deepens as he mortifies his body. I could make out a good case for the opposite being true, granted any spiritual aptitude to begin with. But forgive me," he added with the odd sudden courtesy that was always his. "I have been talking to myself about such matters so much all day that I forget they may bore other people." He put an arm through mine and led me towards the house. "Come in, my dear boy, and tell me what you have been doing."

I followed him up to his study, where he lit the lamp. The room was chilly, but he did not seem to notice that. I told him of my visit to the Littledales, mentally contrasting their pleasant house with this. I asked him if he knew anything of Kitty's books. "Oh, yes," he said. "I've read them all. They make me think of Mary Webb."

I confessed that I had never heard of Mary Webb. He pulled on his churchwarden pipe and looked at me sadly. I hastened to say that I had hitherto had little time for reading, and that the eighteenth-century authors had almost wholly taken such time as I had.

"Forgive my saying, Menheniot," he said, "that a specialist who is only a specialist is the worst type of uneducated brute. The purpose of education is to show the context in which everything exists. A specialist who is aware only of the price of wheat makes life a dust-bowl. The poor fool, usually, doesn't even know that he is doing it. The specialist in spiritual perversion who shuts himself up in a cave in the desert is as ignorant and misguided an ass as any of them. The odd thing is that he is trying to discover the secret of Jesus, who had a weakness for wheatfields, weddings, and a day out with the fishermen. I shall say nothing further about that or about Mary Webb or Kitty Littledale. If you wish to cure your ignorance, the resources are at your disposal."

To turn the edge of his scorn, I said that, so far as Miss Littledale was concerned, I should begin to cure my ignorance at once. I showed him the copy of *Lucky Lucas*.

"Give yourself a comfortable evening," he said. "Go down to the kitchen and have a good blow-out. Then you can light the fire in Will's room and read your book. Don't bother about me. I have eaten all that is good for me to-day."

I went downstairs, remembering that Annie Hocking had promised that supper would be ready, needing nothing but warming up. The table was set for two. A hunk of bread was on each plate, and there was an uncovered pot of the jam that was unlike what Sylvia used to make. On one of the primus stoves was a frying-pan containing sausages that had obviously been half-fried. These were what I had to warm up. A tin thrown into the sink showed whence they had come. I had watched the primus stoves being lit, and was proud when I managed this small operation for myself. The water boiled on one and I made the tea. The sausages warmed on the other. I ate without appetite or enthusiasm, commending Mr. Savage's discernment in abstaining. I washed up the few things and left the place as tidy as I could, taking the sink-basket and emptying it into the dust-bin in the yard. Then I found an old scrubbing-brush and scrubbed the greasy sink with hot water.

In the midst of these occupations, I suddenly paused, asking myself what on earth I was doing here. I was a rich man. I had come into Cornwall to take possession of a charming little house that I had dreamed of for years. I was to settle down on my ancestors' land. I was to be Menheniot of Rosemullion, with beauty about him, service at hand, decorum and propriety ruling his life. And here was Menheniot, scrubbing out a filthy sink in an ugly mouldering house, with no company but the odd creature upstairs who swerved from courtesy to contempt, and was, in any case, a disconcerting companion, with more than a hint of craziness. What on earth, I asked myself again, are you doing here? I could go back to Plymouth, make myself comfortable in the best hotel there, hire a car and a driver to bring me to and fro upon my occasions till Rosemullion was ready for me. It seemed the sensible thing to do, and no doubt I would have done it if I had not called on the Littledales. I went upstairs to Will Savage's room, lit the lamp and the fire, and wrote a letter to the firm that was storing the furniture from my rooms in London. I asked them to let me know when it would reach Rosemullion, and told them to address their answer to the Penmaen vicarage. Then, pleased with what I had done, I settled down to read Kitty's book.

II

I got up the next morning feeling very unwell. I had not been reading long the night before when a queasiness of the stomach overcame me. It seemed likely that this was due to an overheating of the room, for I had piled the fire high. I flung up the window and leaned out, taking in deep draughts of the cool damp air, and suddenly I heaved and vomited. It was a most undignified moment, but it left me feeling better. Even so, I was far from well. I couldn't fasten my mind again on the book, my stomach from time to time gave a feeble surge, and altogether I

decided that it would be best to get into bed and have
done with it. I did so, but I did not sleep well, and this
was so unusual with me that it was a sort of illness in
itself. Half-deliriously, I again and again went over the
situation I was in, calling myself a fool for being here at
all, wondering what had made me ill, deciding that it was
the wretched food I had been eating, and longing for the
ministrations of Mrs. Sara, who understood me and my
stomach so well. The form of that dirty slut Annie
Hocking kept starting up before me, an owl kept on
quavering in a tree near the window, and occasionally I
could hear Mr. Savage's carpeted feet padding in the
room across the landing. Once he gave a hearty laugh. It
was altogether a terrible night. I was exhausted when I
went down in the morning. Mr. Savage was already in the
kitchen, preparing breakfast. His morning service in the
empty church was over. It was nearly nine o'clock. I
declined his offered dollop from the porridge-pot. I
declined the black liquid he was about to pour from the
bottle of coffee essence. I asked permission to make a cup
of tea, and did so. I drank this weak and without sugar or
milk and ate some dry toast. Then I sat back, watching
my stomach, so to speak. It behaved well enough. The
food stayed down. This accomplished, I asked Mr.
Savage's permission to return to bed. I did not feel firm
on my feet. He was at once full of solicitude, but I kept
my troubles from him. I did not want to seem to belittle
his hospitality. However, he was keen enough. "The
trouble is, Menheniot, you haven't become conditioned
to Annie Hocking's cooking as I have. That wretched
woman will poison some of us yet. Well, go to bed. I shall
spend the morning visiting parishioners who will be glad
to see the back of me. While I'm down there, I'll ask Jim
Brokenshire to have a meal ready for you at one o'clock."
  He looked at me and, as it were, sadly at his own con-

dition. "It really is most distressing, my dear boy, that I can't entertain a guest fittingly in my own house. There was a time when you would have been royally looked after. But that was long ago. Dear me, yes; a long time ago. If you could join me over a glass in the evenings, that would be something. But there it is: we must put up with it: you are not a drinking man. Perhaps," he added hopefully, "things will be better when Will comes back. Well, to bed with you. I must be out among the sheep. They're a woolly lot, and they bleat."

III

I slept at once, without dreams or discomfort. At half-past twelve I was awakened by Mr. Savage's hand feeling my forehead. Then he took my wrist and hauled a watch out of his pocket. "Your head is cool and your pulse is normal," he said after a moment. "Up with you now, and away to the Menheniot Arms."

Jim Brokenshire was ready for me. He gave me cold chicken and crisp salad, and alongside the plate was a small glass of wine. I pointed out that I had not ordered this, and he said: "Come to that, Mr. Menheniot, you haven't ordered any of it. It was all written down most carefully by Mr. Savage. What he calls invalid diet. You're his guest, he says, and he's responsible for you. So he ordered just this little glass. Rather special, Mr. Menheniot—Château Yquem. Wouldn't hurt a fly. So just oblige Mr. Savage, please."

Well, I drank it, and I must say it was good. Then there was a fruit pie—a tiny pie made specially in a tiny dish in which it was served. "Mr. Savage says no cream with it. Nothing rich." Cheese and biscuits and coffee followed. "I don't want to deceive you, Mr. Menheniot.

There's just a spot of old brandy in that coffee. Mr. Savage says nothing like it for pronouncing the benediction, and right he is."

There was nothing to pay. Mr. Savage had seen to that, too. Jim left me with my coffee, and I took my time. I had been so used to scampering back to the bank after a snatched meal that it was delightful to make a ceremony of delay. I was feeling good again—as well as I had ever felt. The day was overcast, a pearly-grey day, and presently I would go out into it. At my own time. I had thought earlier of calling on Dr. Littledale to tell him of my upset, but that didn't seem necessary now. Still, I decided, it would be pleasant to call on him anyway.

I read the local newspaper as I sat there, and an advertisement in it caught my eye. Rosemullion had to be furnished; to see to that was one of the reasons for my being here now; and this advertisement of the sale of a country house's contents was the sort of thing I would have to look out for. The sale was to be on the morrow; the house was not far away; and suddenly it occurred to me that it would be a delightfully rash act to ask Kitty Littledale to attend the sale with me. I should probably get the snub that I felt I deserved; but if she *would* come! I know at once that, more almost than anything, I wished she would.

From where I sat I could see the Littledales' front door, and Dr. Littledale came out at this moment. Apart from the footpath by the stream, there was another way out of Penmaen into the hinterland: a road that could hardly be called even secondary but that a car could use if the driver nursed his springs. Littledale got into the ancient car that was standing outside his house and drove off along this road. I gave him a little time, then called good-bye to Jim Brokenshire and walked to the house. My heart was beating rather excitedly as I rang the bell.

The Littledales had no servant. Miss Littledale herself answered the door. She was a woman whose face readily betrayed her emotions. Her confusion was obvious. She coloured and said: "Oh. . . ."

I'm afraid I handled the situation as awkwardly as she did. The beating of my heart did not diminish, and I was suddenly filled with a sense of social sin. After all, it was an odd hour for making a call, even if Dr. Littledale himself had been at home, even, indeed, if I had been an old friend given to "dropping in." And assuredly I was not that.

So we stood there: two middle-aged people blushing like children. The sardonic cackle of the gulls flying against the cliff face seemed well timed. She was wearing a flowered overall. At last she said: "Tom's just gone out. I was washing up our lunch things."

My courage altogether failed me. "Oh," I said, "I'm sorry. There were one or two things we talked about in his study last evening. . . . I must learn more about what times are convenient for him. Well, I'll be off then. . . ."

I turned to go, and I was half-way down the short flight of steps when she said: "I should like to ask you in. But this is a dreadful place for gossip, you know." And as I paused, and then walked up the few steps again, she blushed really furiously, as though the mere hint that there could conceivably be something to gossip about had admitted the possibility that the gossip might be well-founded.

So we stood again, tongue-tied, desperately aware of one another.

"I know this place so well," she said forlornly; and, to give point to the words, Annie Hocking went by at that moment, the eyes in her fat pig-face taking us in with open curiosity.

I felt a great compassion for Kitty Littledale in that

moment, a sense of the spiritual loneliness she must have endured for so long in Penmaen. It was terrible to be so isolated that the mere coming along of someone who understood the things you loved, who *believed* in them, could throw you into this confusion. I dared not think that there was more in it than that. Suddenly I thought: To the devil with Annie Hocking and all the gossips of Penmaen, and I said: "Well, at any rate, let's take a little walk together. Even Penmaen could hardly object to that."

With a touching eagerness she said: "That would be delightful. I'll join you in a moment."

I walked up and down in front of the few houses of the village till she came. Pulled up above the high tide mark half-way across the little beach was the dinghy whereon I had observed some leisurely work. No one was working on it now. We'll walk across the beach, I thought, to the cliffs on the far side, then we'll come back and sit on the dinghy and have a talk. That'll hurt no one's suscepti-bilities. We'll be in everyone's view all the time.

That is what we did. We didn't talk much. One thing I liked about her from the beginning was that there was no need to talk. I felt *with her* all the time, without the need to chatter, and I think she felt so with me. I can't remem-ber even the few things we *did* talk about the first time we were alone with one another. A sense of fitting, of being restful, is all that remains. But I did ask her if she would come to the sale of furniture. I said, with what I thought admirable cunning, that I would like her guid-ance. She said that she would come, that she knew the house and that there were some good things in it. She talked of the outing with a gaiety that made me realize how few such events had broken the monotony of her life.

Dr. Littledale arrived at the house just as we returned to it. We told him of our proposed expedition, and he said: "You can't do this sort of thing, Menheniot. Where shall I be without my dispenser?"

I suppose we both looked crestfallen, for he laughed affectionately at Kitty, and said: "Well, the girl's earned a day off. But don't forget, my boy, the ravages of the National Health Service. In a town, the patients toddle to some multiple chemist's shop with their prescriptions, but they can't do that here. Kitty makes the stuff up. I told you, didn't I, that she's a qualified dispenser? Ah, well, I shall have to put the colour in the water myself for once. Come in, won't you?"

I made my excuses and hurried across to the Menheniot Arms. "Well, Mr. Menheniot, you look as though the invalid diet suited you," Jim Brokenshire said. Indeed, I felt very well. I was going to make a real day of it to-morrow. For one thing, I was going to eat well, if Jim would help me. I felt suddenly sick of the vicarage and its odd ways. And Jim was willing enough. He would have breakfast ready for me at nine. He would telephone for a car to be at my disposal at ten. He would put up lunch for two; and, in the evening, he would have dinner ready for three. No, I amended, for four. I owed that to Mr. Savage. For the first time, I began to enjoy my money. I was throwing it about. The prospect of throwing it by handfuls at the sale exhilarated me.

IV

There are days so unreasonable, occurring so delightfully in a context that doesn't naturally include them, that they lift up the heart. Down there in Cornwall they call such a day a "day lent." The day of the sale was a day lent. It didn't belong to March. By ten o'clock the sun was shining with the warmth of May month, and with

Kitty Littledale sitting at my side and Jim Brokenshire's hamper tucked into the boot, I felt that there wasn't much life could do to improve my situation, especially as the object of the journey was the embellishment of my beloved Rosemullion. And, thinking of Rosemullion, I called to the driver that we would go that way, and we did, admiring the golden sheets of daffodils and the long hedge that elsewhere could have been melancholy privet or laurel but here was camellia: red and white and pink, and every imaginable blending of those three colours. We got out of the car and stood for a moment on the terrace, looking at the far sweep of the country under the warm hazy sunshine and listening to the songs of the birds. They seemed to approve us. They were not like the sardonic gulls of Penmaen. I was an ignoramus in horticulture, and Kitty told me the name of each camellia and daffodil, and of many shrubs that I could only blindly admire. This was pieris, and that magnolia stellata, and this again was wych hazel.

The sense of a vast new world to be discovered was enchanting; and, sitting on the oaken bench where first I had seen Mr. Savage, I watched Kitty who had wandered along the terrace and was bending to examine this and that, tranquil, happily at home with things familiar to her. And I thought, with a sudden movement of the heart, that here, too, was a world, the world of women, that I had not hitherto explored, that indeed I had fled from in fright; and that I had now made, at any rate, my first steps in, and found it not frightening at all, but at once seductive and comforting.

She was given to soft-coloured trailing clothes that carried a whisper with her as she moved. I approved her on the terrace in the mild sunshine. She looked right.

I called to her that we must be off, and she came with a smile as though we were old understanding friends.

"It's very lovely," she said. "I do wish you every happiness here."

"At any rate," I answered, "I've already done something which, I assure you, I've never done in my life before. I've made some friends."

"We are alike in that," she said simply. "I'm afraid I've always lived too much within my own mind. I think perhaps that's why people don't read my books any more. I expect they've lost contact with the stir of things."

I was tongue-tied. I hated to hear her speak of something that distressed her, and I could think of nothing to say. "However," she added, "it's bad of me to talk to you about my worries. Not that they are that any more. I've got over it."

As we went back to the car, I wondered if that were really true. To have known success—something even of fame—and then to have been deserted by it. Did one get over that? It would have been as though at this moment someone snatched Rosemullion from my hands.

How unbearable that would have been I realized when we came to the house we were seeking. I would not agree with Kitty that it was lovelier even than Rosemullion; but it was more ancient: no Lutyens had touched the fabric, which stood as on the day it was built, save that now three centuries of weather had ennobled it. It stood in lovely gardens, serene as though nothing unaccustomed had happened to it; and indeed what was happening now had become but too customary: its owners could afford to keep it no longer. All was going: the house and everything in it.

What things were in it! And what a mad reckless day we had! Now I knew what money was for, and with a kind of pig-headed fury I refused to be outbid. Whatever I set my heart on, whatever Kitty Littledale admired— and she admired nothing that I did not admire myself—

I bought. No doubt this was a reaction from many days in London salerooms when with a bit of hard-saved money, I attended in hope, only to retire too soon. No retiring now. London dealers were there whom I had known in my days of poverty. I rejoiced to leave them standing.

Most of what I bought was furniture, but there were pictures, too. Thomas Rowlandson had been in these parts and much of what he had done was in this house. He was an artist who had always delighted me, and there were three of the drawings that I told myself I must have. They appealed to Kitty, too. I remembered that there were no Rowlandsons on her walls. These were for her.

Though the month was March, the day remained unusually warm. In the saleroom it was even stuffy, and to get into the air during the lunch-time break was a relief. I had spotted a stone seat near a lily-pond in the garden and had told the chauffeur to have the hamper there at one o'clock. We made for the place now, down a sharp grassy declivity, and there was a spot where the grass was oozy from some small invisible spring that no doubt would dry in summer. But now it made the going treacherous, and suddenly Kitty slithered a little and gave an involuntary grab at my arm. It was one of those nothings that are so much, for we were both intensely aware of the contact. She let go at once; and I said, in a voice whose strain she must have interpreted: "I think you had better keep hold just here"; and with a small embarrassed laugh she said: "Yes, I think I had." She released her hold as soon as we were on firm ground, and I wished she hadn't.

When we opened the hamper in sunshine now at its triumphant height, we found that Jim Brokenshire had forgotten nothing. There were two bottles of beer from which I recoiled till I saw a label tied to the neck of each:

"For the chauffeur." There was a package of food similarly labelled, and with these treasures the man retired. For us, there were chicken sandwiches and ham sandwiches and cheese sandwiches. There were two glasses, each packed in tissue paper in a box; and there was a napkin rolled lovingly round an elongated shape. I removed it, and there was a bottle labelled Château Yquem. The cork had been withdrawn and half-pushed back. I looked at the bottle in dismay.

Kitty said: "Jim seems intent on a fiesta. My favourite wine!"

And then I remembered that only the day before, after my qualms and retchings of the night, I had drunk some of this and found it good. "Mine, too!" I cried, recklessly filled a tumbler, and took up the other. But Kitty stayed my hand. She put the cork back into the bottle, poured half the contents of the one tumbler into the other, and said: "Thank you for arranging such a beautiful lunch."

So there we sat, after we had eaten, looking at the sunshine on the water, not speaking, tranquil with one another. Presently a dealer I knew passed by, going back to the house, and he said: "Leaving us the relics, Mr. Menheniot?" I grinned contentedly, and said: "I make no promises. I may come back if the smell of something good reaches me."

He went, and Kitty said: "You know, the sort of thing we've just been looking at would make a beginning for a novel. One wave of time sweeping all the members of that family and all those wonderful things into one place. Another wave sweeping them all out. I wonder if I could make anything of it? I've been terribly lazy for too long."

"Oh, no," I said. "You must have your hands full helping your brother."

"Ah, I see he's been talking to you about me. Poor Tom! He's convinced that he's ruined my life, that I could have been almost anything I wanted if I hadn't chosen to help him. But really, you know, a bit of cooking and housekeeping and dispensing doesn't come to all that. When I had something to write about it was easy enough to find the time. No; it's nothing to do with Tom. I just seemed to go hollow—that's all."

We didn't return to the house. We talked the afternoon through. She told me how, when she was writing, she had always celebrated the finishing of a book by going to London and spending what she had made on the last one. A week of theatres and salerooms. A few water-colours, a bit of furniture, once, audaciously, the Adam fireplace in their sitting-room. But it was some time now since there had been one of these heartening sorties from Penmaen.

Her confidences enchanted me. She got up to look into the pond, and stood there with one foot on the granite sill, a hand on her hip, her head leaning forward. I wished I had Mr. Savage's ancient skill as a photographer. I should have liked a picture of her posed in that way. She must have been almost as old as I was myself, but she had a girl's lissom figure, and her face had a gentle wisdom that seemed to me better than a girl's untested morning shine.

I said with a laugh: "Mr. Savage's study is full of photographs of his first wife, beautifully posed. I think he would find you irresistible."

She came and sat down again. "No," she said. "There was never more than one woman for Mr. Savage."

I said that the high-flown inscription on Sylvia's plaque in the church suggested as much.

"The dreadful thing was," Kitty told me, "that he put the plaque there just after he'd married Annie Hocking's sister—it would be when they'd been married for about a year. What on earth can she have thought?"

What, indeed!

"Tom and I had just come to Penmaen. It was the most satisfying scandal they'd ever had. Mr. Savage had been a widower so long that hardly anyone there remembered him as anything else. Annie Hocking and her sister Mary were always in and out of the vicarage, doing for him, as they say. They were both in their middle twenties then. Their father had just died and left them a cottage in the village and a bit of money. I don't suppose it was more than a few hundred pounds, but they decided to become ladies on it. Mary wasn't a bad-looking girl; even Annie in those days wasn't what she is now, though she was already full of promise. Do you remember the fashion just after the First World War?—skirts hardly down to the knees. They were the only two who wore them in Penmaen. I gather they'd been pretty well kept in hand by their father—one of the local Methodist highlights. I remember Jim Brokenshire's father saying: 'Preach a grand sermon, old Hocking would, on God is Love, an' then come 'om an' belt 'ell out o' they gels with 'is leather strap.' Anyhow, they Broke Out. There's a story that they spent a week in Paris, which, of course, could have only one significance in Penmaen. But some people say they went no farther than Plymouth. Anyway, they were soon through their bit of cash, and then Annie took a job helping Jim Brokenshire's father at the Menheniot Arms. Mr. Savage was in his middle sixties then. He had a housekeeper living in—an ancient who must have been eighty. She died on him; and that was where Mary Hocking stepped in with those knee-length skirts. She didn't live in till he married her, and what happened I don't know: there were so many stories. The air was still buzzing with it when Tom and I arrived. He seduced her. She seduced him. There was no seduction about it. He'd simply wanted to marry again, and about time too. Save him from becoming cracked, if he wasn't cracked already. Anyway, they'd been married for nine months when we came, and one of Tom's first jobs was to help with the birth of young Will Savage."

Well, it was very much what I had imagined. After all, there is seduction and seduction, within marriage and without. Poor old Savage had played St. Anthony too long, and there had come one temptation too many. I felt very worldly wise.

"There's nothing difficult to understand in any of it," I said, "either in his swift marriage or his swift revolt. I expect he soon loathed her."

"Yes," she said sadly. "I expect he did. And yet I felt sorry for the poor creature. Will was a weak child, and Tom was in and out of the house a good deal. Mr. Savage was in a separate bedroom already, and Tom says he treated her like dirt. She mightn't have existed. It was then that he dug out all the photographs of Sylvia and spread them round his study. An abasement before Sylvia, a penance for himself. 'Look on this picture and on that.' And then the plaque in the church! He had it made outside the district and closed the church while it was being set up. Mary never entered the church again after that, and soon she was dead. The boy was about a year old. Annie drifted in and out as she pleased and more or less brought Will up. Mr. Savage took not the slightest notice of her."

"What sort of boy is Will?" I asked.

"Oh, you'll soon see." She got up. "It's getting cold. I think we ought to be moving now." she added as I began to pack the hamper: "He always seemed to me pure Hocking."

I had imagined the pleasant scene there would be when I asked Kitty to accept the Rowlandson drawings. She would protest, embarrassed, that she couldn't take three fairly valuable pictures from one who was almost a stranger, and I would say something rather good: were we such strangers? Didn't a community of taste make us already something to one another? She would be reluctantly overborne, and the small struggle would have established another bond between us.

However, she quite simply accepted the gift. There was nothing wanting in her thanks, but she taught me not to expect our relationship, whatever it might be, to be dramatized. I had for so long been starved of congenial friendship that the expectation of drama was on my side. That night, when the four of us sat down to our dinner at the Menheniot Arms, even the fact that Dr. Littledale called me Roger seemed to me dramatic, and it was with difficulty that I called him Tom.

Old Savage was in good form that night. He had even paid some attention to his appearance. There was a labourer in the village who did a bit of hairdressing in his spare time. He had been called into the vicarage and turned loose on Mr. Savage whose hair and beard shone with unction. His clothes and shoes had been brushed, and there was a touching air of expectancy about him as he came into the room where the three of us stood by the fire. He looked, I thought, like Tennyson all washed and shined to go to the palace to be sworn in as a peer, or whatever it was one did on such an occasion. He took a glass of sherry and stood there taller and straighter than any of us, and infinitely more distinguished. "By God!" he said. "This reminds me of other days! Do you know, my dear boy, that no one has asked me to dinner for fifty years and more? Your very good health."

I don't know what wine Jim Brokenshire provided with the meal: I did not drink it: but clearly it was what Mr. Savage needed to dissolve the years. The rest of us stood out of his way, and an odd young man emerged from Oxford of the seventies, swinging a pick with Mr. Ruskin on the Hinksey Road, riding to hounds, wining and dining, playing preposterous pranks, taking a first in Greats, and winning the Newdigate Prize. This was the young man Sylvia had so briefly known, the young man to whom Winchester had seemed probable, Canterbury not fantastically remote. And then Sylvia had died, and he had chosen to remain with her in this outlandish grave.

It was only of those days—the days of his twenties—that Mr. Savage spoke, as though all that had happened since had been a lapse of meaningless time. "And by God!" he said when we were drinking coffee and Jim Brokenshire appeared with warm balloon-glasses into which he poured brandy for the doctor and the vicar, "by God," Mr. Savage cried, sniffing the brandy, "one becomes less than the beasts. Jim, stay now and listen to this. Here I am, the host of this stranger in our midst"— and he laid a hand on my arm—"who is the representative of a family of some small repute, and I allow *him* to entertain *me*! By detaining him in the vicarage I have overlooked all that is due from host to guest. Menheniot, you must stay here. Shift your gear in the morning. Jim, until Mr. Menheniot is ready to move into his own house, he is my guest under your roof. No," he said, as I protested, "you have brought back to my mind to-night, Menheniot, what hospitality is. I am ashamed of the way I have treated you. It's all very well for my body to wait in that mortuary on the hill until it pleases God to hold the inquest. But that won't do for you."

This seemed like a royal gift to me, and Mr. Savage made it regally. But I was not able to accept it with the simple courtesy that Kitty had shown in accepting the Rowlandsons. I was worried. Probably, I thought in the morning, the old boy was a bit fuddled last night by his unaccustomed festivity, and now he will be repenting of a gesture beyond his resources. Not that he had seemed fuddled as we walked together up the hill to the vicarage. He was silent, but that, no doubt, was because his mind was bemused by the memories that he had chosen to uncover. We both went straight to bed, after he had thanked me again for the night's hospitality. In the morning I put my few things into my suitcase and waited for him to come in from the church in order to say good-bye. But he didn't come in, and when I strolled out to meet him I saw him disappearing towards the hinterland, swinging a stick with one hand and holding in the other what looked like half a loaf at which he took an occasional bite. So I took the suitcase and walked down to the Menheniot Arms.

Tom Littledale came across to intercept me. "Dump that inside, Roger," he said, "and come and eat breakfast with us."

Kitty met us in the hall. "Good morning, Roger," she said, and with my tongue sticking to my mouth I managed to say: "Good morning, Kitty."

"I've no doubt," Tom said, "that Jim Brokenshire would have given you ham and eggs. You'll have to make do with simpler fare here."

The coffee and cereal and toast and marmalade suited me well enough. "I especially commend the marmalade," Tom said. "Kitty makes it."

"Do all good women make their own marmalade?" I asked. And Kitty said: "Yes, when they can get the sugar."

I told them what Mr. Savage had said about Sylvia and the marmalade; and that led me to my doubts about the hospitality he had offered me. "I'm a rich man. I don't want to impose on the old boy. Can he afford it?"

"I imagine he could buy you up and not notice the difference," Tom said. "But he has probably forgotten that by now. Believe me, in turning you out of his own house because he thought it not good enough, he was doing something that would have no relationship to money in his mind."

I felt rebuked, and Kitty, I am sure, was aware of this. She came to my rescue by pointing out how well the Rowlandsons looked on the wall.

"I wonder," Tom said, "what became of the things Mr Savage once had on his walls? And not only on his walls. The place is like the dreariest barrack now, but it was lovely once. There's an old bird living on the outskirts of my beat who often talks to me about it. He's just about the same age as Mr. Savage, but not so spry. His mind's lively enough, though, and he can remember Mr. Savage and his wife arriving at Penmaen. He was the gardener there. The Savages had quite a staff. Every morning, he says, Mr. Savage would come into the garden straight from the eight o'clock service to find one perfect flower to take in to his wife at the breakfast table. This isn't much of a hunting country, but there was a hunt of sorts in those days, and they both followed hounds. I've often tried to find out from him what the Lady Sylvia Savage was like, but he's not good with words. 'Proper li'l madam she were.' That's as far as we get. Somehow I can't see her making marmalade, but I can imagine that she jolly well saw that the cook did. Now that she's unearthly excellence in the old man's memory, that would have to include marmalade. I suppose. Here, have some more of Kitty's."

"You mustn't find flaws in her, Tom," Kitty said. "To Mr. Savage she is what he thinks she was."

"Well, old Bill Rogers likes to say: ''Ad a temper, mind 'e.' And he recalls the day when the boy who worked with him left a rake lying on a garden-path teeth up. The Lady Sylvia put her dainty foot on them and got a smack in the eye with the handle. 'Praaper ole bust-up that were.' She wrote to her father's head gardener for the list of fines in force on the parental estate, and these were pinned up in the tool-shed. Deductions from wages: Rake, teeth up, 1d. And so forth. 'Ah, well, it were the way to learn 'em.'"

It was a strange picture to look on after my experience in the vicarage: a picture of a day when the moss-ruined lawns were green grass, and the slippery paths were raked gravel, and a busy staff filled the house and kitchens, and the gay Oxford boys of whom he had talked last night came down to fill the rooms that were now damp caverns aching with loneliness. "I should think," Tom said, "Mr. Savage's visits to old Bill Rogers are deeply reminiscent affairs. He looks in whenever his walking takes him that way, and there's a standing order for Bill to receive three ounces of tobacco a week and a pint of beer every day. He's the last of what I imagine were once many pensioners. Bill owns his cottage, too. Mr. Savage made him a present of it on his seventieth birthday."

CHAPTER NINE

I

I BEGAN to make heavy demands on Kitty Littledale's time, and Tom was acquiescent. That day at the sale had taught me the joy of spending money, but I still found it hard to break the contriving and considering habits of a lifetime. However, I hired a car for my regular service. The man who had taken me and Kitty to the sale reported every morning to the Menheniot Arms, and Kitty and I began to get about Cornwall.

"Time you had a shaking up," Tom said, when Kitty made one of her frequent apologies. "Why on earth should I expect you to be always hanging attendance on me? You're my sister, not my slave. You've had too much of Penmaen. Get out and enjoy yourself while you're still young."

"Young!" she cried ruefully. "Now, Tom . . . !"

She wasn't young, and I said to myself, "Thank God for that!" I was not happy with young women: I was happy with Kitty. Indeed, I had never been happy with a woman before, young or old. But she wasn't old. I wouldn't have that. She wasn't young, but she wasn't old. I thought of her as a flower, not a bud; but a flower that had not shed a petal.

We were at breakfast in the Littledales' house. It had become a custom, and as a return of hospitality, seeing that there was seldom now anyone to cook for him, Tom took his midday meal with Jim Brokenshire at my expense.

"Well, take her off, Roger," he said. "What is it to-day?"

"Copper dish covers for the kitchen," I said.

They both fell into laughter. "Roger will go down in history," Kitty said, "as the man who put the clock back by two hundred years. What is your Mrs. Sara going to say when she sees that lot? She'll have to do the cleaning."

"She'll have plenty of help," I promised.

"Not in these parts, unless you're luckier than most people."

"I know a nice little dog," Tom said, "that could turn a spit for you."

But I was not to be put off. A row of shining copper covers, nicely graded on the wall from a size that would hide a turkey to a neat little thing for a quail, was part of my vision of the Rosemullion kitchens, and I was determined that so it should be. I was anxious now to have the Saras' domain in order, so that I could recall them to be on hand when the furnishing seriously began. Already the house was full of painters and paper-hangers, carpenters and plumbers.

Searching for specific things like this, or keeping our eyes open in general for pieces that would be happy in the house, Kitty and I spent day after day together. We went with a fine comb through the towns of Cornwall, wherever we were likely to find shops with the things we wanted. And there was more than this hunt to bring us together. There was the midday break. I recall luncheons in the Red Lion at Truro, and the Green Bank in Falmouth, the Angel at Helston and the Queen's in Penzance. In my pocket-book the list was piling up, and soon now the time would come when I would give the word, and all this stuff lying north, south, east and west about the county would begin to move, converging upon Rosemullion.

"Some day," said Kitty, "this will end. There will just be Rosemullion, furnished. I shall miss these days."

We had been to Penzance, and the car was speeding homewards through Marazion. The dusk was coming down over the sea, and a whiff of fog blurred the fantastic turrets and crenellations of St. Michael's Mount. We were nearing the end of March, and it had been a good day for the time of year; but now, suddenly, nature was an old woman huddling a grey shawl round her bones. "I shall miss these days." Yes, I thought, and so shall I. To be in Rosemullion, all at last finished and complete, down to the copper covers on the kitchen wall; the door locked, the fire lit, and myself secluded: oh, this had been the dream not only of these recent days but of weary years. And now this safety that had for so long been the most desirable thing in the world, seemed not so much as though I were locked in, but rather as though some lovely things were locked out. Kitty's hand was lying on the seat between us, and I wanted to take it in mine, or at least give it a reassuring squeeze. But I hadn't the courage to do either.

II

All through that journey home the wind freshened from the south, and after I had eaten my evening meal I wandered out into it, on to the beach where the tide was coming in sharply, a tumble of white in the darkness. I walked as far as the cliff beyond the beach, and I sat down there on a tussock of sea-pinks, listening to the surge of the water, watching the stars that the clouds covered and unveiled and the cluster of humble lights half a mile away that was Penmaen. I felt lonely. My body was warm, but I was chilled to the soul's marrow. This was the oddest feeling I had ever known: this loneliness. Aloneness was something else. I had sought it eagerly, welcomed it when found, but I had never been lonely in my aloneness. Now

I was so lonely that I could stand it no longer. I set off at a good lick back to Penmaen. Tom Littledale's surgery hour was past. Unless he had been called out, there he would be—someone to talk to. And there was now something that I wanted to talk about. In these journeys through Cornwall I had found much that I wanted for Rosemullion, but one thing I hadn't found was pictures for my walls. That would need a visit to London, and seeing that Kitty had helped with everything else, why shouldn't she help with this, too? The hardihood of inviting her to visit London with me made me tremble, and I fairly rushed across the dark beach so that I might speak before my resolution cooled.

Tom opened the door. He was smoking a pipe and wearing a dressing-gown and slippers. He was a man for whom I already felt affection: a solid character. The wind blew in with me, bringing the wet briny smell of the night. He took my arm, drew me within, and shut the door. He looked at me standing under the light of the hall lamp, and suddenly smiled. "What have you been up to, Roger?" he asked. "What have you been doing to Kitty?"

I suppose the unexpectedness of the question made me look a dithering idiot. He took my arm again, and said: "Come up to my den. I was just settling down to an evening with *The Lancet*. You will be better, at any rate, than that."

A fire of driftwood was burning on the hearth in his untidy comfortable room. Blue and green and orange tongues licked about the logs. He stood with his back to the flames, looking down at me sitting in a leather chair, and I thought he was like a child with a happy secret that he longed to reveal. "She's At It again," he said. "She's said nothing to me, mind you, but I know the symptoms." He rubbed his hands. "I'm pretty sure she's At It."

Now I understood his gleeful mood. He was a man who was not light with what he considered his own offences. I recalled the story he had told me of the German soldier. It would for ever be a wound in his mind. And it was on his mind, too, that Kitty had been made a sacrifice to his own well-being. A willing sacrifice, perhaps; but that didn't lessen his perpetual feeling that, but for him, she could have cut a figure in the world.

"You've done what I could never do," he said. "How could I, with this damned drudgery round my neck? You've shaken her up, given her things to see and think about. It's been heartbreaking, Roger, to see her caged up in this hole for year after year."

He sat down opposite me and refilled his pipe. I didn't agree with his view of the situation. I wasn't an artist of any sort, but I thought I knew something about how artists' minds worked, and I didn't believe that to change an external situation had much to do with it. It was what they did with whatever was lying about that mattered. I said so, hoping to lessen his feeling of guilt. "What about the Brontë girls?" I said. "They lived in a narrow world if you like."

But he came back at me at once. "Did Charlotte ever do anything better than *Villette*?" he asked. "And wasn't it Brussels that set her off on that? Wasn't it her falling in love with a middle-aged professor?"

Now that remark was altogether too much for me. I am sure Tom Littledale did not mean it to have a personal implication, but it scared me badly. I had come intending to make my ties with Kitty closer; now I recoiled like a frightened boy. The thing, however unintentionally, had been put into words; and I said: "Well, I'm glad Kitty's started on something. I came in to apologise and make my excuses to her. We had arranged to see some stuff in St. Ives to-morrow, but that will have to wait. There was a

etter when I got back to-night that means I shall have to
ravel up to London to-morrow. I may be away some time.
Make my excuses, Tom."

III

I did not write to the Littledales while I was away, and
hey did not have my address. My absence prolonged
tself, for this was the first time I had been able to visit
he galleries and salerooms with money to spend. I found
London more agreeable than I had expected it to be, but
hat was only because I passed my time wholly in the
pleasant places of my choice. My stay drew out from a
week into a fortnight, and then half-way through another
week. It was now mid-April, and the weather was good.
The parks and florists' shops were gay with spring flowers,
and had these not stirred in me a sudden wish to see the
gardens of Rosemullion, where I had left three gardeners
wrestling with the years' neglect, I would have lingered
still. Then I wrote to the Littledales, but merely to
announce that I should return to-morrow and that I
hoped Kitty would be able to visit Rosemullion with me
on the day after that. I had been feeling contented
enough, but I was surprised how the writing and posting
of this letter, brief and factual as it was, lifted up my
spirits. During these few weeks I had slid back, though on
a grander scale, to the self-contained life I had lived with
he Saras. Now the frightening glimpses I had had at
Penmaen of the possibility of another kind of life returned
to my imagination. As I was falling off to sleep that night
in my hotel, I was obsessed with a recollection of the low-
ering evening when we motored through Marazion and
Kitty's hand was lying on the seat, waiting for me to pick
t up. I was quite sure of that: it had been placed there

intentionally, waiting for me. In the morning Paddington seemed a glad place: the place of return to the Little-dales. Well, I said to myself honestly, to Kitty.

IV

During the journey I thought so much about meeting her again that to find her away was startling. I had thought of her as a fixture. Jim Brokenshire handed me a note in which Tom said that he and Kitty had accepted an invitation to spend the afternoon and evening with what he called a "brother medico" in Newquay. They would not be back till late. Kitty would be pleased to join me on the morrow.

Jim said he would have a meal ready for me at seven and there was some time to go before that hour. I felt loose-ended, desolate almost. London afforded distraction Penmaen did not. There was only Kitty.

I decided to walk up along the stream and call on Mr. Savage. I had been neglecting him, taking his bounty for granted. But that was something, I had the sense to know that he would be the last to worry about, even to notice. However, here again I was unlucky. I walked through the open door into the chill of the house and up the stairs. I tapped at the study door, and, getting no answer, peeped in. The room was empty—save for Sylvia. She was every where. I stood for a moment looking at the photographs, wondering what this enchanting creature would look like now, had she, with Mr. Savage, survived the long years' vicissitudes. Anyhow, I thought, there would be no young Will Savage, that elusive ever-expected prodigal. If there were children at all, they would be old—older than I was myself. I wandered into the room opposite to gaze again at Will's many representations, and as I stood there I heard steps come up the stairs and enter the study. In a moment or two I moved out to the landing, thinking to go across and greet Mr. Savage. But I stood arrested, for it was not Mr. Savage. The study door was open, and I returned quietly to Will's room. Pulling the door to behind me, I could look through the crack on the hinge side. Annie Hocking stood with her solid back to me, her grey hair disordered, a piece of sacking tied round her thick waist. She moved about the room, picking up the pictures of Sylvia one by one, studying them with an intent evil look, as though ill-wishing them; and then putting them down again. The sight of the beautiful girl in those red heavy hands, under the scrutiny of those close-set peering eyes, revolted me. There was venom in every second of the picture unfolding before me. She held the last picture for a long time, glaring balefully, then suddenly spat full into its face. "There!" she said and chuckled. She watched the saliva for a moment sliming down the glass, then wiped it on her sack, raising her knee and rubbing. She put the picture down and walked out of the room. I felt nauseated, as on the day when I spewed through this window.

I stayed where I was for ten minutes, then stole quietly down into the hall and went to the kitchen door. I opened it, shouting: "Anyone in?"

Annie was at the sink, stirring a brew in a bucket. More than ever, in the darkening room, she looked like a witch at a cauldron.

"Good evening, Annie," I said. "I'm looking for Mr. Savage."

"You won't see 'e for a bit," she said. "'E's over old Bill Rogers' way. Plenty of chin-wag for the pair of 'em to-day. They'll be talkin' about she." Annie jerked a thumb vaguely in the direction of the study.

"A lot 'e cares about Will so long as there's she to talk

135

about. I'm the one to make things decent for Will. 'Ave 'e seen them ole paths?"

I shook my head.

"Praaper shambles the place be," she said. "Weeds, weeds. I bet they kep' the weeds down for she."

I gathered that her brew was to spread on the garden paths, and I left her stirring and slopping at it with a ladle. I went down to the Menheniot Arms full of foreboding, though of what I could not say. But Annie Hocking, I felt, was the sort of woman who would never forget the cool affront thrown to her sister by Sylvia's plaque in the church.

v

What fools we are! I had a twinge of resentment against Kitty—I, who had vanished for nearly three weeks, leaving no address! Tom's letter said they would be back late, but it wasn't so late as all that. My room at the pub, to which I retired after supper, looked towards the Littledales' house. I saw the car arrive soon after nine, lights spring up in the house. Now she and Tom will come to say How d'you do, I thought. I so much wanted them to do this that I couldn't go on with my reading. But they didn't. I went to bed disgruntled. I had spent fifteen hundred pounds on four pictures. I'll think of them, not of her, I told myself, and at last went to sleep thinking of not thinking of her.

Penmaen is mixed up in my mind with so much sorrow that my tendency, when I think of it, is to associate it with the first evil night when Mr. Savage and I walked through the rain beside the roaring stream out into the wind howling off the sea. With that, rather than with the many lovely days there, such as this April day when Kitty and

136

I went to Rosemullion. It began beautifully, and it ended in a perfection of which now I can hardly bear to think. I took up at once my old habit of going to breakfast with the Littledales. They were expecting me: my place was laid: it was as though I had not been away at all. Except—or did I imagine this?—that there was about Kitty some new quality, or some deepening of an old quality, that was hard to define. It would be too much to call it gaiety, but it was as though her gravity had become warm from some inward resource and satisfaction.

"We got back last night sooner than we expected," Tom said. "There was a sad ending to our day."

He told me that when they were on the way to visit his friend they overtook Mr. Savage striding along and smacking with his stick at the hedgerows, as was his custom. They stopped and talked to him, and he said that he would eat his bread and cheese under a hedge and then go on to see Bill Rogers. Tom mentioned that he would be spending the day with Dr. Richards, and that was how Mr. Savage knew where to find him. There was a wayside telephone box near Rogers's cottage, and Mr. Savage telephoned from there at about seven o'clock to say that old Bill had suddenly collapsed while they were talking. "I can't understand it," he said. "He's no older than I am—a bit younger, if anything. Do you think you ought to come?"

The old boy was dead when Tom and Kitty reached the cottage. "I had been expecting it," Tom said. Mr. Savage was sitting in the dusk, holding Bill's cold hand. "An extraordinary sight," Tom assured me. "He needed only a scythe to be Father Time himself, waiting the moment to reap us all."

Kitty sat with him while Tom arranged with Bill's daughter, married to a farm labourer living nearby, to take charge of things at the cottage. "She's sixtyish," Tom said, "just become a grandmother. Bill always called her 'My li'l maiden.'"

They had some difficulty in persuading Mr. Savage to come away. "He's an odd type, you know. The affairs of mortality don't normally have much effect on him, so far as one can see; but last night he really was bowled over. You see, however frail a thread old Bill was, still he *was* a thread tying up with the Lady Sylvia. And he was the last one. There'll never be anyone again that Mr. Savage can go to and think 'He knew her.' There'll be nothing now but what's in his mind, and God knows what a queer lot of stuff that is."

They invited him to come home and eat with them, even to spend the night, but he would do neither. He was very quiet as they put him into an easy chair in his study. Kitty asked if she should make him a meal, and he said gravely: "No, thank you. I still have some bread and cheese in my pocket. Just give me a drink, Doctor, if you please." So Tom mixed him a brandy and water, and he sat there sipping it and looking at the photographs. At last he said: "Please go now. This place isn't fit for you to be in. Slugs have been here. I can always *feel* when the slugs have been near her."

"So we left him," Tom said. "I shall go up and have a look at him as soon as I've done breakfast."

I wanted to tell them of seeing Annie Hocking in the study, but I simply *could* not. What point was there in disturbing anyone's mind with that disgusting affair?

VI

This sad tale of Mr. Savage could not dim the brightness of the April day. I especially remember Kitty's parasol. The sunshine was so brilliant that it was not out of

138

place, except in so far as a parasol has become out of place anywhere. Women now don't shade themselves from the sun. They court it. Even women of Kitty's age go forth all biceps and buttocks, with black glasses on their eyes, giving their faces an inhuman anonymity.

I liked Kitty as she was. Her faded silken clothes whispered down to her feet, and when we got out of the car at Rosemullion she opened her parasol, and that, too, was of faded silk. Her face, in the half-light of it, seemed to me that day to be beautiful. There was, I felt, as I had done at breakfast, something new, or something deepened, about her.

"Roger," she said, "you wouldn't believe how happy it makes me feel to be writing again."

So it was that. I felt a little crestfallen.

"And to have you back," she said. "And a day like this! Oh—I——"

But what she felt she couldn't say. She gave a sigh of happiness; and I said—so insufficiently—"Well, it's good to *be* back." But how happy I suddenly was!

It was a Saturday morning. The men working in the gardens and the house would be knocking off for the day at one o'clock. That would be in an hour's time. We spent the hour inspecting the work in the gardens. The paths were all in order, newly spread with fine crushed granite, and the sun sparkled in it here and there, catching the points of mica. The weather had been fine enough to permit the lawns to be mown. Straggling overgrown bushes had been trimmed back and herbaceous borders and rose-beds weeded. Everywhere the camellias were blooming; on every sloping bank primroses of many colours grew in thick clusters, and aubrietia and snow-on-the mountain—never could I call it arabis! —flourished in spready cushions. From down by a little pond in a hollow we looked up at the house standing on its plateau, with all about it trim and kempt once more, backed by trees new-greened, and with a lazy plume of smoke rising from one of the chimneys into the blue air. I suppose the workmen inside were burning rubbish, but the effect was as though contrived to give the last touch to the scene—a touch that animated the house with a sense of habitation. I watched the smoke curling against the screen of elms and beeches; and my eye, travelling up from the ground at my feet to that distant point, saw nothing that did not seem perfect. Rosemullion re-created! The old dream come down like the new Jerusalem and dwelling among men.

But in the old dream there had been no woman. So rapt had I been in my contemplation of the house and the scene about it, I had forgotten Kitty; and now I turned to see her looking steadfastly at me.

"How you love it!" she said.

And to me she looked a part of it. It didn't belong to these days we lived in, this tranquil house, built of stones so old, this ordered, settled beauty. It had nothing to do with the rush and ruin and disorder of the time; but neither had I; and neither have you, Kitty, I thought, you with your faded silk, and your parasol, and your face that is as quiet as this pond, but animated by thought and feeling as the pond is by the reflection of these slow spring clouds.

Her waist was so small. I put my arm round it, shaking with sudden apprehension. I could feel her shaking, too. Her whole body trembled at my touch, out of control. For a moment she held her face away, then looked at me as if across a distance of wonder and unbelief. I kissed her, and at that she shuddered again with great violence, so that I had to hold her up. The kiss did not last long. She said: "I must sit down."

There was a low stone wall, and she sat upon it, with

er head bowed, her large, floppy, old-fashioned hat
iding her face, the parasol, which she had hung on to,
ilted back over her shoulder. She spoke with difficulty,
s if breathless: "I'll see you at the house presently."

So I walked away and left her there. The men had
one from the gardens and the house. There was no one
bout but my chauffeur, and I took the luncheon-basket
rom him and told him to be back in an hour or so. Then
was alone on the terrace. Looking down, I could see
Kitty still sitting, bowed, on the wall. Everywhere about
ne cascades of birdsong were falling through the sun-
ight, and here was my house, here were my gardens; but
felt nothing save apprehension, almost despair. I could
not take my eyes from that far-off bowed figure. This
morning she had said in happy excitement: "And to have
you back!" Now she looked as if I had brutally struck
her to the ground. I am an inexperienced lover, God
knows, I thought. But should the very touch of me make
her shudder?

She got up at last, and came slowly to where I was
standing. We stood side by side for a moment without
speaking. Then she said: "One does not do that sort of
thing lightly."

"No," I said.

She said: "Kiss me."

I put my arms round her. She dropped her parasol,
and this time it was she who kissed me, and with a passion
that took me by surprise. Her mouth was soft and hot,
and it was with all of this, not with the grave lips that I
had admired, that she was kissing me. It was my turn to
be shaken, and when, with a deep sigh, she let me go,
I could only stand there looking at her in foolish amazement.

CHAPTER TEN

I

ON MAY day the Saras went into Rosemullion. Their part of the house was in order; arrangements had been made with tradesmen; I had found a full-time gardener, a crusty widower who was well content to live alone in the lodge and eat at the house; and bit by bit the things I had bought were being assembled under my roof. But I lingered on at the Menheniot Arms. I could not go on accepting Mr. Savage's hospitality, and one morning I walked up to the vicarage to tell him so, and to thank him for all he had done for me. He was in the yard behind the kitchen, his coat off, his sleeves rolled up, working away at the sawing-horse. The weather had become warm and settled. Even that dreary house had a more cheerful air. The trees about it were in happy green, and the haphazard and ill-conditioned garden was full of such flowers as look after themselves.

When I stood before him, Mr. Savage stopped sawing, wiped his forearm across his brow, and looked at me for a moment without recognition. I had been neglecting him, but I had heard from Tom that he was in poor shape since Bill Rogers had died. He seemed to me now much as usual physically, but his vacant glance was disturbing. At last he said: "Ah, yes—Menheniot—the last of the Barons. How are you, dear boy? How is Jim Brokenshire looking after you?"

We shook hands, and he said: "Let me get you a drink."

I declined, and he took my arm and led me through the kitchen and upstairs to his study. He pulled on a coat and gave himself a brandy. "I forget you are not a drinking man," he said. "There aren't many of them left now—not the real drinking men. I began at school. We had beer at breakfast—poor stuff, but it set a man on the right road. Well, your very good health, dear boy. Not a soul in church this morning—five last Sunday. I wonder what God thinks of it all?"

He sipped and meditated, put down his glass, and began cutting from a plug of tobacco into the curl of his hand. When his churchwarden was going, he said: "I'll have to order Bill Rogers' tombstone, and that, of course, means an epitaph. Have you any ideas?"

I said that that was hardly in my line and that, anyway, ad not known the man.

He pulled together a few scattered sheets of paper on writing-table, and said: "I've been trying over a thing two. This is the one that pleases me best. I'll have to unt out the dates, but this is the gist of it: 'Sacred to e Memory of William Rogers, gardener at the vicarage djacent hereto throughout the life in this parish of the Lady Sylvia Savage. He remained for many years in the service of the Rev. Henry Savage, his wife's unhappy survivor, but left him in the week preceding his second marriage. Well done, thou good and faithful servant.' "

He looked at me with a gleam of humorous malice in his eyes. "I'm afraid it's not very good," he said, "but perhaps I can polish it. There was a time when I could turn a pretty epitaph. How d'you like this one? I wrote it at Oxford when a pompous Balliol don died. For some reason he loathed Jesus men.

> *Here was a Balliol don, now called to Heaven*
> *To introduce true learning's needed leaven*
> *Among those saints who mightily displease us*
> *Because they spent their earthly days with Jesus."*

His mind seemed already to have left Bill Rogers. "In

those days," he said, "policemen carried bull's-eye lanterns. One of them gave me a glim from his bull's-eye as I put this on the grave one winter's night. It was painted on a board nailed to a stick. There was a bit of a row for form's sake, though I was never discovered, but on the whole, I think, the thing was appreciated. It deserved to be," he added complacently. "I had given the policeman a half-sovereign—gold in those days—and when we passed one another in the streets after that he would put a finger to his forelock and wink. Ah, well, I wonder what young men do at Oxford now? Work like moles, I fear, throwing up little tumps with neat state-aided paws."

He refilled his glass, sipped, and said: "How good t[h]is on an empty stomach!" We sat side by side, looking of the window, listening to the murmur of the stream, the sudden glad cries of thrushes and blackbirds.

"So you are getting cracking," he said, "—forgive expression, dear boy: it's one of Phil Menheniot's— Rosemullion. And I hear you intend to perpetuate t[h]e dynasty."

Well, I suppose in a place like Penmaen nothing is unseen, nothing left without comment. Still, I was surprised. Kitty and I were constantly together, but we were a middle-aged couple, nothing flamboyant about us, and I hoped our association would be seen as a friendship natural in the circumstances. But now I gathered that gossip was expecting more than this of us.

"Not," said Mr. Savage, "that I attach too much importance to Annie Hocking's nods and hints. Still, it would be natural enough in the circumstances. And if you do marry Miss Littledale, don't go in for one of these furtive little chats in a registrar's office. Look at those two words, my dear boy. Registrar! A man who keep a register, which is to say a list. Is that all you want—to put your name on a list? And office! Why, bless my soul, bookmakers have offices! No, no. You must come and speak up manfully in the sight of God and the congregation. It would give me pleasure to do you proud."

I assured him that no word of marriage had passed between me and Kitty, and that was true—so far as it went.

"Oh, words, words!" he said, emptying his glass with a swig. "What do words matter? Was there ever a time in human history when more men got together to talk more words? Conferences, congregations, councils, committees —words, words, words! They fly about the world to-day, the clever little men, dropping a word in Europe this morning and a word in America to-night, like birds dropping their turd as they fly, and never were men so far from any sort of understanding. Don't let words have too much importance with you, dear boy. God has an unwritten constitution. Well," he added casually, "did you know Will was on the way home? He's written at last."

At that, I sat up. Will was rapidly becoming in my mind a myth, one of those talked-of people one never meets, and I said sincerely: "Well, I *am* glad to hear that."

"We shall see," he said shortly, and shouted: "Annie!"

Annie Hocking came shuffling across the landing from Will's room.

"Annie, would you let Mr. Menheniot see Will's letter?"

She was wearing her sack-cloth apron and big boots. She looked at us suspiciously. "It's my letter," she said.

"Yes, I know, Annie," he said patiently; and to me he explained: "Annie received the letter this morning. I haven't read it, but she has kindly communicated the sense of it to me."

"I haven't got it with me," Annie said. "It's my letter."

Her fingers were crinkling something in the pocket of her apron. It was obviously the letter. She wanted us to know that it was there, and that there it would stay. "I haven't got it with me," she repeated. "It's simply that —what I told you. 'E calls me Dear Aunty, and says 'e's on the way home an' 'll be 'ere any time now. That's all."

"All right," Mr. Savage said politely. "Thank you— dear aunty."

She smiled with malicious triumph, crinkling away in her pocket. "I'll get on with his room," she said, and muttered cryptically, sidling out: "Blood's thicker'n water."

He stood with his back to me, looking out of the window, then turned, and said with a smile: "All gall is divided into three parts. Added together, they make Annie Hocking. Well, good-bye for now, dear boy. You're sure Jim is looking after you properly?"

I couldn't come back to the question of Jim's bills, so I raised it with Jim himself. As I expected, Mr. Savage had forgotten to pay any of them, and I put the matter right.

11

In the evening of this same day Kitty and I went for a walk. It was high time, I told myself, that I left Penmaen and settled down in Rosemullion, but before doing that I wanted to ask Kitty to be my wife. I had no doubt that she would say yes, but all the same it was not going to be an easy question to ask. I remembered the kiss she had given me on the terrace. She had never kissed me like that again, and I had never been able to kiss her like that. We kissed at meeting and at parting, and I had a feeling that, having given me a cue, she was waiting for me to follow it up. But I could not. I could not commit myself to what I should almost have considered an assault upon her. She was so ideally the sort of woman I wanted to share my life, the sort of woman I had never thought I should meet, had,

146

indeed, hardly thought to exist, that, now I had met her, I hated the idea of rough and tumble. It seemed to me altogether unbecoming to any relationship I could have with this serene and gracious woman. In the course of a walk one evening we took the cliff path at the end of the beach, came out on to the wild open space there that gave an immense view of the sea, and, before we knew where we were, had reached a point which overlooked a hollow full of last year's bracken. It had been beaten down into a bed on which a boy and girl of the village were in the unmistakable process of copulation. I was so shaken with disgust that I stood still, trembling, outraged that a woman like Kitty should be compelled, however accidentally, to cast a glance at such a spectacle. She took my arm and continued to walk, impelling me firmly past the spot. When we reached the upthrust rock from which we could see all round us, and which was my favourite place because there we *could be seen*, whoever might wander by, I was sweating and shaking and glad to sit down. But we did not sit long. As soon as I was recovered, I got up and suggested a return to the village. I could not remain in her company with even the thought of that episode between us, and I took care, as we went back, to avoid the hollow. Somehow, I could not kiss her at all as we parted that night. She looked at me sadly as she stood on the steps leading to her house, and said: "You mustn't let that sort of thing worry you, you know. That's how life is."

That she had even mentioned the matter filled me with dismay, and I almost rushed from her to the Menheniot Arms.

III

And so, on the evening of that day when I heard that Will Savage would soon be home, I was resolved to put an end to all these complications. It was a beautiful evening, and we took the usual walk, up the cliff path and on to the headland. The sun was going down. The sea was quiet and full of colour. We reached the place where the path skirted the bracken hollow, and I took Kitty's arm to steer her along a way that would give us no reminding sight of it. To my surprise, she resisted, and continued to walk towards that spot. On the brink of the hollow she paused, and said: "Let us sit down here for a moment." And she began to go down into the bracken.

I watched her go, but stood where I was. At the bottom she turned, and called: "Aren't you coming, Roger?"

"Kitty," I said, and the words stuck in my throat. "I've got something very important to say to you. Let's go on to our old place."

What I had to say I couldn't say *there*!

She came up slowly out of the hollow, and I offered a hand to help her over the brink. She did not take it, or look at me, and we went on side by side to what I thought of as "our rock."

Just to be there with Kitty was good. I was in no hurry to say what I had to say. I liked to be quiet and to feel her tranquillity flowing out into me. I knew her so much better now that I had read all her books. There were six of them, and I could see why they had never had large sales. They were so full of her own spirit, her sensitive understanding of the ways of birds and beasts, her hatred of cruelty and violence, her preference for country people living simple lives. It is true that in two of them were scenes that had bewildered me. I found it hard to believe that those few pages flowed essentially out of Kitty. No doubt, they had been necessary in order to portray the worst as well as the best of the people under her hand. I could see that a novelist might well have to do that; but I did not believe that when Kitty wrote those pages she did

148

anything but call on her recollection of other writers' work. Certainly she could not have entered imaginatively into the moments she described. I wished she had somehow been able to write the books without touching pitch. That was how I thought of it, and the pages, whenever they came to my mind, as they often did, were between us like that disgusting scene in the bracken hollow.

She was very quiet as we sat on our rock that night. Not so much as a murmur came up from the sea below us. It was a just-moving quilt of shot purple and violet. Even the gulls, often so noisy, were content to float and wheel soundlessly on the air. I was so full of happiness and peace that I could have wept. This, here and now; and a few miles away beloved Rosemullion, waiting for me and Kitty. I thought of the drawing-room, painted a parchment colour picked out in gold, and of the pictures I had bought in London now hanging there. On a night of spring like this it would not be too warm for a fire. I could see the light of it glowing on the walls.

Kitty said: "It's a bit cold sitting here, Roger. Let's be getting back."

"I was just thinking," I said, "that on a night like this we would have a fire in the drawing-room at Rosemullion."

Kitty got up. "*We?*" she said.

The word had slipped unintentionally out of my mouth, and I felt glad. It had spoken for me, said what I wanted to say.

"Yes—we," I repeated, with an emphasis that she could not misunderstand. I got up and stood by her. On the top of that thrusting rock, with the sea below us and the wild rough land behind us, we were lifted up for all the world to see us if they liked and to hear her answer.

"No, Roger," she said. "No."

It was so unexpected that I felt as though I had been

149

shot. I crumpled down on to the rock again as if I had literally received a heavy blow. I was aware of Kitty standing over me, pulling on a coat that I had carried up for her, and of the grey and gold splotches of lichen living on the granite into which my fingers were clawing. I could not believe that those two words, spoken so decisively, were all that she had to say, and I waited for her to speak again. When she did, it was simply to say: "Are you coming now, Roger?"

I didn't answer, I couldn't answer, and she began to move slowly away. Once she stopped and looked back at me with a sort of wistful speculation, then went on and was soon over the curve of the land, out of sight.

I stayed there till it was quite dark, then got up and started off at a furious pace, full of anger and frustration. Down in the bracken-hollow as I went by I heard murmurs and saw a white flesh-gleam, and increased my speed to take me past the horrid place. And *that* was where Kitty had invited me to go! Disgust flamed up in me, and I said I had been lucky to escape from such a woman.

IV

That night I met Bella Thoroughgood for the first time. I have explained how Dr. Littledale's house was the one building of distinction in Penmaen's ragged street, and how a lane ran back on either side of it, leaving it detached. Down one of these lanes, and thus crouched right behind the doctor's house and a little to one side of it, was Annie Hocking's cottage. It was minute, built of whitewashed mud, with a slate roof that had again and again been washed over with liquid cement, so that the gradually increased weight thus imparted caused the roof to sag and ripple. It was a witch's den if ever there was one, with tufts of ragwort sprouting in the gutters, blocking them up, causing the frequent rain to overflow down the sides of the cottage, mottling them with patches of damp green. You would see Annie's vast width edging itself into the lane and disappearing like some monstrous creature retreating into a den too small. When she emerged, you would see her pause, nose and eyes seeming to sniff and squint before she would decide to entrust her precious being to whatever might be abroad in the world.

When I got back to Penmaen that moonless night, the lamp hanging outside the Menheniot Arms cast the only light there was. It showed me Annie Hocking coming down the street with one hand carrying a suitcase and the other tucked into a girl's arm. They had just drawn level with the entrance to the lane and Annie was about to squeeze into it, when the girl looked across at Jim Brokenshire's and asked: "Is that a pub?"

"Yes, midear," said Annie.

"Then for God's sake let's have a drink before we do anything else."

They crossed over the road and went into the Menheniot Arms.

I had not seen this girl before, and I suppose I had been in Penmaen long enough to have acquired a village curiosity. The lamp outside the pub did not give much light, but it had shown me a young woman shapelessly wrapped in one of those near-white duffle coats fastened with wooden toggles that one saw in the towns at that time. She was wearing dark-blue trousers and red shoes, and a square of gay silk was tied about her hair. The few words she had spoken were in a clear and rather penetrating voice that did not belong to the district. Who she was, what on earth she was doing in Annie Hocking's company, I could not make out. I followed them into the pub.

I learned all too soon who and what Bella Thoroughgood was, and I might as well put down the outline here.
She was an only child, and her mother died when she was
seven or eight years old. Her father was a well-to-do trades-
man. He owned three or four grocers' shops in London
districts. He was a man of rigid religious beliefs, a deacon
of some Nonconformist sect. Faced with the upbringing
of the child, he solved his problem by sending her off to
a boarding-school. She appears to have been a lively little
creature from the beginning. She loved to sing. The head-
mistress of the school was attracted to her and suggested
to Mr. Thoroughgood that when Bella's schooldays were
over she might well be trained as a concert singer. Mr.
Thoroughgood was not much impressed. Public singers
seemed to him little removed from actors and actresses,
and he could imagine nothing nearer to the devil than
that. However, when Bella's schooldays were in fact
ended—she was eighteen then—it chanced that a "sacred
concert" was being arranged to benefit the funds of Mr.
Thoroughgood's chapel, and Bella was given a place on
the programme. She sang "Jerusalem, Jerusalem, lift
up your voice and sing," and other even more regrettable
ditties, as she herself put it; but they brought tears to
Mr. Thoroughgood's eyes, and made him think that, after
all, God had perhaps entrusted Bella to him for purposes
of His glory. No one could fail to be a better man after
hearing Bella sing. He was not hasty, and pondered the
matter throughout the following winter and spring,
encouraging Bella during that time to sing her "sacred
songs" wherever opportunity offered. He then wrote out
a document in which Thomas Lofthouse Thoroughgood
of the one part undertook to provide the means whereby
Bella Thoroughgood of the other part should receive

"reasonable vocal tuition" with a view to public appearance as a profession singer conditional upon the said
Bella Thoroughgood hereby giving her solemn oath and
promise that she would sing only such songs as would
"redound to the honour and glory of God."

I have seen this extraordinary document. Bella carried
it about with her. "I was shattered," she said. "It wasn't
so much the honour and glory of God stuff as the idea of
going back to a teacher. I was always a lazy little bitch."

She turned down her father's offer; and he, greatly
annoyed by the rejection of what he thought a magnani-
mous gesture, told her that she had better, then, find something else to do. She would not be allowed to "eat the
bread of idleness." She must go to a commercial college
and learn to look after the books of his firm. Bella replied
to this by simply refusing to do anything of the sort. She
loafed about at home, doing nothing.

In this impasse, Mr. Thoroughgood remembered his
sister, Mrs. Mince. Mrs. Mince had not prospered like her
brother. She had married a poor man endowed with every
qualification for making himself poorer: bad health, a
dislike of work, an addiction to tipsters and tapsters. Since
her husband's death, Mrs. Mince had found life easier.
She kept a boarding-house in a south-coast seaside town.
It would do Bella no harm, Mr. Thoroughgood decided,
to spend a summer with her aunt. It would show her
which side her bread was buttered on, and perhaps she
she would come back in a more reasonable frame of mind.
The financial arrangements were soon made, and Bella
was glad to go. That was in 1938. Davy Trimble's concert
party appeared on the beach every afternoon, and Davy
Trimble lodged with Mrs. Mince.

No one would have imagined Mrs. Mince to be either a
sister of Mr. Thoroughgood or a widow with a gruelling
marriage behind her. She was fat and full of laughter,

and she liked Mr. Trimble to take his meals at her own table because he was a man of jokes and nonsense. Never had Bella had a happier time. Every afternoon she sat in a free deck-chair on the sand, and though she soon knew every song and every joke and every word of every sketch by heart she never failed to enjoy it all. Mr. Trimble could skate over the thinnest ice, beneath which, so to speak, was very hot water indeed, and Bella enjoyed that, too. She found herself waiting for it. And then came the day when she went up on to the platform.

On Wednesday afternoons the audience was allowed to take part in the show, almost to run it, with Mr. Trimble as *compère*. They could sing, dance, recite, or, if they liked, stand on their heads. Then there was a prize for whoever was voted the best performer of the after- noon. Bella had long wanted to go on to the platform, and on a July afternoon she overcame her not formidable scruples. She was good to look at. She had that sort of fair hair which is almost white, and blue eyes, and, she said, with the frankness she practised on me from the begin- ning, "I had learned the importance of a tight sweater." Of all things, she sang "Jerusalem, Jerusalem, lift up your voice and sing."

Nothing gets an English audience like a mixture of mush and religiosity, and the applause from the cigarette- smokers and chocolate-munchers in the deck-chairs left no doubt at all that Bella was going to be voted the prize- winner that day. The audience called for more, and Bella gave them more, and people drew near from all over the sands and stood in a semi-circle behind the deck-chairs. It is not difficult to imagine that the crowd and the golden sand and the sun pouring down and the jolly colours of blinds and awnings on the front all swam together that afternoon in a haze of glory for Bella; and the bags shaken under the noses of those who were not paying for deck-chairs were satisfactorily filled for Mr. Trimble.

It was so usual for these enterprising amateurs to be figures of fun, keeping the show going on the humour of their own ineptitude that Meg Merril must have spent an unhappy afternoon. She was the young woman on whom the show depended for its singing, and her singing never got this sort of response. And what should she do the next week but get herself knocked down by a motor car. A fractured pelvis, and what the local paper called facial contusions and abrasions, put an end to her for that season, and when the hospital had done with her she was taken back by ambulance to Battersea, to be plain Enid Hopkins.

It is not surprising that Davy Trimble decided to use what was to hand. Bella took her first professional job, and as, in a company of that sort, everyone is expected to do a bit of everything, she was soon acting—very badly, she said—in the little sketches that helped to make the programme. They were not modest pieces, and she began to learn something of the ways of the world. What she didn't learn from the programme was imparted to her by other members of the party, especially by Trimble. She became his mistress. "That was the happiest summer of my life," she told me.

Mr. Thoroughgood, of course, knew nothing of these goings-on. He had troubles enough of his own. This was the summer of Munich, and Mr. Thoroughgood decided that Europe was wholly given over to perdition and that clearly God's purposes for the future would be entrusted to the people of the United States. He made a clean sweep, sold his shops and other properties, and prepared for departure. When all this was safely settled, he went down to see how Bella was getting on. He gave no warning of his coming. When he reached Mrs. Mince's house an over-worked little slattern told him that the mistress was out and would not be back for an hour. He strolled down to the beach and was in time to be delighted by Mr. Trimble's riskiest sketch in which Bella played the part of a servant-girl having an "affair" with the master behind his wife's back.

Bella loved to read her father's letters aloud to me. She kept them as one would keep some favourite pieces of literature for bedside reading. "A blackness as of hell descended upon my soul," he wrote of that moment when he stood in his free pitch on the sand behind the sixpenny deck-chairs watching his daughter's performance.

He may not have been putting it too high. It may have been like that to him, though he did not know, and never knew, that the little mistress on the stage was a mistress in fact.

There was a show-down at Mrs. Mince's. Seeing that Bella had chosen her career and was earning her keep, she would no longer need his support, Mr. Thoroughgood said. He would continue to pray for her: that was one thing, he said, she could always count on, and though the world might say he was abandoning her, that was not so, for the prayer of a righteous man availeth much. He would always be side by side with her at the mercy seat. A long time afterwards she received a letter from him bearing an American stamp, an illegible postmark and no address. Whether he was alive or dead at the time I met her, she neither knew nor cared.

VI

After this, things were not so cosy at Mrs. Mince's. She had been well aware of all that was going on between her niece and Mr. Trimble. It was one in the eye for that stingy and sanctimonious humbug, her brother. Still, he had been paying her generously enough for Bella's board nd lodgings, and now Bella found that she must pay for erself. Her wages, not excessive, could no longer be rittered away. She suggested to Mr. Trimble that he hould meet the bills, seeing that she was "his wife." He ughed, and asked: "Since when?"

Altogether, that was an eye-opening summer; and when he leaves began to fall in the promenade gardens, and he deck-chairs became emptier, and the wind-clattered uckets and spades disappeared from the shop fronts, and he landladies began to thank God that that lot was one for another year, Bella disappeared with the other ligrants and left the beach and the town to the sea and he winter wind. The girl who watched the photographs f the concert party unhooked for the last time from the oard by the pitch on the sand—her own among them, vearing the short skirt and the goffered cap of her scandalous little scene—this was a different girl from the one vho had hopefully arrived to spend the summer with unty Mince.

Mr. Trimble at the seaside in his concert-party clothes. arning a modest income, was one thing. Mr. Trimble in ingy London lodgings, with nothing coming in regularly, as another; not at all so amusing a companion. "My gent" became his theme song. It was incredible to Bella ow many hours Davy spent with his agent, to come back reary, depressed, and often enough quarrelsome. Sometimes his agent found him a minute part in a film or with ome B.B.C. show, and once or twice Bella herself was in "crowd scene." But it was a miserable winter, and how ley kept body and soul together she never knew. When was over, she didn't like Mr. Trimble very much, or he er; but they were becoming a habit to one another.

The spring of 1939 brought more cheerfulness, for the acker who had financed the show in which Davy and ella first met asked Davy to get another show together for a North Wales seaside town. They opened in May, and, with steady work in the sunshine and sea breezes, the neurotic quarrels of the winter became fewer, and Bella had a fairly happy time till Mrs. Davy Trimble appeared one day on the promenade with the twins in a perambulator. She told Mr. Trimble it was time that they either got together again or arranged a divorce.

When war began, Bella found herself, without Davy Trimble's backing, such as it was, almost penniless, for she was never a saver. As a last favour, he got her a job with a party of entertainers who went about the country delighting the toilers in forges and factories. Bella sang "Jerusalem" to them with great acceptance, and later she transferred to another party which went overseas. She sang in the Middle East and in the North African desert and saw with her own eyes Arabs and camels and tanks. Also, when the party was invited after a show to an officers' mess, she met Lieutenant Will Savage for the first time.

So the war went by, and when it was over she again had no money and could get no work, but a generous government decided to make her a grant for a course in a London dramatic school. This, she was convinced, like thousands of others, was all that was needed to put her in line with the Vivien Leighs and Celia Johnsons. But somehow it didn't. She began to know "My agent" with the same dour persistent intimacy that had marked Davy's association with that gentleman. She at last got a job with a repertory company in a small provincial town and learned for the first time in her life what work was. But she never got anything but negligible parts, and, seeing that the British public despises the theatre and doesn't really want it, she soon had no parts at all. The company was disbanded, leaving the small provincial town to its true love, the cinema.

She had occasionally helped the scene painter to dab

away at canvas flats, and found that she had a certain aptitude with a paint brush. Poor Bella! She had a certain aptitude at singing and acting and painting, but it was all amateur aptitude without guts or conviction. However, the generous government was there again. It was pathetically eager to come to the help of the dabblers, and this time Bella found herself grant-aided into an arts-school. She cut little pictures into little bits of linoleum and walloped about with oil-paint and produced in water-colour runny little scenes that the vicar's daughter of Victorian times would have been ashamed to show to her drawing-master. But in our more generous era they were enough to wheedle the taxpayers' money out of the paternal exchequer. There was always hope of one more teacher on the endless belt of teachers to teach teachers to teach.

"Of course," said Bella. "I couldn't *live* on the grant. And one *has* to live, hasn't one? I mean, not just *exist*."

It was incredible how innocent she could look when she said a thing like that. The appearance of innocence was her most devastating quality. Her blue eyes would look at you with the candour of a child's.

"Why should I *pretend*?" she said. "I *liked* it. From the first time with Davy, I was mad about it. If I'm *made* that way, what am I to *do*?" She looked like a kitten talking of milk.

So the government deficiency was made up, and at last the government grant came to an end, and Bella was once more faced with the question: What had it all done for her?—her singing, her bits of pert acting, her nibbling at squares of linoleum. She was living with an advertisement copy-writer, playing with the idea of becoming a commercial artist, when she met Will Savage again. Her young man had been asked to a fashionable hotel: as it happened, the hotel where once I had dined with Phil

159

Menheniot. He was to meet a client there, and he too
Bella along and left her sitting in a lounge with a drin
when he went up to the client's room.

I could imagine the scene. I had watched it enacter
I remembered how Phil had been seeing me off, and
passing the girl, had said familiarly: "I'll be right back.
And Will Savage, who, Mr. Savage had reminded me
had as much Menheniot blood in his veins as I had mysel
had been sitting there where Phil had sat, eyeing this gir
drinking alone; and presently he had gone across, an
said: "Hallo! Haven't we met somewhere?"

VII

They soon remembered where they had met and tha
gave them plenty to talk about. Will said: "I'm stayin
here. Have pity on my loneliness and dine with me."

I imagine it was that phrase "I'm staying here" tha
settled the matter. I don't think Bella Thoroughgoo
ever loved anyone in her life, ever felt so much as con
mon affection for anyone. She had now reached the poir
where it wasn't any good to pretend to herself any mor
None of her half-developed little bits of equipment woul
ever give her more than a chancy existence on the edge o
poverty. She would either have to give up pretending an
work or find someone who would do it for her. Bett
still, someone who, without working at all, could mak
life pleasant for both of them.

It didn't take her long to decide. She had been sittin
there with her drink, dreamily absorbing the atmospher
of luxury, looking enviously at other women who seeme
at home there, lulled by the carpeted soundlessness, th
quiet lighting, the soft coming and going of uniforme
servants. Only the chance that her young man had

wealthy client to interview had brought her fleetingly there, and she knew enough about the young man to be aware that he was not likely ever to be there in his own right. It was not a thought that would have meant much to some women, but it meant a lot to Bella.

So she agreed to dine with Will Savage, and he said: "I think a little intimate meal in one's own room is so charming, don't you?"

Bella agreed, and they went up in the lift, and her feet dreamed along the quiet corridors.

"I say—I'm not stealing you, am I?" Will asked. "You weren't waiting for someone?"

"Oh, no," Bella said. "I find the place so restful. An actress's life is pretty hard. People think it's all glamour, but really it's nerve-racking. I often come here just to be quiet—just to be myself."

"What are you in now?" Will asked.

"Nothing, you silly, or I'd be at the theatre, wouldn't I? I simply *had* to turn things down. I'm resting."

Will opened a door with his key. He was blueing his gratuity, giving himself a good time while it lasted. When it was gone, he would think about going back to the old man. Meantime, life owed him these few weeks. He had hated the stinking war and wanted to forget it. "Well, how d'you like it?" he asked proprietorially, as though this were his for ever.

Bella walked across the sitting-room and stood at the window, looking down on the traffic sliding by far below, and at the lights coming on, throwing rippling snakes of flame on to the water of the river. She liked it very much. It was oddly unlike digs shared with Davy Trimble.

Everything was so quiet. She turned, almost startled, on hearing voices in the room, the carpets were so thick, the waiter so soft-padded. Will Savage was ordering drinks, and he ordered the dinner to follow them, and when the drinks came and the waiter was gone they sat sipping them and smoking on a couch drawn up to the window. The hum of the town came up to them, and Bella said feelingly: "This is heaven." Will's head was against hers. "After dinner," he whispered, "are you going to be an angel?"

He hadn't learned then how unnecessary a question that was.

VIII

She loved to talk of such episodes. I hated her and hated myself as I listened: hated her as a victim of Circe must have hated that bitch. But so long as she lived I was powerless, and now that she is dead I sometimes wake up in the night sweating from her embraces, and even in the daytime live them over. "From the first," she said, "I did what I liked with Will Savage."

That night there could be no going back to her young man. "I'd given Will something to remember. He saw me off positively fawning." She called on a friend, another actress who was "resting," and shared her room for the night. She never bothered to recover her poor bits and pieces. She had arranged to meet Will Savage for lunch; and she was already so sure of "where she had him," as she expressed it, that she could afford to be frank in her blue-eyed innocent way. "Look, darling. I'm not really resting. I expect you've guessed that, haven't you? A girl's only got to look at you to know you're a pretty experienced type who doesn't need to be told that when an actress says resting she means rusting. I haven't had a job for months, and heaven knows when I'll have one again. London's absolutely lousy with little half-baked turn-outs from the drama schools. Still, that's lucky for you, darling, isn't it?

162

We could go anywhere we liked, couldn't we? We wouldn't be disturbed by a telegram calling me back to play Juliet at the Old Vic."

"Why go away from here? Don't you like being in London?"

"I'm thinking of you, darling. I think a girl *should* think of a man, don't you? Why waste your money? This place must be horribly expensive. And actually"—all blue eyes again—"I *prefer* it in the open air."

So Will Savage bought her a few clothes and a day or two later they booked as Captain and Mrs. Savage at an hotel on the fringes of Dartmoor where there was plenty of open air. They stayed there for a fortnight, and then Will decided that the time had come to go home. "I think we ought to be married, Bella, don't you?"

Bella was not so sure. She had had time to make some discoveries about Will. His apparent riches were merely an officer's gratuity flashing brilliantly in the pan. His father was nothing but an old parson in some God-forsaken country place at the back of nowhere, and altogether there didn't seem, in her phrase, much future in it. If she had known that Will's father was a rich man she might have taken a different view; but Will himself didn't know this. The only father he had ever known was a queer ancient who had long since ceased to think of such matters, much less speak of them.

IX

I know a good deal about Will Savage now, and I think of him with the sympathy one extends to a fellow victim of calamity. Like me, he had never known the care of a mother, and he had missed, too, what I had enjoyed: the companionship and support of a loving father. Old

163

Savage, embarked so late on a marriage that turned to nothing but an occasion of disgust, must have had subconscious feelings of aversion from the child who was there to remind him of it after it was happily done with. I doubt whether the old man was ever aware of these feelings. He was already old and full of unusual quirks and idiosyncrasies, and it would seem to himself that these alone formed a barrier between him and the boy. But I am sure there was more in it than that, and that Will was aware of not being loved.

He was packed off to a prep school as soon as could be, and then to a public school, so that from his earliest years he saw his father only at holiday times. These were not such holiday times as other boys knew, when a family would pack up—brothers, sisters, parents—and be off as a happy clan to some change of scene. They were solitary occasions within the shadow of the old man. Mr. Savage's courtesy to the boy was faultless; but what boy wants courtesy as the primary thing? He would prefer the rough edge of a tongue, perhaps even a blow, now and then, so long as there was an occasional tickling of the ribs and laughter and loving indignity. It is courteous to respect a fellow-being's right to privacy by providing him with a room of his own; but it can be torture to make him feel that that room is where he is expected to be, out of one's way. It is courteous to concern yourself with a boy's progress in his studies; but when it is clear that to you, a distinguished scholar, he is, in such matters, little more than a dolt, then your courteous abstention from worrying him about them can seem bitterly like contempt.

So young Will kept out of the way as much as he could during the holidays, amusing himself in the summer by going out with the fishermen and sailing his own small boat and lying in the sun on the beaches or swimming in the sea. There was not much wrong with that. It was perhaps a better holiday than some of his friends were having on stylish yachts or at fashionable resorts. Will loved it all; everybody in the village knew him and liked him, and he needn't go home till bedtime. He would potter about, mending or painting someone's boat, repairing someone's fishing-tackle, digging lug-worms for someone's bait, and his aunt, Annie Hocking, liked to be about on such occasions, chatting of this and that, especially of the virtues of her sister, his mother. "Not that you need mention 'er to 'im."

Such occasional remarks deepened the boy's sense of separation from his father; for he had already learned in odd indefinable ways that his mother was not someone to be spoken of at home, and that the beautiful woman whose photographs crowded his father's study was nothing to do with him.

During the winter holidays life was not so easy. The long nights kept him indoors; his father remained in his study; he himself kept to his room, for nowhere else in the house, that was more mouldy and decayed with the passing of each year, offered a gleam of comfort. So he would pile his fire, take out the pipe he was learning to smoke, and yawn till bedtime over his infantile books. I could not wonder that, once he was in the army, he did not spend a leave at home.

I don't read much modern fiction, but I have read a few novels about the two world wars, and in all of them soldiers break down into moral ruins, drinking and leching and cursing themselves blue. I don't think these are true pictures. The astonishing thing to me is not how many men do that, but how few. Certainly Will Savage didn't do it. He learned to drink, he had adventures with women; but these things were episodic, not fundamental. If the war had turned him into a creature disrupted by evil, he would not so easily have been Bella Thorough-

good's prey. And surely he would not so innocently hav
brought her home to Penmaen. It would have been
dangerous experiment even if he and his father had bee
in accord. As it was, it was disastrous.

X

I never saw this young man who had so great an effec
upon my life. It was from Annie Hocking and Bella tha
I learned what happened when he brought the girl t
Penmaen. Annie was at the vicarage when they arrived i
a taxi-cab as dusk was beginning on that May afternoon
It was the usual Annie, girded with a sack, wearing he
hobnailed boots, pottering about with her weedkillers o
the garden paths, giving the impression that had alway
been so powerful in my mind that she was there not s
much doing things as watching things. It was a mild an
beautiful evening. The dusk was lit by the glimmer o
blossom on the neglected apple-trees, and already th
march of the year had thickened the foliage all about th
house so that the sense of being imprisoned there wa
strong. Mr. Savage had been taking his afternoon walk
and at this moment he returned and stood looking abou
him, seeming to be in a softened mood, saturated, I shoul
guess, by the memories of all the May months he had see
come and go there, thinking, perhaps, of the girl he ha
photographed under one of those apple-trees, with on
arm lifted to a branch and a big hat trailing to the groun
from the other. He did not speak to Annie, who covertl
watched him standing in reverie, leaning on his stick
Even she was impressed by the quiet of the moment,
sense of everything standing still, waiting. She stopped he
pottering and raking, and, without turning to her, M
Savage said: "Thank you, Annie." Now that the silenc

was complete, she was the first to hear it broken a moment later by the sound of the taxi-cab's approach.

Bella said to me: "He terrified me the moment I set eyes on him," and I am sure he did. The taxi was gone, and there were those two advancing towards Mr. Savage up the path. His son, who had never been loved, was now not even familiar. He had gone away a first-year undergraduate, hardly more than a schoolboy, and he came back tall, tough, moustached. And with him was this girl in the duffle coat, with a square of red silk on her head, wearing trousers and with shoes that extruded the painted nails of deformed toes. She was smoking a cigarette. I can well imagine the obscene effect of this apparition upon Mr. Savage, and his effect upon her, as he stood, tall, black and doomful, leaning upon the stick and watching her approach. She and Will stopped before his gaze, as though it had frozen them. Then, without a word, he turned and walked into the house.

All the misery of remembered winter holidays must have broken in a wave over Will's mind. He said, like a snubbed schoolboy: "What's wrong *now*?" and that was Annie's cue to take him to her heart. "Well, you've got a kiss for your old aunty, haven't you, midear?" and she drew him in an embrace upon her sack.

She, too, must have seemed odd to Bella. The girl threw down her cigarette, crushed it with her foot, and looked about her. The dark, decaying house, the press of trees about it, a coldness now that the night was coming on. "God!" she said. "What a ghastly place! You never told me your old man was like that. More like your great-grandfather."

"It'll be all right, Bella. It'll be all right, I tell you," Will said with a hopefulness he could hardly have felt. "Here's aunty, anyhow. Aunty, this is Bella. We're going to be married."

167

And now it was Bella's turn to be hugged and kissed by Annie, who was rejoicing at being on the side of evident disruption.

As they stood there talking, a light appeared in a window above them. Mr. Savage had lit his study lamp. They heard the study window open, and looked up. The apostolic head was thrust through the window. "Aren't you coming in, Will?" Mr. Savage asked reasonably. "It's a long time since I've seen you, my boy. You may bring the young lady with you."

"You go on up," Annie Hocking said. "Go an' get it over. I'll be in the kitchen. My, it's good to see you again, midear. Lookin' such a man, too. Don't be afraid of '*e*.'"

Will must have felt a good deal short of a man as he and Bella dropped their suitcases on the stone flags of the hall and began to climb the stairs. Bella shivered. This was so unlike the suite in the London hotel. She may have been a little reassured when Will, having knocked at the study door and been bidden to enter, stood aside for her to go in. Mr. Savage had lit the lamp and put a match to the fire. He now shut the window and pulled the curtain across. The room at once seemed human and comforting in its rough and ready way. Even Mr. Savage without his stick and sombrero was not, in her eyes, so formidable. He was standing up with his back to the fire in an attitude I knew well, cutting tobacco into his palm.

If there was one thing Bella prided herself upon more than another it was that she knew how to deal with men, old or young. She believed in direct attack, in doing something that would at once put them on easy terms with her. And so now, one swift glance having shown her the array of photographs in the room, she stepped to Mr. Savage's writing-table, picked up the one that was propped there, and cried: "Oh, what a beautiful lady! This must be Will's mother!"

168

Old Savage must have felt that his gods had been outraged. He took the photograph from her hands, and then walked round the room gathering up the pictures of Sylvia from tables, book-cases and walls. He placed them all carefully out of sight in a cupboard, as though to save them from defilement. Then he filled his pipe, lit it, and at last said: "Now, Will, who is this lady whose intuition is so grievously at fault? Sit down, madam."

Bella sat down, threw one leg over the other, presenting the unpleasing picture of her painted callouses.

"Will was standing up all the time," she said, "like a little boy. The old man never even shook hands with him. You'd think they'd met only yesterday. Old man! Old devil, I call him!"

Will had indeed miscalculated in laying that long absence, and that long silence hardly broken by a letter, between himself and his father. Mr. Savage had been left for too many years alone with his fantasies. They had become more real to him than flesh and blood.

"Father," Will said, "this is Bella—Bella Thoroughgood."

The old man, standing up by the fire, bowed towards the duffle coat. He said nothing, as though he felt that there was nothing to say until something more than a name had been given to him.

As Will added nothing to this, Mr. Savage said: "Your aunt had the privilege, denied to me, of being informed that you were on the way. Did she expect this lady?"

Mr. Savage turned a long considering look upon Bella. He looked at her toes, her tobacco-stained fingers, her trousers, her toggled coat. He drew hard on his churchwarden and blew out a cloud of smoke. "Why?" he asked.

The word, so simple and devastating, threw both Will and Bella into consternation; and, seeing this, Mr. Savage began to laugh. I had heard that laugh, and it was very

unpleasant. It would come when he had recited to me one
of his scathing epitaphs. No doubt he felt now that he
had composed Bella's epitaph in a single word. This
would account for his repeating to himself with enjoy-
ment, as he did: Why? Why?

The word and the laugh gave Will some fibre at last,
and he said angrily: "Well, for one thing, because I love
her, and for another, because we've been living for some
time as man and wife."

Bella, with a shaking hand, took a cigarette from her
case. Mr. Savage bent towards her courteously with a
match. "Where were you married?" he asked.

"We are not married," Will said.

Mr. Savage straightened himself, considered the burning match for a moment, then blew it out. "Then you are
not living as man and wife," he said. "You are living as
man and whore."

"Very well," Will said defiantly, "you should be the
first to want such a situation rectified."

"Oh, no. The sin is yours. *You* should be the first. I
shall be pleased to give you any spiritual direction you
ask for. It's not merely a question of getting married. That
would be shoving a sacrament on top of a sin. There is
first the question of repentance."

Bella said: "Well, of all the damned home-
comings——" But both Will and his father ignored her.
As though this were the most usual discussion in the
world, Mr. Savage turned to a cupboard, took out his
brandy bottle and two glasses. "You will join me?" he
said to Will; and Will said hotly: "No, I won't."

Mr. Savage poured his brandy. "Your very good health,
my dear boy."

Will shouted in anger and exasperation: "Look,
Father, for God's sake try and see this with my eyes."

"For *God's* sake?"

"Well, for common humanity's, then."

"The same thing in the long run, my dear boy, if common humanity would only realize it."

("I mightn't have been there," Bella said; and I am sure that for Mr. Savage she no longer was.)

Will said desperately: "I give you one last chance to act as a human being. Since you appear to find us objectionable, Bella and I will remove ourselves as soon as possible. May we stay here to-night?"

"You may not. This house is sanctified to me by blessed memories. It would be most unseemly to turn it into a brothel."

"I've never seen such a look of horror on a man's face," Bella said. "Poor Will! He was rather a weak-minded type, you know. He had a very thin skin. When the old man said that, he looked as if he were being flayed alive with hot knives. Oh, but that was a wicked old devil, wicked down to his heart's roots. He knew how to say just what would make Will hate him, and hate himself and hate me. He was absolute hate all through, old Savage was." She could not forget that except for "Sit down, madam"—almost a command—not one word had been spoken to her by Mr. Savage.

Will almost leapt from the room, seizing Bella by the wrist and dragging her with him. In the kitchen he sat down on a wooden chair, panting. Annie Hocking was hovering, awaiting news. He was unable to give her any. He sat there with his face in his hands for a time, then jumped to his feet. "Aunty," he said, "look after Bella. Take her to your place to-night. I'll write to you as soon as possible."

Without another word, he ran into the hall, picked up his suitcase, and left the house. The two women had followed him, but he would not speak to them. They watched him go, and then Annie said complacently:

"I could 'ave told 'im 'ow it'd be. Well, if you're ready, let's go."

They went down beside the stream towards the hamlet, and as they came under the light of Jim Brokenshire's lamp I saw Bella for the first time. On that night when Kitty said she would not marry me.

CHAPTER ELEVEN

I

I FOLLOWED the two women into the Menheniot Arms. When I first came down to instal myself in Rosemullion, two months before this, I was a teetotaller as near as makes no difference. But Jim Brokenshire, Mr. Savage and Tom Littledale between them had given me a taste for a little liquor now and then, usually wine. But I had not taken to sitting in Jim's bar. I drank my wine with my meals, and they were usually eaten alone. But that night, so miserable did I feel, the cheerful-looking room attracted me. The fire was burning, the lamplight fell on the fully-rigged model ships that Jim liked to make and that stood on wall-brackets, and on the red curtains, and on the gleaming brass of a ship's bell that customers struck if they wished to call Jim from the back premises.

Tom Littledale was there. He liked to stroll across and drink a pint after surgery hours. He and three fishermen were playing darts, and a few other people with drinks before them sat near the fire, stolidly ruminant as cows couched in a field.

The quiet friendly atmosphere attracted me. For the first time in my life, I wanted—needed—the companionship of my fellows. Jim and Tom greeted me; the game of darts went on, and I sat down as far as I could from everybody, but glad to see them there. Annie Hocking and Bella had gone up to the bar. Annie ordered a glass of port and Bella a dry Martini. They picked up the drinks and, to my discomfiture, carried them across the room and sat down near me. Jim said: "You joinin' the happy throng to-night, Mr. Menheniot? What can I get you?"

I ordered a half-bottle of wine, and as I sat there waiting for it I was aware of the interest Bella's arrival had awakened. The frequenters of the bar were a pretty constant lot. Any stranger would have been carefully inspected. A stranger like Bella, ten a penny in any sizeable town, given away *gratis* in London, was something they did not often see in Penmaen. You could almost hear their brains ticking. At that time of night, it was unlikely that she was a passer-through. She would be staying in the village, for the night at least, and Annie Hocking was with her. Who on earth could she be? Chairs were carefully adjusted to bring her into view: her trousers, her painted fingernails and toenails, the sleek white-gold hair that fell to her neck and then curved inward. She was sitting there under my eyes, and I was as interested as anyone. I had seen Bellas by the score trotting about in London. Here, it was different. She didn't "belong," as the Cornish say. Her effect was disruptive.

The wine warmed me, made me even more appreciative of company than I had been when I came in. Annie Hocking, sitting so near to me, did not seem as disgusting as usual. When she said good evening to me, I was able to reply amiably enough. She did not introduce the girl.

Presently Tom Littledale called across the room: "What news from the vicarage, Annie? Anything more from Will?"

I suppose Annie had been waiting for that moment. To be the only possessor of news that will interest many people is always to be in a powerful position, and Annie was not going to part with everything at once. She sipped her port and chuckled. "News from the vicarage? You'd be surprised!"

Jim came to take away the women's empty glasses, and Bella said: "Same again, please, for both of us."

It was the first time she had spoken. The hungry ears

snapped at her voice. Not a Cornish voice. Not a voice with any accent or individuality. A voice divorced from locality.

Jim renewed the drinks, and everyone was waiting for Annie Hocking to embroider her bleak hint. She didn't oblige.

Presently someone asked: "What'd surprise us, Annie midear?"

"Plenty," she said, sipping. "Not that it surprises *me*. That old devil."

"Ay," an ancient encouraged her. "You know'n, Annie. None better. What be 'e up to now?"

"My own sister's son," Annie said. "'Im that I brought up more 'Ocking than Savage. Me 'e belong to—not to that old devil. Me 'e ought t'ave come to, if I 'ad my rights."

One of the fishermen passed a wink to his companion. "Ay, we know your rights, Annie, midear. It's you ought to be up to Rosemullion—not Mr. Menheniot 'ere."

I blushed to find myself pulled thus suddenly into the discussion; but there was happily an impatience because the matter had been switched from whatever it was that Annie had to tell.

"Ay, but what be Mr. Savage up to now?" insisted the ancient.

Annie took up her glass. "You'll know soon enough," she said. "It's not to the likes of me you should be comin' for high matters."

"But, Annie, midear. . . ." someone started, when to the surprise of all Bella spoke in her clear voice. "Of all the palaver!" she said. "Why make a mystery out of it? Will came home to-night, and I came with him. He wants to marry me, and told his father so. But apparently Mr. Savage doesn't like the cut of my jib or something. So there was a dust-up, and Will walked out. Where he's gone to and when he'll be back, don't ask me."

Having made this crisp statement, as much to my surprise as everyone else's, Bella got up. She was tapping a cigarette on one of her long red fingernails. There was an ash-tray on my table with a few matches in the attached holder. I struck one and stood up to give her a light. Our faces were very close together, and I looked into her innocent blue eyes. She cupped both her hands round my hand to take the light, and I was aware that for a moment her fingers were subtly and secretly stroking mine. Then her eyes suddenly did not look innocent. They had a meaning that I could not mistake, and when she drew away, blew out smoke, and said abruptly "Thanks," she had forged the first link of the fatal chain that was to bind me.

II

I have said that it had become a pleasant routine for me to take breakfast with Tom and Kitty. The next morning I did not do so. I could not face Kitty. I was in a great trouble of mind. My sleep is usually sound and refreshing, but I had awakened out of a confused night. The story told by this girl whose name I did not yet know had set me thinking of the scene at the vicarage. Knowing Mr. Savage so well, I could imagine his implacability when faced by such a woman; and knowing Will Savage well enough through his revealing room, I could see how he would crumble and surrender. Then I thought of the girl herself, and to my horror found myself warming to her image. When at last I fell into troubled sleep, I was goaded by dreams. I was down in the hollow among the bracken with Kitty, and she was stroking my fingers. I woke sweating, in a disorder of mind and body.

When I went downstairs, I asked Jim Brokenshire to

give me some breakfast, and he did so. "I suppose we'll be losing you soon, Mr. Menheniot?" he said. "From what I hear, things are shaking down up to Rosemullion."

"Yes, Jim. You'll come and see the place, I hope, when you have a chance. I'll be away soon now."

"The doctor and Miss Kitty'll miss you. Not much for making friends, them two aren't. Especially Miss Kitty. The doctor likes to look in here of an evening, but that's for companionship, not friendship, if you see what I mean."

"Well, I'm not sure that they need much friendship, Jim. They give a lot to one another, you know."

"Ay," he said reflectively. "They've got pretty set in their ways. It'd need a block-buster to put 'em apart now."

I drank my coffee, comforted by that remark. That's what it is, I told myself. Kitty and Tom have been so close together for so long that they have entangled like two wistarias growing for years side by side. Kitty knows that it would be destructive to pull apart that intertwining. It's nothing to do with your deficiencies. And I knew how I was lying to myself.

Jim was disposed to hover. He said with a laugh: "Well, when you're settled down in Rosemullion, look out for Annie Hocking. She thinks the place belongs to her—by all good rights, as she says."

"Yes, Jim, I've heard about that. What good rights has she in mind?"

"God knows. It's just some damn' old tarradiddle she's got into her noddle. Been a trouble-maker from time immemorial, Annie have. An' gets worse as she gets older and uglier. I've heard my old man say that, if it had'n' been for she, there was just a dog's chance that her sister could've made a go of it with Mr. Savage. Not that I'd accept that, knowin' Mr. Savage. An old man's last bit

177

of skylarking, and then he wakes up an' sees what a bloody fool 'e been. As simple as that, I'd say it was. Not big enough, Annie isn't to make Mr. Savage do one thing or another. Everything that old cock does comes out of what he is himself, if you get my reference."

That was my own view, and I wished Jim would go, but he pottered around, flicking at things with a duster. He was by the piano now, on whose stand the same song was open at the same page as on that stormy night of March when Mr. Savage first brought me to this place.

"But they're not all like Mr. Savage," Jim said. "Most folks round here are terrified of Annie Hocking. All of 'em, I should say, except Miss Kitty. Cor' stone the crows! She didn't 'arf blow up with Annie once. We're a bit remote 'ere, you know, for fancy things like district nurses an' so forth, and some of the women who was too stingy to have the doctor used to call Annie in when a kid was coming. Dirty old slut. Two kids died under 'er 'ands, an' one mother. Miss Kitty was livid. I've never seen 'er fly orf the 'andle before or since, but she met Annie in the street an' told 'er that if she laid 'er dirty 'ands on another woman in labour she'd be 'ad up for manslaughter. Told 'er in front of 'arf the village, an' wondered whether Annie wasn't doin' other things on the side. She's a trained midwife, you know, Miss Kitty is, and sometimes she 'elps Dr. Littledale with that sort of thing—all free, gratis an' for nothing. Extraordinary, when you come to think of it, an old maid like that all mixed up with the mysteries of life an' death. I've known 'er 'elp a farmer with a difficult calf when the vet couldn't come. You'd think she'd be squeamish, but bless your soul, not she. I once ventured a gentle 'int, like, an' she burst out laughing. 'When we're all saints in 'eaven, Jim,' she said, 'p'r'aps the good God will spare us the embarrassment of having rather complicated insides. Till then, it's as well to understand what

178

they're for an' 'ow the complications work.' Ever been in that cottage of Annie Hocking's, Mr. Menheniot?"

"No. Haven't had the pleasure, Jim."

"Pleasure! A bloody pigstye. I wouldn't let Annie deliver my canary of an egg. Not that I've got a canary. Noisy little bastards."

I had got up early after my troubled night and had worried Jim for breakfast at so unaccustomed an hour that I owed it to him to allow his chatter to flow. When the meal was done and he was gone, it was only half-past seven. I decided suddenly to do what I had not yet done: attend eight o'clock service at church. This was not from piety, but from a discreditable curiosity. I wanted to see how Mr. Savage was bearing himself after the explosive meeting of the night before.

It was a superb morning. I walked up the lane with the singing water on my right hand, and in the fields on my left the whalebacks of rock were shining with dew amid the green undulating grass as though they were indeed monsters just risen from the sea. Overhead everything was now in full leaf, so that I was walking through a verdant tunnel from whose roof flicks and spurts of water fell as the birds stirred there. I met no one, and it was difficult to believe that this ferny fecund track was in the world whose strain elsewhere frightened me with apprehensions of a breaking-point. This feeling was deepened when I came out to the level land where the church and vicarage stood. I stopped and looked at them girded with trees, mouldering, almost rotting, as another year rushed to its climax, to carry the spores of more ferns into the interstices of the stones, to put more ivy into a strangle-hold, chiselling out the mortar, drying the unpainted wood, prising another point of entry, some minute conduit for rain and dew.

With the lush wet grass of the graveyard soaking my shoes, I stood there quite beaten down by a feeling I could not dismiss: a feeling that what had happened here last night was final and fatal, that whatever it was that Mr. Savage's loves and hates had been tending to through so many eccentric years had now reached its fullness, for good or ill. A flock of jackdaws rose with a sudden quarrelsome chatter from the church's squat tower. I pushed open the door and went in. It was exactly eight o'clock, and, knowing Mr. Savage's precise habits, I expected to find him there before me. Or had my apprehensions already told me that he would never be here again?

What called my attention to the girl was the pale-gold gleam of her hair, and my first thought was of how this would outrage Mr. Savage. She was sitting in a pew under the Menheniot memorials, her face lifted up towards them as she looked at the carved and coloured coats-of-arms and read the suave lies about these long dead and done for Rogers and Richards. I walked towards her, and a stray gleam of the morning sun, falling through the colour of a window, put a rosy stain upon her face. I saw only the face, abstracted from so much that was tawdry and repulsive about her: a face, as I have said, that had an almost angelic innocence. The blue eyes seemed to swim in a milk of innocence, and the hair near her ear was like spun silk caressing a pink shell.

My dreams of the night before recurred to me—dreams so erotically confused that I did not know whether it was she or Kitty that I had possessed.

I shuddered, went up to her, and said harshly: "You should cover your hair. Mr. Savage will be here at any moment. He will insist on it."

I had edged into the pew. She got up and stood facing

me so closely that I could see the gleam of her perfect teeth as she smiled. "What a pity," she said. "I think it's one of my best features. It's so soft, too." She seized my hand, raised it to her hair, and stroked the hair with it. All of last night rushed suddenly upon me, tingling through my fingertips into every vein of my body. I took hold of her fiercely, pressed her body hard upon mine, and could not make an end of kissing her. They were such kisses, given and returned, as I had never known with Kitty Littledale. At last I sat down, exhausted, and buried my face in my hands. She stood above me, ruffling my hair. Then she sat and put both her arms round me. "Let's go somewhere," she said.

I was filled with horror. "Go away from me," I said hoarsely.

"All right," she answered. She was quite calm. "Don't think I came here to look for you. I didn't sleep very well —that's all it was. When I woke, that woman was still snoring like a pig, so I got up and made myself a cup of tea and strolled out to enjoy God's fresh air. That's all."

That she should now—at this moment when she had shattered me—go into this humdrum of the question, seemed to me so grotesque and inappropriate that I began to laugh as though I were crazy.

"Well," she said easily. "I'll leave you to it. I'll be seeing you."

IV

It was a long time before my trembling ceased and I was able to stand. I walked out of the church on legs like jelly. And I knew that this morning's misadventures were not yet ended. I went, full of foreboding, towards the vicarage to find out why Mr. Savage had not appeared in the church. As ever, the cold of the house was a mor-

tuary's. Mr. Savage's surplice hung on its nail in the hall;
there were his sticks and his big uncleaned boots. I was
about to go into the kitchen to see if he was at breakfast
when his voice startled me. I looked up, and he was
leaning over the banister. "Ah! it's you, Menheniot.
Come up, my dear boy. You can do me no harm. You are
no part of my polluted flesh."

I cried good morning, with a desperate attempt at
normality.

"Good?" he said. "How good is this morning? Come
up and tell me. How good is it, my dear fellow?"

He disappeared towards his study, and I slowly climbed
the stairs and joined him there.

"Tell me, my dear Menheniot," he said, "have you ever
entertained angels unawares?"

There's no doubt about it, I thought, it's the finish of
him this time. His eye was glittering. He was alive as a
flame is alive that is consuming itself and must soon end.
He looked as dry and brittle as last year's kexes, bleaching
amid this uprush of springtime sap.

"I don't think I have," I said as smoothly as I could.
"Let me get you some breakfast."

He ignored this attempt to by-pass whatever mania was
on him. "No," he said. "I don't suppose you have. How is
Jim Brokenshire looking after you? Remind me to settle
with him. It is given to few people to entertain angels. I
was one of them. That's a matter for my epitaph. Remind
me to write that."

"The devil of it is," he said after a moment, "that it's so
long ago. It must be months, at least, since Sylvia died.
You didn't know her, did you?"

"No," I said. "But I've heard she was very beautiful."

He turned to me eagerly. "Do they say that down in the
village?"

"Yes," I assured him. "Everyone says so."

182

"Good," he said slowly. "That is very, very good."

He poured himself some brandy and sipped it, looking through me. "You are Menheniot, are you not?" he asked, coming to with a sudden start.

I assured him that I was, and he said: "Remind me to show you the memorials in the church. It is very good of you Americans to come to help this old land of ours."

"You are thinking of Phil," I said. "I am Roger."

He began to laugh. "Yes, indeed. You are Roger. A different kettle of fish. Nevertheless, your very good health."

He raised his glass. "Be a good fellow, Menheniot, and do me the favour of lighting the fire. I am a little cold."

There were logs in the grate and some dry kindling wood. I soon had the fire going. He pulled his chair up to it and stretched his hands to the blaze. "Who is the ruler of this realm now?" he asked.

I said it was King George the Sixth.

"That doesn't help me," he said. "He would never do it. I have been thinking of the saintly Bishop Ken. He wrote a good hymn or two—'Awake my soul, and with the sun. . . .' Well, you know he was at Winchester when Charles the Second came there with a raggle-taggle that included Nell Gwyn, and, for what that may matter, one of my ancestors. Charles wanted Ken to lodge Nell in his house, and the good doctor refused to have the holy premises polluted. So, you see, I have an excellent precedent, my dear boy."

He reached towards his brandy, and I moved the little table it stood on near to his chair.

"Thank you. This solitary drinking is inhospitable."

I took another glass and poured myself a small tot. This cheered him up. "Your very good health," he said. "Well, now, the point is this. A year later the see of Bath and Wells was vacant, and Charles asked: 'Where is the good little man that refused his lodging to poor Nell?' And, damme, he made Ken a bishop."

He began to laugh. "It won't happen to me," he said. "There have been in the course of history various reasons for making men bishops and archbishops. Nowadays, the chief commendation is sound business sense. His Grace, F.S.A.A. Well, well. Stoke up, Menheniot."

I threw on more wood. We had a proper roaster now.

"This is very jolly. I love company, you know, but so little of it, fit to keep, is left in this world. And now, adverting to angels, unawares or otherwise. I had a visitation during last night. Did I ever tell you that I had married twice?"

Without giving me time to answer, he went on: "My first wife never approved of my second. She was right about that. She was a woman of faultless taste. The longer I lived the more I saw that I had been guilty of a gross desecration. But last night it all ended well. I drove out the last reminder of my betrayal, and in the early hours of this morning I had a visit of approval from my angel. These visits are becoming rare. There was no fire. It was rather cold for her. However, she was pleased with what I had done. That is the main thing, my dear boy. She couldn't promise me a bishopric, but she promised me the end of all this." He waved a hand vaguely round the room. "So we must make ready. Let's clear the decks."

I had missed the photographs that usually stood about the room. Now he got up, took them from a drawer, and threw them one by one into the flames.

I had seen Annie Hocking spit upon one of Sylvia's photographs. That nauseated me; but this burning made me wince to the marrow as though these pictures were flesh being thrown upon the flames. I watched toes crinkle, and thighs blister and breasts blaze and disintegrate. Face after smiling face was licked by fire and obliterated to a trembling curl of charcoal.

Mr. Savage sat watching intently till nothing was left but the black crackling paper, played upon here and there by dots and lines of vivid red, as though something of life lingered there that refused to be utterly destroyed, some veins of pulsing blood and sparks of sentience. He took up a log from inside the fender and vehemently crashed it down, as one might, sick and revolted, crash down one's heel to kill a sorely wounded animal whose life yet desperately pleaded from the eyes. Then he got up, and said: "Mr. Menheniot, I am not well. Do me the kindness, please, of asking Dr. Littledale to call."

V

My mind was blinded by the carnal image of Bella as I stumbled down towards Penmaen. I was terrified by the thought of coming face to face with Kitty while this obsession was upon me. She was so far removed from all that. I craved her presence as that of a deliverer from everything that the hour had so ruthlessly projected upon me, yet recoiled from it while I was so unfitted to look upon her quietude and grave sobriety. Chance spared me the meeting. I met Tom Littledale coming towards me where the path opened out into the beach.

"Good morning, Roger," he hailed me. "What have you been up to? We missed you at breakfast."

"I had a very restless night and got up early. Jim gave me breakfast at seven. I should have asked him to send a message."

"Well, you didn't miss much. Kitty was as glum as a broody hen. I'm feeling a bit worried myself. What we heard in the pub last night didn't sound good to me.

There must have been a terrific emotional disturbance at the vicarage, and God knows what that could do to Mr. Savage at his age. It'd be enough to send him round the bend. He's been odd enough lately as it is. The last time I was up there he talked to me under the impression that I was a man he had known as Oxford."

I told him then something of the morning's adventures: nothing of the girl in the church, nothing of the burned photographs: simply that I had looked in and found Mr. Savage behaving oddly, and that he was asking for Dr. Littledale.

"Then he *is* behaving oddly," Tom said. "He hates doctors on principle. By now, he's probably forgotten that he asked for me. Well, I'll look in casually in the course of the morning, as though paying a friendly visit. So long."

I walked on to the Menheniot Arms and went up to my rooms to think. There was plenty to think about. After what had happened last night, I couldn't go on imposing my company on Kitty. The breakfasts would have to stop, and that meant I should have to leave Penmaen. She was my only reason for staying. But for her, I should already have been in Rosemullion. The house was furnished; I had nothing to do but walk in; and I marvelled that a change had come over me so great that I had been able to resist entering upon an inheritance I had so long dreamed of as an exiled angel might have dreamed of paradise regained. Until I now consciously turned the matter over in my mind I had been unaware that this incredible treachery to Rosemullion had come about. It was a week since I had so much as set foot in the place. The Saras had seemed puzzled. They had the golden snare shining with allure, but I was rejecting it. I was happier in this poky room of Jim Brokenshire's than I should be amid the treasures I had been so long and covetously assembling. It was Kitty Littledale who had done this to me—cool, soothing Kitty.

I had been lying extended on my bed, and as I thought of Kitty I got up and walked to the window. There was the girl who had accosted me in the church, coming out of the lane that led to Annie Hocking's house. The square of scarlet was on her head: a cigarette hung from her scarlet lips. I thought of her hoarse and hurried invitation to me in the cold church, and drew back behind the gauze curtains. But she had seen me. She raised a hand in salute, and walked on towards the beach. There was something so insolently casual about her as she went by that I raged with anger, and with shame, too, that she had so easily overborne me, caused me by a mere gesture to take her as I had never before taken a woman, holding her with such sensations rocking my body as terrified and disgusted me. I watched her trousered legs and red shoes disappear and felt I could gladly have killed her.

This encounter finally settled the thing for me. I would leave Penmaen to-morrow for the quietude and seclusion of Rosemullion, where a man's mind could shut out what it did not wish to entertain.

VI

I spent the morning in my room, compelled by a perverse resolution to have nothing to do with human-kind, man or woman. I ate my midday meal alone, and told myself that for the rest of the day I would dodge all encounters by wandering where no one was likely to come. I crossed the beach and climbed the cliff-path I had often climbed with Kitty, but I went on for miles beyond the haunts that were accustomed to us. The path petered out and I found myself in a beautiful desolation of heather and granite, with the May sky tender above me and the sea reaching beyond sight, moved by nothing but its own quiet breathing. I sat down in the sunshine. A semi-circle of grey rock enclosed a small lawn of rabbit-bitten turf and sea-pinks. From the edge, the cliff shelved down to the sea. This charming pleasance and the opal water beneath was all I could see. I could hear the sighing of the water and the piping of curlews and the heaven-high singing of skylarks. For the first time that day I felt content, I felt myself untroubled. For an hour I lay in sheer happy surrender to my recovered quiet. Then for an hour I read *Urn Burial*, which I had brought from Rose-mullion the last time I was there, and then I fell asleep.

I was awakened by a tickling sensation on my face. Without opening my eyes, I brushed lazily at it with my fingers. But it persisted, and at last I sat up rubbing my eyes sleepily. Then they opened wide in terror. A pair of innocent milky-blue eyes were laughing down into mine. Between a finger and thumb the stem of sea-pink that had tickled me was twirling. At first I did not recognize the girl who was kneeling there. Had she been wearing the scarlet scarf or the trousers or the toggled jacket I might have known her. But all these things lay under a rock. She was wearing nothing. I looked at her, too stupefied to speak. She looked back at me, smiling. She said: "You wanted me this morning, didn't you? Well, here I am."

At that, she got to her feet, spread her arms wide, and stood looking down at me, offering herself unabashed to my eyes. My heart was pounding. She lay beside me and pulled me down.

VII

She used to laugh about my first surrender. "It was like undressing a baby," she would say. "My goodness, you didn't half leave everything to me."

But that was later, when I was like a baby no longer,

188

when my innocence was gone, when day and night were continuing slavery to desire. It was, from the first, as though she had pulled a stone out of a dam: all that had been piled behind it rushed down with increasing vehemence. I am not writing this to whitewash myself and to pour the blame for my sins upon Bella. She, indeed, consciously set me on that way; but how ardently I trod it, and with what insatiable appetite! At last I came to hate her, but that was the measure of my hatred for myself.

That May afternoon, when she had done with me, I fell again into a profound sleep, but now with my arms about her. I awoke dazed, staring up into the blue where gulls were wheeling and crying, and slowly remembrance of what had happened returned to me. My heart leapt with a frantic happiness, and finding my arms empty, I sat up in sudden consternation, thinking her gone. She was standing a few yards away, pulling a garment of silk over her head. "Don't!" I cried. "Please don't!"

She looked at me with smile, her silken rag trailing in her hand. "Don't what?" she asked.

"Don't dress," I pleaded, not knowing then how little need there ever was to plead with her. "Let me see you." I added, half-ashamed, "You are the first I have ever seen, the first I have ever. . . ."

She looked at me with frank amazement. "What!" she cried. "At your age!" She sat beside me, and said: "Well, that explains a lot."

But I didn't want to talk. I wanted only to look at her. She had a beautiful body, and there was no temptation to consider the blemishes of her toes. I wanted to look at her and to fondle her, and presently I wanted more than this. This time it was I who took the upper hand. She laughed up into my face. "You're a quick learner, Mr. Menheniot," she said.

189

I put my mouth over hers to stifle her words. "Don'
talk," I said. "Don't talk."

It was one of her oddities that she *would* talk. She
would say flippant, or irrelevant, or sometimes shocking
things, in the very heart of what I at first thought of a
sacred moments, but later as moments of disgust.

When we sat up again the sun was still shining. She
walked to the edge of the little lawn and looked down
the declivity of rock to where the water lapped lazily on
to a minute beach that was the corn-white colour of her
hair. "I'd love a swim," she said.

"You mustn't."

She turned on me, flashing. "What do you mean—
mustn't? Don't say mustn't to me."

"I'm sorry," I said, enslaved, pleading. "But the
water'll be terribly cold. It's never properly warmed up
till July."

She put her feet into her shoes and began to clamber
down the rocks. "I'm strong," she boasted. "A drop o
cold water won't hurt me, and I love swimming." She
stopped her scrambling to look back and say: "I need to
be strong, I can tell you, to put up with all that men
have done to me."

She was like that from the beginning. She never made
any pretences. Indeed, she loved to say things and to use
frank words that made me wince. There is no excuse for
me: I knew what she was, even in the days when I pre
tended that she might become what I wanted her to be

On the little beach she kicked off her shoes and, withou
any preliminary shrinking and toe-dabbling, plunged
into the water. It deepened sharply there, and she threw
herself forward upon it and struck out boldly. Then she
swam slowly back, and, close inshore, turned over, lying
upon the water with her fingers finning. I watched her
filled with well-nigh unbearable ecstasy and desire.

"Now rub me down," she said, when she had clambered back. I did so, using my handkerchief and the square of scarlet silk and finished her off with my woollen shirt which was warm through lying in the sun. It was an exquisite, disturbing task.

We dressed ourselves, and she brought a leather satchel that had been lying with her clothes. It contained a Thermos flask of hot coffee and some biscuits. "The coffee's safe," she said. "I made it myself. I wouldn't let that Hocking woman touch it. Ugh! What a messy old slut!"

She leaned against the rock, glowing from the swim and the rubbing, looking to me heartbreakingly beautiful. She lit a cigarette and blew rings into the now withdrawing sunlight. She sighed with content. "Christ!" she said. "Isn't life good! This beautiful open air, a swim, and a man!"

I wasn't repelled by a remark that would have seemed to me unbearable only a few hours ago. I put an arm round her and began drawing her to me. "What is your name?" I asked. Odd that we had gone so far without my knowing even that.

"Bella," she said. "Never mind the other for the moment. Just Bella, Mr. Menheniot."

That was a trick she continued to develop. She would never call me Roger—always Mr. Menheniot, with a smile, as though in me and my name there was something absurd that tickled her.

She resisted my attempt to take hold of her. "Steady on, Mr. Menheniot," she said. "The trouble with you is you've waited too long. When the starving shipwrecked mariner gets picked up—repeat picked up—the cook in the galley knows better than to turn him loose all at once. You'll have to be rationed, Mr. Menheniot. Take it easy now. I'll be seeing you."

191

She screwed the cup on to the Thermos flask, put it into the satchel, and got up. "So long."

I got up, too. "I must see you back," I said.

"Don't say must to me—don't say must or mustn't. Stay where you are for a bit. We'd better not be seen together till we know which way the cat's going to jump."

With that she left me.

VIII

Why had she bothered with me in the first place? I often asked myself. I was ageing and nothing to look at. Such qualities as I had—the qualities that had appealed to Kitty Littledale—could never have meant anything to her, and, in any case, she could have known nothing of them that night when she fumbled my fingers over the light I held for her in the Menheniot Arms. And, of course, that was it—that name that tickled her. In the bar she had heard me called Mr. Menheniot. She had noticed that the pub was called the Menheniot Arms, and a pub isn't named after a family unless the family has some significance. There would be enough in that to make her want to cultivate Mr. Menheniot, stranded as she was, for her instinct told her—and rightly—that she would not see or hear of Will Savage again.

Annie Hocking was not so sure of that. Will had said he would write, and, anyway, it would be one in the eye for Mr. Savage to keep Will's girl here under his nose and to whisper tales of the vicar's abominable cruelty in turning his son from his door. "Son! Treated poor Will more like a dog than a son. There's a Christian for you! There's an example to the flock! Not that Will was ever a Savage, come to that. My own dead sister's son—dead of that old 'oly savage, if ever a woman was—an' my own sister's blood, too. So I'll look after Will's little girl, never fear."

It was only later that odd ideas concerning Rose-mullion, the place that should be hers "by all good rights," began to stir in Annie Hocking's head. But for these ideas, there is no doubt that, as week followed week and no news came from Will, Will's little girl would soon have been sent packing. Especially as now there was no Mr. Savage to annoy.

When Tom Littledale called on him, the old man was calm and reasonable. The glittering excitement of the early morning seemed to have been consumed with the photographs. He was smoking in his study and had forgotten that he had asked Tom to call. "I must have slept uncommonly late, Dr. Littledale," he said. "Here it is— half-past ten and I haven't conducted morning service. This is the first time in my life that such a thing has happened. I shall begin to suspect soon that I'm past my prime."

All that had happened while I was there seemed a blank in his mind—all, too, that had happened when Will came home. At any rate, he never spoke of those things.

"He looked starving," Tom told me, "and I persuaded him to come down to my house and have a bit of food. He was charming with Kitty and me—he *can* be charming, as you know. There was a hint of condescension in him. He was an eighteenth-century aristocrat receiving the attention that was no more than his due, but paying for it with a display of exquisite manners."

When he had eaten, he said: "And now, if you and Miss Littledale will permit me, Doctor, I must do my pastoral duty. It really is shameful. I have been a most neglectful shepherd. Penmaen is almost foreign territory to me. Well, I must get out and see what is happening *in partibus infidelium*."

It was almost noon when he began to tag here and here—through the one street and the few scattered cot-

tages. The news of Will's return and rejection had go
about. There can hardly have been a soul in the plac
who had not heard of it, and it would have lost nothin
of its flavour in repetition. Will had been liked in Pen
maen. He had belonged to the village rather than to th
vicarage, and it is not to be wondered at that feelings o
outrage and resentment were smouldering.

So many stories were current afterwards that it is im
possible to piece together exactly what happened. Ever)
body had a tale to tell of the witty or bitter or cuttin
thing said to Mr. Savage that day; but most of it, I
imagine, was excogitated after the event. Fright, I shoul
think, was the emotion he chiefly aroused. That ta
bearded figure with the clattering boots and the heav
walking-stick, the black sombrero crowning the plent
ful hair, must have been pretty daunting, and not man
people in Penmaen would have dared to say much. Bu
undoubtedly he was met by doors opened a few inche
and then firmly closed, and by doors not opened at al
and by a growing sense of rejection. And undoubted)
one hag, shaking mats through her bedroom window, di
continue to do so as he stood stumping with his stick o
the door beneath her. She shouted to him to be gone. H
stood back from the door, looked up at her, and raise
the hat soiled by her filth. Then he walked away.

He went down to the beach. Pulled up on the sand wa
a dinghy that had belonged to his son. A fisherman, one o
Will's friends, had kept it painted and watertight a
through the years of Will's absence. This man was sittin
on the gunwale of the dinghy, and Mr. Savage asked if h
might borrow the boat to go out for a row. It was surpri
ing suggestion: no one had seen him on the water durin
all his years at that place: but the man called anothe
loiterer and they ran the boat down to the water's edge.

That is not an easy place to embark from. The tid

lways makes a bit of a surge there, and the beach has a hallow shelf. Mr. Savage was wetted to the knees in getting aboard, and so were the men who pushed him out nto deep water. They saw him lay his stick and hat on the loor-boards, take up the oars and begin to row awkwardly. He shouted: "Haven't been in a boat since I was t Oxford. This one seems a bit different somehow."

They watched him for a while. He seemed to get the ang of things pretty soon, and when he was a few undred yards out they went back to the village for their nidday meal. Away from the bobble on the shore, the sea vas as flat as a dance-floor.

Already, when the men got back, the village was full of tories of Mr. Savage's pastoral calls and of the way he had een received. Putting two and two together, the men night have been alarmed had they not been conscious hat there was "no ha'm in the weather," and not likely o be any for a long time. That Mr. Savage had decided, t his age, to go for his first row in a dinghy was thought musing. Just like the old crackpot.

There was no sign of the boat when they returned to heir loafing on the beach, and it was not till late that fternoon that news of the vicar's voyage reached Jim Brokenshire. Jim, I should say, was the only person in the village, apart from the Littledales, who had some admiration for Mr. Savage and some understanding of what his ctions might portend. He owned a large dinghy with a notor; and he went to Tom Littledale and suggested ursuit. Tom and Kitty joined him at once in the boat nd they chugged away seawards. It was an hour before hey saw a speck that soon turned into a dinghy, and their earts must have thumped with apprehension when they aw no rower. The boat was floating idly. They could read er name, *Tiddler*, painted on the stern. When they ame alongside they found Mr. Savage extended on the floor-boards. He had inserted his thin length somehow beneath the thwarts. His coat was off and rolled into a pillow beneath his head. The oars were gone. Whether he had thrown them away or lost them, who knows? They did not try to move him from his awkward couch, but tied a painter to the ring in *Tiddler's* bows. Kitty got aboard to keep the sleeping man company, and Jim's boat started for home. I was told that Mr. Savage looked peaceful, even happy, as though in sleep out there on the gently moving water many knots had been untied and perplexities resolved.

By the time the boat got in there was a bunch of people on the beach, eager to haul *Tiddler* out of the water, and thus have a hand in drama. It was only when the boat was high and dry and Jim and Tom were easing him out from under the thwarts that Mr. Savage's face lost its serenity. He woke up, and to be awake in life seemed too much for him. He began to cry, and when he was out of the boat he went on crying. Annie Hocking was there. "Ay, 'e've got plenty to cry about, 'e 'ave," she shouted. "But it's too late now." Even those who had rejected Mr. Savage that morning were horrified, and she was hustled away, shouting vindictively. Mr. Savage noticed none of it. He collapsed upon the sand and sat there, knees up, his face in his hands, crying still.

He was carried to Tom's house and put to bed and went on crying till an opiate sent him to sleep. He awoke quiet, gentle and childlike, but clearly out of his mind. A week later he was housed in the asylum at Bodmin.

CHAPTER TWELVE

I

I DID not carry out my resolve to leave the Menheniot
Arms and take up my quarters at Rosemullion. I was
spending the greater part of every day with Bella, and
was fool enough to persuade myself that such an association need not be discovered. We were never seen together
in Penmaen. If we passed one another in the street we
would nod and say good day; and so, too, we would
casually greet one another if we met in the pub bar.
Bella liked to look in there for a drink or two in the
evenings, and usually Annie Hocking came with her. This
gave the place a note it had not been accustomed to. It
had been a man's pub, and now the men's tongues did not
wag so freely. Jim didn't like the female intrusion, but
there was nothing he could do about it. For me, there
was a high excitement in sitting in the bar, saying nothing
to Bella as though I knew no more about her than the
next man, while my imagination was reliving the events
of the day we had spent together. Sometimes, passing my
chair, she would flash me a wink which said as clearly as
though she had spoken: "If they knew!" Tom Littledale
obviously loathed her and would not so much as say good
evening when she came in. The others would greet her
with a few words, and it gave me a perverse satisfaction to
notice their covert desiring glances. She, too, must have
got the same satisfaction. How otherwise explain her
action one night? Usually she came to the pub in her
slacks and duffle coat, but that night she wore a blouse
that was taut upon her breasts, a silk skirt and silk stockings. She propped one leg over the other, displaying her

197

calves, and smoked her cigarette from a long holder. Till then, I was the only man there who knew what wa beneath the disguising shapelessness of her clothes, bu that night she intended that everyone should know. Th women of Penmaen tended to be short and wide. The would have made good models for Hogarth or Rowland son. Bella's experiment caused an excitement that coule be felt.

The next day I remonstrated with her. She was annoyed with me. She hated must or mustn't. "You don't thinl I did it to please *them*?" she said. "If you do, you mus be greener than I thought. I did it to please myself. got a kick out of it."

We would leave Penmaen at different times and ever by different routes, and meet at some place we had agreed on. Then we would walk till we found a spot that pleased her. She was restless and errant, and disliked making lov in the same place and the same way. "Leave it to me," she would say. "I'll find a place. I've cultivated a good eye for country." And as she walked she had a way o looking about her as though nothing in all the wide world existed except as a secret cover for love-making. A wood, a hollow in the moors, a cave, a bend of wall "Look! Here! Here's a place." Even as we lay together she would prattle of her obsession, telling me of other occasions and other men and other places. "You wouldn' believe the odd places where you can do it if you take chance, Mr. Menheniot."

I soon gave up trying to restrain her chatter. She had become indispensable to me like drink to a drunkard and I was glad to have her on her own terms.

II

At first, Annie Hocking was enchanted with Bella. To

198

be the custodian of something so rich and rare by the standards of Penmaen gave her great satisfaction, and "my nephew Will's little girl" was rarely off her tongue. Soon after Mr. Savage's departure, I found her wheeling a barrow down from the vicarage. It contained a lot of junk, including the assortment of jars and tins that used to stand on the filthy shelves over the kitchen sink. Annie was confident that she would soon hear from Will and that this would be to her advantage. She was to be seen painting the woodwork outside her cottage, and when she was at work on the bedroom windows, standing on a ladder, passers-by were treated to a sight of her calves bulging like Chianti bottles. She attacked the weeds in the cobbled lane leading to her dark front door, slopping her weed-killers about and grubbing between the stones with a kitchen knife.

Bella detested her, and never to me called her anything but Fat Annie, though she spoke to her smoothly enough when face to face. One day she said, as we relaxed on the sand of a small cove flooded with sunshine: "Fat Annie's getting restless. I think she's beginning to develop doubts about Will's intentions. She asked what about paying for my keep. I haven't a bean."

That was the first time money had been mentioned between us. I don't think I ever persuaded myself that what Bella was doing was being done for love. In my heart I knew that she was doing it because of fathomless lust, and that her lust had contaminated me, too. But I had never allowed this knowledge to come to the surface. Physically, I had found such release that I moved in exultation, and it wasn't difficult to deceive myself with the thought that I was involved in a memorable experience of the spirit. And so my first reaction to Bella's words was a feeling that a small chill wind had come over a glorious relationship, a mercantile wind at that, sullying what was between us. I did not blame her. I blamed myself. I should have realized her poverty and taken steps to deal with it. But I hadn't done that, and now she had virtually asked for pay.

"If it comes to paying for your lodgings," I said, "why stay in that filthy hole?"

"What memorable thoughts you have, Mr. Menheniot," she mocked me. "Where am I to go?"

"Anywhere. Anyone would be glad to have you."

She laughed outright. "D'you think the women love me in Penmaen? Actually, I've sounded one or two of them. They wouldn't touch me with a barge-pole. They have wonderful noses for moral lepers."

"I'd like to hear one of them insult you!" I said hotly.

She laughed again. "Pipe down, Mr. Menheniot. You're as bad as any of 'em. You're a proper old woman yourself."

I dared not answer that. I feared a quarrel—something that might separate us. I sat up and looked at her extended on the beach, one hand curling into the warm rippling sand, the other still, with a wisp of smoke rising from the cigarette it held. All the sunshine and the swimming had beautified her skin, still further bleached her fair hair. It was a golden creature lying there, and this middle-aged man with the thick pebble glasses could not get over the wonder of his situation. Indeed and indeed he feared to say anything that would separate him from this.

I bent down and kissed her breasts. She unveiled the innocence of her eyes and smiled at me. "Thank you, Mr. Menheniot," she said lazily. "Help yourself."

Still, it was hurtful to be called an old woman and to know, as I did, that this was a grotesque touch of humour in our situation that tickled her fancy. She had said that she "got a kick" out of titillating the men in the bar, and I knew that she got a kick out of my inexperience,

out of shocking this "old woman" with her frank words
and with ever new revelations of the body's rapture. She
could set me trembling and then laugh at me, so that
there were moments when in my humiliation I could
have killed her as I loved her.

III

That night she and Annie Hocking did not come into
the bar. I was aware of a sense of disappointment among
the drinkers. Every time the door opened eyes would
switch round, the darts players would pause. I could have
sworn I saw a sour amused grin on Tom Littledale's face.
Beyond a good evening, he had not spoken to me, and
the greeting had been brusque. For some time he had
been avoiding me.

Presently one of the men said: "Don't look as if Annie's
coming to-night."

Tom laughed. "Annie?"

"Ay—Annie."

"I didn't know she had the same name as Miss Hocking," Tom said; and in the uneasiness that followed this
remark Jim Brokenshire said: "Easy all. Easy now."

Tom finished his pint and got up. "Coming for a stroll,
Menheniot?" he asked. Not Roger.

I got up and followed him out, and, without speaking,
he led the way to the beach. We walked in silence half-
way across it. Tom filled his pipe and stopped to light up.
With his hands cupped round the glow of the match, he
said between puffs: "Making a proper fool of yourself,
aren't you?"

I was terrified. I have always loathed a scene of any sort,
and had no idea how to handle this one. I said stupidly:
"What are you talking about?"

He threw down the match and crushed it into the sand

with his heel. "About you and that little bitch who's go[t] you on a bit of string."

Still I could say nothing to the point, and he burst ou[t] angrily: "You don't deny that you're going about wit[h] her?"

"Why should I?"

"Why? Well—good God, man! A cheap little trollo[p] like that?" He looked at me in exasperation. "Haven'[t] you anything to say?" he demanded. "Don't you thin[k] you owe me an explanation?"

"You?"

"Yes—me." And as I still did not answer he added: "You're so dumb I wonder what even a girl like that see[s] in you!"

Then I said the supremely silly thing of my life. "Wha[t] did Kitty see in me?"

He looked so terrible when I mentioned Kitty's nam[e] that I thought he was going to lay hands on me. He turne[d] towards the sea, out of which a full moon was risin[g] clenching his fists, struggling with himself. At last h[e] said: "All right. Go through with it, Menheniot. G[o] through with it to the end."

In his agitation, he stuffed the still-burning pipe int[o] his pocket, and strode away.

I didn't know what to do. Bella had been more realist[ic] than I. "Things don't stand still, Mr. Menheniot. The[y] move one way or another sooner or later. We can't go o[n] like this for ever, you know."

I had asked her what she meant. "Oh, anything," sh[e] said lazily. "A couple like ourselves on the prowl for [a] good spot. Someone with a telescope." She laughe[d] "You'd be surprised at the things that are seen throug[h] telescopes."

But I had preferred to stay in my fool's paradise, an[d] now the crumbling had begun. I walked miserably bac[k] towards the pub, and then, at a venture, turned into the lane that led to Annie Hocking's house.

I never knew who had seen us and taken the news to Penmaen. But it spread quickly, as such news would in such a place. Tom was not the only one to have got hold of it by that night. Annie Hocking had heard it, and when I arrived at her house I was to witness her reaction to it. It was dark in the little lane, and her windows were shrouded. It was characteristic of Annie that, summer and winter, she ran down the linen blinds at all her windows and pulled the curtains as soon as dusk came. Her life was so much a peeping and a prying that she could not believe an eye existed that did not wish to peep and pry upon her. And so there was nothing to see that night but the grassy tufts growing in the roof gutters, sharp against the moon-lighted sky. A bush of verbena that had taken hold in a crevice under the wall and flourished there exhaled a perfume that seemed incongruous in that place. There was no bell or knocker. I rapped timidly on the door with my knuckles. Some time passed, and I had had to rap again, before there was a response. Then feet shuffled in the stone passage. I heard a chain released, a bolt drawn back, as though this were a fortress besieged by an enemy. The door opened half a crack, enough to allow a voice to speak but no face to appear. "Who's that?" Annie asked, distrustfully.

"Mr. Menheniot."

To my surprise, the door flew open in joyful welcome. "Come in! Come in, Mr. Menheniot. This *is* a pleasure."

I stepped over the threshold and waited while Annie readjusted the bolt and chain. Then she took my arm and led me into a living-room, crying: "Bella, midear! It's Mr. Menheniot. Aren't we a pair of lucky women?"

"It was just the same with me," Bella said later, when I told her how stupefied I had been. "I went back expecting to be thrown into the street, and the old bitch was all over me. She'd got a slap-up supper waiting and she'd actually laid on beer and cigarettes. Spending money on me! I couldn't make it out at first. Then after we'd eaten she took me into the sitting-room. I'd never been there before. She keeps the door locked and we live in that filthy kitchen. Well, then, there we were, with that oil lamp lit, hanging from the ceiling, and the whole place stinking like a mouldy grave that's just been opened. Fair gave me the willies. All those doilies and moth-eaten plush and bamboo whatnots! And the photos of Fat Annie and her sister as juvenile smashers!"

I saw them, too, that night: the pictures of this incredible pair of Hocking sisters in knee-length skirts and cloche hats, and there were some without hats, showing the bobbed hair that must have swept Penmaen at that time with a revolutionary violence. I looked particularly at Annie's sister who had whirled old Savage into his moment's madness and life-long disgust. It was possible —just possible to understand it. Odd, when I look back at it, that I—I of all men—should have made this gracious gesture of understanding.

"Well," said Bella, "there we were, all lashed up with this pampas grass and Woolworth flowers and the mantelpiece crowded with shells all demanding What are the wild waves saying? and Fat Annie cooing, 'Well, midear, are you quite comfortable? What do you think of my little drawing room?' I said I thought the Victoria and Albert Museum would pay her a fortune for it, and she said she dared say they would but they were not going to have it. She knew the value of antiques as well as the next one. She handed me cigarettes in a box with a picture of Plymouth Hoe on the lid, encrusted all round with varnished cowrie shells. 'Don't you think that's beautiful?' she asked, and I said it was stunning. It pretty nearly stunned me. She actually lit my cigarette for me, and even the match came out of a fancy bit of stuff with a poker-work motto on the lid. 'See how great flame aspires, kindled by a spark of grace.' The fat one said: 'That's a line from one of Charles Wesley's hymns, but we thought Mr. Savage wouldn't mind, though a churchman, being as he was so deep in love with my sister. We bought it soon after the engagement. Not that he was any great catch for her. We may have been comparatively poor, but by all good rights it was up to Rosemullion we should have been living then, and I should be living now.' "

This was the first Bella had heard of Rosemullion. I cannot remember that, till then, she had ever asked a prying question, and she was utterly unmercenary. As I have said, I imagine that the name Menheniot had engaged her fancy, but she never questioned me about my life or circumstances, though she was ready to prattle unendingly about her own. She lived like a gay frank animal, without either the vices or the virtues of a calculating mind.

But she heard plenty about Rosemullion that night, and about me, too. "So you've hooked Mr. Menheniot?" Annie said. "My, but you're a deep one! I wondered what you were up to, out and about from morning to night! And *him* of all people! Such a quiet one—you'd think butter wouldn't melt in his mouth. Well, still waters run deep. Aren't you the clever one? You'll be up to Rosemullion yet."

And now the real fiesta began. Annie produced a bottle of port and two glasses and launched upon the story of the Hocking family's "good rights" to Rosemullion. I had not known that I had a competitor, that through the years when I had been collecting pictures of the house, I had not been the only one. Annie had been at it, too, and I arrived that night in time to find the book outspread and Bella's history lesson in full flow. One fantastic detail of the evening was Annie Hocking's dress. I was so accustomed to her charwoman's outfit that I was fascinated as I looked at this figure splodging itself upon an easy-chair: this maroon velvet flowing down to the feet, this white fichu fastened by a cameo brooch at the neck. The cameo depicted a willow weeping over a tomb; and the dress was weighted all over with so many beads that some old-timer could have used it to do a year's trading with a tribe of Indians. Annie, I imagine, was rehearsing a domestic evening at Rosemullion. For that was the idea that had stuck into her small pig brain. She might not achieve Rosemullion by her good rights, but if Bella arrived there, who could say what might not happen to one who had been kind to Bella?

v

I had not had a clear thought for weeks. I had been living in a whirl of self. As I stepped out of the lane that night into the serenity of the moonlight I felt suddenly as though I had come out of a cage foetid with wild animals into the crystal smell of air. There was not a soul about, not a light in a window. It was past closing time at the Menheniot Arms. There was nothing but roofs that looked wet with this silent rain of moonlight, and the sleeping houses and the sea's breast rising and falling with tranquil breaths. Coming into this from that over-crowded, overheated room, stinking with tobacco smoke and the stale, damp exhalation of imprisoned years, infected by the devious working of Annie Hocking's mind,

I was suddenly appalled, like a sinner who turns a corner sharply and finds himself face to face with God. I wanted to fly, to go quickly to the door of the pub, enter, and rush to my bed, so that sleep might at once blot out these new stirrings that were in me. But after a moment of standing still, receiving the benediction of the night, I walked down to the beach. I had to face the fact that Bella would not arrive at Rosemullion through marrying me. I had no intention of marrying her. Very well, then. What was I doing?

There were always a few dinghies drawn up there, where the sand petered out in rough grass and tufts of sea-pink and sea-holly. I sat down between two boats, and though I was obstinately telling myself that I must face the facts, as if I were capable of some clear $x = y$ reasoning that would put everything straight, I knew that there was no need for any such thing. What I ought to do was already as plain as a pikestaff: the only question, as always, was would I do it?

So there was no thinking, but only a welter of emotional waste, an inability to say the yes that the moment demanded. It was of no use to pretend that it would be easy, that I would be giving up nothing worth while. During these weeks I had been enjoying something that certainly must come to an end at last, but, equally certainly, not without a wrench and a sense of loss. Enjoying was the word. However dubious her means, Bella had achieved the end of freeing me from physical fears that had tormented my life. I had experienced joy in deepest measure. I would never again shrink from my own flesh. All the same, Tom had been right. She was a cheap little trollop.

So my mind tossed to and fro amid the arguments until I was sick of them, and I got up to go back to the pub. And I was face to face with Kitty Littledale. She gave a small cry, and stopped dead in her tracks, her hand over her heart. I had risen like a shadow out of shadows; and, for her, her footsteps had been soundless as she came across the sand, going home from her moonlight walk.

We looked at one another for an astonished moment, and then she began to walk on towards the village. To see her go untied my tongue, and I called urgently: "Kitty!"

She stopped, stood still for a moment, then turned round and came slowly back. Her tall shape was outlined against the moon-glistering water. I longed for all to be as it had been between us. I longed to talk with her, but could do no more than ask stupidly: "Where have you been?"

She answered tonelessly: "I have been walking."

"At this time of night?"

"It is very beautiful at this time of night."

It was very warm, and I noticed that she had removed her shoes to walk barefoot on the sand. I stared at the beautiful feet, mother-of-pearl in the moonlight, and Kitty, shifting restlessly, said: "I must go. Good night." She spoke like a stranger.

Before she could move, I threw myself upon her. I forced my kisses on her—such kisses as she had never before had from me. She resisted me. I forgot her beautiful feet and trampled them. She cried out in pain. My hands were upon her breasts, and she placed her hands on my chest and pushed me away with great strength. In doing so, she fell. Then she lay still for a moment, as though exhausted, and I got down beside her and began to fondle her feet, and then her calves. She endured this in silence for a moment and I could hear her hard breathing and the sighing of the sea. Then she pulled herself together as if with a supreme effort, and struck me a blow in the face with her flat hand that left me dazzled and sick. She got up and made the first remark that had not been an answer to one of mine. Panting heavily, she said:

"You learned your lessons in the wrong shop. You mustn't try them out on me." She went quickly away, leaving me to think that over.

Even this experience, which left me feeling dazed and shamed, might not have been decisive in itself. To have encountered Kitty again, even in such shocking circumstances, might have helped me to free myself from the mere carnality of my situation. But at the pub a new blow awaited me. The bar had been closed for some time, but one or two of the cronies were drinking privately with Jim Brokenshire, or rather drinking at his expense. Jim was not much of a drinker. They got up when I entered, looked at me uneasily, and soon were gone. It was clear that they had been talking about me, and there was only one thing about me that could have interested them. Jim was as uneasy as the others, and I knew what was coming. I was sorry. I liked Jim, and I had enjoyed being here. Even if I had never met Bella Thoroughgood, I should have left the Menheniot Arms reluctantly. It had done me good to be among men. The attraction of my beautiful cloister had weakened, and there had been some talk between me and Jim of his finding a small boat for me and teaching me to sail.

"Mr. Menheniot."

"Yes, Jim."

"D'you remember that artist feller from London I mentioned to you?"

"Yes."

"He's been down here now every June for the last few years. There's a telegram from him to-day, asking if he can come at once. Stay if you like. But it'll be a bit awkward if I have to refuse him, seeing he's a sort of regular. And there's only the one spare bedroom."

Jim had put it as kindly as he could, but he had asked me to go.

"I'll get out as soon as you like, Jim," I said. "There's nothing stopping me really."

"Thank you, Mr. Menheniot. It'll be a convenience. 'V'you noticed old Green hasn't been in this last few evenings?"

I had. I was getting to know them all.

"I'm told his missus has been playin' old harry. Seems the women don't like their men comin' while that girl bobs in and out."

"Why don't you stop her from coming?"

"You can't, Mr. Menheniot. It's a matter of the law. You can't refuse refreshment to anyone."

"I see. A pity. Well, good night, Jim."

So I was spoiling his trade and I must go. All right, I said to myself. Tom, Kitty, Jim: they had all tried to get at me that night. All right, let them try!

CHAPTER THIRTEEN

I

THE SARAS were delighted that, at last, I was in Rosemullion, but I was not delighted. I found the evenings
intolerably tedious. If one can imagine anything so
fantastic as a sentient fly in amber, that is how I was. I
felt imprisoned in the immovable, longing to be free of
my self-created incrustations. I remember how, the first
evening I was there, I wandered from room to room and
experienced nothing but desolation. The pictures, the
furniture, the ancient curtains that had been newly hung,
the cabinet of early Staffordshire figures: they meant
nothing to me, nothing whatever. In the drawing-room
I drew the curtains to create the sense of night and seclusion that I had always loved. I turned the light on in the
chandeliers, and the dripping lustres might have been
stalactites hanging from the roof of a cavern of ice for all
the warmth and joy they brought me. I could have cried. I
thought of Annie Hocking's sitting-room. I thought of the
pub bar. I thought even of the bank where I had worked
with men about me. And I was terrified by the knowledge
that I would have preferred to be in any of these places
rather than where I was. I let in the daylight, put out the
lights, and went into the garden. It was a beautiful evening, utterly quiet. The roses and jasmine on the house
front filled the air with perfume, and the scent of newly-
cut grass came up from the lawns. There was no bird-song,
only now and then a scuttering cry as thrush or blackbird
went long-leg-hop across the grass. The sky was a clear
luminous green, fading in the west to a dusky mauve.
Far away—so far that I could not hear their clamour—

homeward-drifting rooks were setting down towards invisible trees. It was all how I had imagined such nights would be, except that I had imagined myself in tune with the night, and this night was existing in a beauty that rejected me.

I did not linger long on the terrace. It was haunted by the memory of Mr. Savage whom I had first met there, and the old ghost induced a tumult of thought about all that had been born from that pregnant meeting. That he was now in a madhouse did not help. It gave a tinge of insanity to my thought of what had followed our encounter.

So I left that place and climbed up behind the house to the ruins of the keep. I was looking eastward now, and the dark tower was blocked against the dark sky. The twiggy hair sprouting from the uneven top of it had a witch-look that was the most forbidding and rejecting thing of all the night scene. The last bit of the Menheniot stronghold. And the last Menheniot drawing near. But with no sense of acceptance. I felt no more Menheniot than Tudor or Plantagenet. I was nothing but a lonely man, frightened by this night's sense of rejection. I did not seem to belong to anything.

I went through the gap that had held a door, stumbling in the darkness amid the fallen stones. Bats flapped about for a moment, then swirled skyward through the tube. The heavy charnel smell of elderberry flowers was on the air. I was tempted to go back, but pressed on, found the stairway and slowly climbed. Here and there falls of rubble cluttered the steps. More than once they made me trip and pause, holding my breath at thought of the jumble of vast stones into which a fall would send me flying. I avoided the edge by keeping my shoulder pressed into the solid ashlar, and at last reached the top.

It was dark now. Far off, the moon was climbing out of

the sea beyond Penmaen, but it was too low to light what lay below me. However, I knew what it was: the wood of small scrub oak rising towards the foot of the tower, and then an open space full of tumbled stones. A horrid place. A mangling place to fall into. I clutched the edge to peer down into that chaos, and drew back with a sharp catch of the breath. The great stone my hand rested on shook and trembled, so delicately had the undermining of wind and weather poised it. One sturdy shake, I felt, and down it would go, and the quiet night would be broken by the sound of its smash and mangle.

Out of the tower, in the air again, I found myself sweating and trembling. I hurried down to the house and went straight to bed. It was a beautiful bed: a four-poster whose hangings were of costly brocade. For all the sleep it brought me, it might have been a fakir's plank of nails. Like everything else that night, it seemed to imprison me. Where was the happiness I had promised myself at Rosemullion? What was I *missing* here? And suddenly I knew what it was. Here I had become encrusted with layer upon layer of self; and I was missing those adventures out of self that had begun when I met Mr. Savage. They had been timid enough; after Bella came they had even been shameful; but what there was between me and Bella now came fully into consciousness and I wondered whether even that shameful thing had not been better than the virtuous dream that had brought me to Rosemullion. I remembered some words of Francis Thompson:

> *Virtue may unlock hell, or even*
> *A sin turn in the wards of Heaven*

and feeling excited, as though my mind were at last on the track of something real, I fell asleep.

I awoke to a sense of happiness, but for a time I did not know what caused it. My bedroom had an eastern window, and the sun was flooding through it, making me feel stuffy and ridiculous in my curtained bed. I got out and went to the window and looked at the light lying low on the fields and woods and flashing on every jewel of a spider's web that trembled from one branch of a rose to another. The dew drops were like beads upon the beautifully arranged filaments, and each bead blazed with the morning's fire. It pleased me more than my chandelier had done the night before, and surely, I said to myself, it must have been from looking at some such sight as this that the notion of a chandelier first entered someone's head. "But don't sentimentalise it, Mr. Menheniot," I said to myself. "Remember it's just a spider's clever trap for catching his breakfast. Now go and get your own."

Before leaving the Menheniot Arms I had written letters to Bella and Kitty. To Bella I said that I would let her know as soon as I had made arrangements for our meeting again. I felt that she would be safe enough with Annie Hocking in Annie's present mood. My letter to Kitty had been formal, an apology for what had happened between us on the beach. I didn't think that she would bother to answer it, but while I was eating, Mrs. Sara came in with a letter. I knew Kitty's writing: tall, thin and fragile-looking like herself. I turned the envelope over in my hand, looking with pleasure at the address: Roger Menheniot, Esq., Rosemullion. It was the first letter that had come to me here, and the association of the two words—Menheniot: Rosemullion—pleased me. They seemed to establish me in my place. But some residue of the thoughts that had troubled me in the night came sanely back and said: Don't be a fool. Don't wrap yourself up in *where* you are. Come out of your parcel and look at *what* you are.

It was only a flashing thought; but it was the first time in all my life that Rosemullion had seemed, if not unimportant, at any rate, not so important as all that. And this was not depressing. It increased the blitheness of my mood.

Kitty's letter made me feel happier still. I hesitated to open it, fearing that she would flay me, but to my incredulous joy it was a light-hearted letter.

DEAR MR. MENHENIOT,

The solicitude which I am sure you feel for my welfare prompts me to assure you at once that I reached home without further molestation. Penmaen is quite a safe place—normally. You may fall into its ways when your present abnormal phase is ended. Whether or not you were attempting to pay me a compliment is such a tangled question that I haven't been able to straighten it out; but I hope you will agree that, the circumstances having been what they were, it would have been possible to carry the doctrine of non-resistance too far.

Yours very truly,　　　　KITTY LITTLEDALE.

I don't know why this letter made me feel cheerful. The more I read it, the more I felt I was handling a stinging-nettle. But it wasn't a whip or a scorpion, and I had been expecting one or the other.

III

My first unhappy night at Rosemullion had an important consequence. I could not face the thought of loneliness. And the more I examined this revulsion the more I hoped that there was something in it beyond that. There was nothing wrong with loneliness in itself. I was

215

as convinced as ever that it was a great need of the human spirit, but I began to think of the loneliness as a time of refreshment for something else, not as a condition in itself. My small and timid contacts in Penmaen had made me aware of my need for sharing the life of men, for ceasing to use loneliness as self-fullness. I began to fear the madness that self could lead to, as it had done with Mr. Savage, blazing at last into that rejection of Will and Bella. My own shameful association with Bella was, it seemed to me, a flaring out towards a release from self that would not have been disastrous, perhaps might not have happened at all, if self had not been damned to such awful depths.

It was a strange few days of meditation that I passed, days in which physical need for Bella troubled me not at all. I began to see that I could do without her. But could she do without me? She was friendless, penniless, and who knew what insane notions Annie Hocking might be putting into her head?

One thing I had done during these days: I had ordered a motor car. Billy Polwheel, the sour old codger who lived in the Rosemullion lodge and was supposed to look after the gardens, wasn't much of a gardener. He wasn't much of anything: one of those people who take up job after job without ever having bothered to learn how to do them. At one time he had called himself a chauffeur, and he could, at all events, make a motor car start, proceed and stop, which was more than I could do. A new car was not to be had, but I had heard of a good second-hand one, and now it had been delivered. Billy was delighted to be a chauffeur once more.

It had been my intention, once I had finished my rushing hither and yon with Kitty in search of furniture, to have done with cars and retire into my lovely shell. What did any man need more than Rosemullion? But now here the car was: I looked on it as my link with the world. In my new frame of mind, I thought how pleasant it would be to go down to the Menheniot Arms in the evenings, have a drink and talk with the men, and come back taken out of myself. I might even learn to join in the game of darts. I can smile now at the thought of darts as a stepping-stone to salvation. I had ever been a naïve sort of person, and I am afraid my philosophic—could I call them religious?—gropings were as naïve as the rest of me. But I was sure—I am sure now—that isolation was sin.

I suppose it was a measure of the extraordinary self-centred way of my life till then, and of my joy in beginning to come out of it, that this small scheme gave me a disproportionate feeling of elation. Penmaen was the back of beyond, but what did that matter? See what it had already done to me!

Throughout these few days when I did not see her, and when I found to my joy that I did not desire her, a sense of responsibility towards Bella grew in me. I began to see her not as an instrument of pleasure but as an unfortunate young creature in whose fate I had become involved. What to do about it I was not yet clear. Enough, I said to myself, that I accepted the position. When I met her, we should see.

It was of Kitty now that I most often thought, and especially I thought of the night when she had gone down into the bracken hollow and called to me to come down to her. All the tangles of my knotted self had filled me then with horror. I had had to learn, as she said, in the wrong school; but now I saw what a world of giving might have come from that moment, rightly understood. All the same, I could feel no bitterness towards the teacher in the wrong school, only a great tenderness.

It was in this mood that I went down to Penmaen the next night. I walked, and told Billy to be there with the car at closing time. I enjoyed the walk through the evening, and took my time about it, going down alongside the stream that had roared in flood when Mr. Savage first led me that way, and that now slipped with hardly more than a tinkle from boulder to boulder beneath the dense midsummer canopy of the trees. I loitered for a while on the beach, my face freshened by the southerly breeze that was bringing a small sailing dinghy inshore. It was so light that the boat was hardly moving, and the man in it was helping its progress with the oars. Presently, he pulled up his keel, ran down the red sail, and the boat grounded. I had strolled down towards it, and as the man jumped ashore and took hold of the gunwale and began heaving the boat up I gave him a hand. He unstepped the mast, wrapped and tied the sail round it, laid this in the boat, and hauled his anchor over the bows. Having given this a grip into the sand, he tied a line round the flukes and carried the end of it to a bollard among the sea-holly, where he made fast. He seemed knowledgeable, and did things neatly and quickly, as I had hoped Jim Brokenshire would teach me to do them. He sat on the bollard, pulled out a pipe and lit it, and said: "Thank you." After a moment he added: "What a wonderful place this is. My God! I'm glad to be back! London!"

"So you're not a stranger in Penmaen?"

"Not altogether. I've been here every summer for the last few years. I stay with Jim Brokenshire. Know him?"

"Pretty well."

"Do you live about here?"

"Not far away—a few miles. My name's Menheniot."

"I'm Raymond Swithinbank."

Jim had not told me his name. He had spoken now and then of "this artist feller" who came down in the summer. I had thought he was using this as an excuse for levering me out of the pub, and I was glad to find that I had been mistaken. Not that Jim hadn't shown clearly enough that he was getting tired of my ways.

Anyhow, it was interesting that the visitor was Raymond Swithinbank. His painting was not of a sort that I liked, but during my visit to London in the spring I had looked into an exhibition of his work and been impressed at some point of myself that was not within my understanding. Whatever the picture was called, it was a variation of the same picture, and to me the titles seemed no more than pointless jokes. Each picture was a riot of swirling voluptuous paint. As colour, even as colour in harmony, I liked them; but I feared I would never get beyond my preference for pictures than contained recognisable objects. I remembered that what had looked like a stormy sunset exploding among pithead machinery was called in the catalogue "Nude arising," and I don't get that sort of thing. However, plenty of people did, and when I returned, somehow attracted, to the exhibition on my last day in town, there was an impressive number of red tabs stuck to the pictures.

I said nothing of this to Raymond Swithinbank, and, for his part, he had told me his name with no sort of pride or boast. No doubt, he reasonably thought that Penmaen was not a place well up in *avant-garde* painting.

He looked a man in his mid-thirties, and I knew he had had a distinguished naval career during the war, commanding some type or other of small craft. It may have been a submarine. Perhaps it was then that he began to cultivate his strong black beard. He wore a dirty old blue turtle-necked sweater, flannel bags, and blue canvas shoes, stained by sea-water. The hand that held the pipe was by no means what people mean when they talk about "an artist's hands," as though an artist's hands were always like those praying hands that Dürer drew. Swithinbank had the fists of a heavyweight boxer, and altogether he looked a robust man, virile and handsome. Virility was perhaps the thing above all. I had always prided myself on being sensitive to the aura of the people I met. Bella's lust. Swithinbank's virility.

At that thought, I looked at him with a sudden quickening of interest. But what had Bella, now, to do with me? I was finished with that.

"Well," Swithinbank said, "what about joining me in one? Or two or three?"

We set off together for the Menheniot Arms.

IV

The usual crowd was there, and they greeted Swithinbank with a heartiness I had never myself evoked. As soon as he walked in, he was the principal thing in the room. I had nothing to complain about so far as my own reception went, but as my overpowering desire now was to be accepted wholeheartedly by my fellows, I was a little depressed by the thought that, having come in with Ray Swithinbank, I was receiving only the overspill of his ovation. I was like some local mayor walking on to a platform in Wales behind Lloyd George. Hardly a man there failed to offer Swithinbank a drink, but he declined them all, walked to a seat evidently regarded as his, and was followed by Jim Brokenshire carrying a pint tankard of beer. It was clear that his needs were understood and were supplied without his having to express them.

"What's your, Menheniot?" he asked.

I said I would have a half-pint of lager beer, and when Jim had brought this, Swithinbank took up his tankard, said, "All hail!" and half-emptied it at a draught. Then he filled his pipe and sat back. "Jim," he said, "did I ever tell you of the dog-fight between the thoroughbred and the mongrel?"

"No, Mr. Swithinbank, I can't say I've heard that one."

"Well, this mongrel belonged to a chap who was having a drink in a pub one day. A very nasty-looking type it was, too, a huge mangy brute lying down by the bar. Presently in walks the local squire and with him a posh canine that takes one look at this roll of matting by the bar and then lifts his leg on him, full of contempt. The ugly brute just opened one yellow eye and said a few words, deep down in his guts. His owner said to the squire: 'I don't advise that, guv'nor. Better tell your dawg to lay off. Askin' for trouble he is.' 'Trouble,' says the squire. 'Trouble from *that*! Why, my good man, this is a thoroughbred. He could stand up to anything. If it came to a fight, he'd make rings round that brute.' 'Orlright,' says this chap. 'Betcher a fiver. Let 'em 'ave it out.' Well, after a bit of an argument, out they go, and the squire holds his dog on one side and this chap on the other. Then the landlord says 'Go!' and they loose the dogs. In about half a minute the squire's dog was a bloody mass of skin and sinew. 'Well,' said the squire, 'that certainly is some dog. What's his breed?' 'Breed? 'E ain't got no pertickler breed. 'E's just an old dawg my brother sent me from Africa. Before we could get 'im into the kennel we 'ad to cut a damn great mane orf 'im.'"

Swithinbank drained his tankard amid the laughter, and Jim came forward to refill it. "Same again for Mr. Menheniot," Ray said, "and for anybody else."

"A peculiarity in natural history," Ray said, "was the case of the young rat that was adopted by a hen and grew feathers, even on the tail...."

It went on for a long time. Now he was telling stories, now taking a hand in a game of darts, now singing songs with scandalous double meanings. It was at about nine o'clock that Bella and Annie Hocking came in.

I had drunk no more than two glasses of mild lager beer, and as I had eaten a good dinner before coming out, these could not have affected me. But I was feeling more and more unhappy. Nobody took the slightest notice of me. Tom Littledale had paid his strictly regulated visit, as perfunctory almost as though he had come to take the temperature of the bar, and, having done that, to go. He had nodded to me without even speaking. Everybody was now in Ray Swithinbank's grasp. He seemed to be making no effort to do it, and to be unaware of what he was doing. It was a measure of the absurdity of my way of looking at things that I was surprised to find a man, distinguished in his own line, so easily able to forget all that, to make no demand for recognition because of it, but all the same to be given recognition so freely for qualities that flowed out of him like scent at night from jasmine.

The fact is, I felt Swithinbank to be my opposite, and yet he was the sort of man I now deeply desired to be. An extraordinary mingling of admiration and dislike filled me as I found myself, like all the others, subjugated by him.

Moreover, to my surprise, I was disappointed that Bella was not there. As the evening wore on, I felt a crazy wish to see her. I had thought during my few days of philoso-phizing in loneliness at Rosemullion that I had done with her, that nothing remained now but a friendly arrange-ment to part. But it wasn't so simple as that, especially in this atmosphere of nothingness, of being no more important than the pot of pampas grass on the mantel-piece or the varnished fish in a case on the wall. To Bella, at all events, I was someone. Yes, by God, I said to myself, indeed I am! She could tell them something about Mr. Menheniot!

When she came in, she did not speak to me, except to say good evening. This was not surprising. As I have explained, we maintained a careful public face of indifference, and though Bella must have known now, as well as I did, that our secret was out, it seemed to me natural that she should continue in the way we had established. What interested me at once was that her coming was almost unnoticed. The maleness of Swithinbank dominated the room. He had just finished a game of darts and had carried his tankard to the counter to have it refilled when Bella went to order drinks. They stood side by side. He was about six foot tall and so broad that his height seemed diminished. She was no more than five foot. I can see them now, standing there in the room thick with wreathing tobacco smoke, the scarlet of the silk on her head contrasting with the rough blue wool of his sweater. I was aware that Bella, so unobtrusively that no one would notice it who didn't know her ways as I did, was nestling her head upon his shoulder. I could see, too, that Swithinbank was aware of this deliberate titillation, and as he turned to walk away with his beer one look flashed between them. I knew the look so well that it stabbed me. It was the look that she and I had so often shared in this room, the look that was not an invitation for the future but a reminiscence of experiences already shared.

Where was my philosophy now? It had not prepared me for the torment I endured. My wanderings on the cliffs and moors with Bella had filled my mind with a hundred vivid pictures that rose before me with a difference: the difference that I was not an actor in the scene and Swithinbank was.

I sat there in silence and suffered till closing time. I watched them go one by one, Annie and Bella with the rest, and there was no one but Jim, collecting glasses and mopping the bar as he whistled between his teeth, Ray Swithinbank and myself. I was trembling with fright at what I had to do, which was have this out with Swithinbank. I didn't know what to say to him, or how to start saying anything. He was sitting in a chair, his legs stuck out before him, his hands in his pockets. Suddenly he opened his mouth in a colossal yawn that dug a wet red hole in his black beard. I could see his tongue and his white teeth. He looked voracious and lustful, like a wild animal relaxing after effort. Then he got to his feet, beat his fists on his blue woolly breast and padded on his rubber soles soundlessly about the floor.

"What a stink!" he said. "I'm for God's fresh air. Coming for a turn, Menheniot?"

I bade Jim good night and we went out together. Bill Polwheel was rubbing down the car like a stableboy cherishing a horse. I told him to wait. Swithinbank and I went along the beach, lit by a half-moon that didn't give enough light to dim the stars in their sparkled myriads. The sea was quiet. We said nothing till we were half-way across this beach which seemed to me to be entering more and more into my most intimate emotions, and then Swithinbank said: "God! How lovely!" He looked up at the sky and cried: "Oh, God, I wish I could paint, Menheniot."

This knocked me off my perch. It was not what I had come to talk about. I hadn't allowed for men's variable minds, for the opposing ingredients in them, that jostle with this now to the top and now that. I couldn't imagine how a man who had just been literally rubbing shoulders with Bella could think of anything else.

So I was silent, and we came to the bollard to which he had tied up the boat a few hours ago. The boat was now rocking on the risen tide. Swithinbank stood looking at it for a moment, then said impulsively: "Let's go for a sail!"

"You haven't eaten anything," I said. "You must be starving. You've done nothing but drink all the evening."

"We can soon deal with that," he said. "Will you come?"

My mind rebelled at his dominion. This was not the sort of thing one did. At night one went to bed, not on to the sea, and, anyway, I had never been in a boat in my life. But, all the same, I wanted to go with him.

"All right," I said.

"Good. Let's go back to the pub."

It was Swithinbank who quickly arranged everything. Jim Brokenshire cut him a hunk of bread which he doubled over on to a slice of corned beef and began to munch right away. He gave Jim a hip-flask to be filled with brandy, and he borrowed some blankets and took them out to Billy Polwheel. "Here," he said, "pack yourself up in these and go to sleep. Mr. Menheniot may be away for some hours." I would not have dared to do it, but Billy took it from Swithinbank. He grinned, and at once began arranging himself in a cocoon. Ray went back into the pub and was soon out again, carrying in one hand the loaf from which Jim had cut his bread and in the other a blue sweater like the one he was wearing. "Put that on," he said. "It'll be pretty cold." I obeyed, and we set off.

I was nervous in the boat. There wasn't much room for two, especially when one was as big as Ray Swithinbank. He stepped the mast, but left the sail dangling. Till we were beyond the headland, he rowed. When we began to feel a bit of breeze coming out of the south-west, he shipped the oars, hoisted the little sail, and sat with the sheet in his hand. An extra puff came into the breeze. We leaned over, and I had a moment of panic, holding on hard to a gunwale. The boat began to run smoothly through the water with a sighing sound, and I realized that this was how one sailed.

"We can go a long way out on this tack," Swithinbank said, and he secured the sheet and sat back to light his pipe. I had never known anything so peaceful as this. It was a deeper peace than any I had known on land, somehow a different peace. Ashore, a hundred sounds could be heard, if you listened, on the quietest night, and you never lost the sense of belonging to them, of being involved in whatever of struggle or exaltation or despair they represented. For the earth was your element; you were chained to it; and it was precisely the feeling of having slipped the chain that soothed me now.

We were far out from land. I looked at Swithinbank. "How peaceful it is!" I said.

"All right," he answered. "Why break the peace? Why start a riot?"

He was slumped back with his eyes closed. I didn't need to be told twice. "Very well," I thought. "We'll shut up till you please to speak."

He spoke very little that night. Now and then, as we went on a new tack, he gave me an order, made me change over from one side of the boat to the other. There were hours of this dream-like gliding, disturbed by nothing but these small necessities of the job. By the time the east was paling we were nearing land again. I was pretty cold and that helped me to shake off the mesmerism of the night, and I was thinking that I had said nothing to Swithinbank of the matters I had intended to open with him.

Penmaen was some miles to the west of us as we drew to the shore. We lost the wind, and Swithinbank came fully awake and active. He dropped the sail, pulled up the centre-board, and took the oars. We ran ashore on a small sandy beach, and this at once brought everything back to my mind. It was the beach—twenty or thirty yards of sand—where I had so often watched Bella swimming.

"We needn't pull her up," Swithinbank said, "the tide's still ebbing a bit."

From a locker he took the loaf of bread, and jumped on to the sand. "Let's climb up here," he said. "I know this place."

I'll bet you do, I thought bitterly.

We scrambled up the rocks to the little lawn. It was soaked with dew, and we remained standing.

All the east now was a ferment of changing colour. Round about us, mist was already rising from the land, and the sea was smoky. I am not going to try to describe a midsummer dawn. I couldn't do it; and somehow it was Ray rather than the scene that held my attention. When the sun at last blazed through, he looked, standing there bareheaded, with the loaf of bread in his hand, so much a part of what was happening that he seemed to have been created to worship the moment. His hair and the frieze of his sweater were shining and there was a condensation of drops on his beard. "God almighty!" he said, and this sounded to me not like an oath but like a falling upon the knees.

Soon the sun was warming us. He took the brandy-flask from his pocket, swigged, and handed it to me. "Here," he said, "this'll put some guts into you."

The fiery stuff stung my throat and warmed my stomach. Ray pulled the loaf apart and gave me half. We sat on a rock and began to eat.

"Now about this woman," he said. "All night I've felt a glum animosity flowing out of you. I suppose she's the cause of it."

I must have looked staggered by his percipience, for he went on: "There's nothing surprising in my knowing about you and her. You must have discovered that she's a talker, and you know as well as I do what it is she loves to talk about. I expect you've been told the physical peculiarities and odd practices of every man she's ever been with. And no doubt of a few she hasn't."

This was true, and I had nothing to say to it. Swithinbank went on, after another mouthful of brandy: "Very well, then. You don't imagine, do you, that she's the sort of piece that'd make an exception in your case? Believe me, you've given her a lot of amusement. She'll be able to sleep out on her stories about you for a long time to come."

He handed me the flask, and I drank again. My stomach glowed. My mind was ardent with anger. I felt naked before Swithinbank, who must have shared Bella's laughter at my expense, and this produced in me a murderous fury against her.

"Well," Ray was saying, "if you want my apology you can have it. Naturally, I knew nothing about you when I began to go with her. Not that that, possibly, would have made any difference, because, believe me, Menheniot, she's not any man's woman: she's every man's woman. I shouldn't have felt I was robbing you. If you want Mistress Bella, you must be content to take your place in the queue. However, if you'll permit a man of experience to drop a word in your ear, you'll give her the go-by. You're a serious type, not made for casual affairs."

I should have been thankful to him; he was being kind to me; but that a man so much younger than myself should talk to me in this almost pitying way, that a man I had met only a few hours before should so obviously be aware of all my most secret doings, filled me with such a blaze of anger as I had never known. Violent language was shocked out of me for the first time in my life.

"What the bloody hell . . ." I began, and my temples were throbbing.

"Pipe down, messmate, and listen to Ray," Swithin-

nk said. "The bad boy of the family feels qualified to
fer a word of advice to dear old uncle who never left
me."

He laid a hand on my knee. The wide bangle on his
rist caught the morning light. Gulls were cackling and
ewing as they flew overhead, and he began tossing pieces
bread that they caught in mid-air. "With women,
ncle," he said tolerantly, "I should say you know your
ay about as much as one of those bits of bread among
ose ravening beaks."

One of the gulls landed almost at our feet and began to
ream. "Look at that eye," Ray said. "Hard as a ten-per-
nt moneylender's. Look at the beak." He picked up a
bble and threw it at the bird. "Get out, Bella, you
eedy bitch," he said. "Vamoose!" The gull flew away
That's how to treat 'em," he said.

He had torn out all the pith, and was now holding the
ncave crust of half a loaf. He bit into it with relish and
id as he chewed: "You should stop all the jaw that's
ing on about you in that pub by marrying a nice
spectable woman. But if you *want* Bella, you can have
r so far as I'm concerned. This evening a car will arrive
the Menheniot Arms in time to take me to Plymouth.
n catching the night train to London. Tomorrow I'm
f to Paris. Did I tell you I was a painter?"

I said nothing of what I knew about his work. I simply
swered: "Jim Brokenshire told me so. And last night
u said: 'I wish I could paint.'"

He laughed. "Did I? I must have been in one of my
re humble moods. Well, I had an exhibition in London
t long ago, and a Paris dealer saw it. I've just heard that
 wants to stage a show over there. I'm going to see what
s all about."

He was silent for a long time, and the gulls came back,
d he began to tear up and throw to them what was left

of the crust. Suddenly he said as impetuously as a boy:
was in the Navy. And d'you know what used to keep r
going? Dreams—just dreams. Especially of a Paris sho
I can't believe it!"

It looked as though he had no more to say about Bel
His mind had wrapped itself round its master-bias. I h
a feeling that if I said "Bella," he would look at me li
someone roused from a deep preoccupation and sa
"Bella? What Bella?" I got up from the rock, shaking t
breadcrumbs from my lap, and the greedy birds car
about my feet, screeching and trailing their wings. I he
out my hand to Ray. "Well, good-bye," I said. "I think I
walk back and wake up that man of mine. I hope you
have a successful exhibition."

"Thank you, Menheniot," he said. He scrambled
down the rocks, and I watched him push out the boat a
get under way. Then I began to walk along the path, :
familiar, so evocative of things I now wanted to forget.

But you can't forget at the word of commar
Especially, looking now and then out to sea, whe
Swithinbank's red sail shone in the morning light, I cou
not forget the things he had said to me. So I had given I
a lot of amusement. She would be able to sleep out on ta
about me. I was a figure of fun in the Menheniot Arr

I didn't feel tired or hungry. I felt alive with nerve
excitement. The sun was now quite warm, and I sat do
to watch the boat beating out to a place where she cou
tack for the run-in to Penmaen beach. She looked a vi
triumphant little spark of a thing, using immensities, t
sea and the wind, to take her where she wanted to be. S
seemed a symbol of the man she carried, off eagerly in
life's morning to challenge his fate. He had dreamed
this show, and here was the dream come true, because
had made it come. What had I ever dreamed of except
be tucked in under a warm blanket of safety? And wl

ad I ever done to make even that true? Nothing.
Nothing but accept a quixotic gift from a dead man.
Could anything that Bella might say of me, anything that
might be said in the Menheniot Arms, show me meaner
than I was? Bella herself was worthier than I. She had
faced a hard life in her own way, with something of
courage, with gaiety; and because I thought of her as
naming me, I hated her the more.

CHAPTER FOURTEEN

I

I HAD expected the Saras to be alarmed at my all-night absence, but Billy Polwheel, more intelligent than I had run the car back to Rosemullion to tell them that they might expect me when they saw me. Then he had returned to Penmaen. If they were not alarmed, they were surprised. Their manner when I returned suggested that they had joined the growing body of people who disapproved of me.

I went at once to bed and slept the day through. I awoke refreshed. I bathed and went down to my dinner. Mrs Sara confronted me with a glum face. She had received a letter from her brother-in-law, a railwayman in Truro to say that her sister was very ill. Here she had been, her tragic resignation said clearly, waiting to tell this dire news while slothful Menheniot slept through the summer day. Billy came at that moment to ask if I would be using the car that night, and I sent a message to say that I wouldn't, but that he would. He could take the Saras to Truro. They could stay there, all three of them, for the night. They could leave everything to me. I was quite capable of washing a few dishes and getting my own breakfast.

By the time my coffee came, the Saras were ready to depart, and I shoo'd them off. I was glad to be alone. My high humanitarian resolves, my intention to know more of my fellows, had evaporated. I didn't care if I never saw Penmaen and the Menheniot Arms again. I had had a sickener of the whole place. Much joy it had brought me. I drank my coffee, looked with satisfaction at the picture

232

I had bought in London, and thought of them all. Insane Mr. Savage. Dirty, prying Annie Hocking. Nympho-maniac Bella. Sermonizing Swithinbank. Contemptuous Tom Littledale. What a doctor! A man who could stand apart and watch a German soldier die. In what, I asked myself, was any one of these my better? I would stay where I was, which was something I should have done from the first. Let them try and get at me here!

And there's Kitty. What's your adjective for Kitty?

Never mind Kitty, I answered. Kitty's well able to look after herself. You do the same. I stacked the dishes in the scullery and went out for a walk in the garden, fully restored to my best running-away form.

This was the evening of midsummer day, still and sultry. Clouds were banking up. Even a townsman like me could smell a coming thunderstorm. I walked on the terrace, rejoicing at my aloneness in all this. From this terrace of stone, steps led down to a terrace of lawn, and under the retaining wall, which was hidden by coton-easter, there was an oak seat or two. I went down the steps, and Kitty was sitting on one of the seats. I was aware of no sense of shock or surprise. I walked to the seat and sat down beside her.

"Well, Kitty," I said, "how did you get here?"

"I walked. It's not much of a walk. Tom's gone to London for a day or two, and I was lonely."

This seemed explanation enough, and we sat without speaking while the light grew feverish and threatening, and a few bats began to flitter in the air.

"I thought you might be lonely, too," she said pre-sently. "Forgive me, Roger, for knowing it all. You can't help hearing every mouse-squeak in Penmaen. I mean about this girl of yours and her new man."

How happy I felt! Lucky Menheniot. I just had to do nothing at all, and things flowed my way like this. Saying to myself that the Bella business would have to end some time or another, I had added that there would then be the Kitty business. I would have to get back to Kitty. Even in the moments of my most abandoned idiocy with Bella, at any rate, after the vertigo of the first week, I knew that Kitty was the end of my meaningless life, the only thing that might give it communion and so make sense of it at last. That attempt to violate her on the beach had been a brutal overflow of this feeling, and among my recent agonies had been the fear that it had separated us for ever.

Why, then, had Swithinbank's casual intervention made jealousy flame in my heart? Should I not rather have been grateful? I don't know. My emotions were so confused that I was beyond all endeavour to disentangle and understand the springs of my conduct. I was like a shellfish that had been awash in the delights and agitations and terrors of the tide; and now the tide had withdrawn, and the shell was shut tight. Or so I thought. But tides are recurrent.

Anyway, there it was. I should not have to solve the problem of getting back to Kitty, for Kitty had come to me.

After all that had happened, it was odd to be sitting there like that, with this peace between us. Peace was something I had never known with Bella. It had been an alternation of stress and relaxation: never peace. I did not want to disturb this happy feeling of oneness that flowed between me and Kitty, and so I made no answer to what she had said about Bella. I said: "I'm surprised that Tom can go away like this and leave his patients."

"Penmaen is a disgustingly healthy place," she answered. "I don't know how he makes a living out of it. It would be absurd of him to have a *locum* for a few days' absence. Dr. Renner is only a couple of miles away, and

234

if anything goes wrong I can ring him and he'll be there almost in a matter of minutes. As for merely renewing the medicine, I can do that. I always have done it."

Then we said nothing at all for a long time, and I don't know how long we should have sat there if a sudden sound had not brought her to her feet. It was a heron, ripping the silence with his harsh cry. As Kitty got up I heard again the soft flow of her silk. It came upon my ears like gracious music that I had forgotten. "Well," she said, "thank you, Roger."

"Oh, for heaven's sake, why?" I asked. "You've got little enough to thank me for."

"I wonder." She looked at me earnestly, as though seeing in me something I should never see myself, and she repeated: "I wonder."

She took up her parasol—that piece of antiquity that I always found so endearing—and, looking up at the sky, said: "I'm afraid this won't be of much use."

Indeed, at that moment the rain began. We ran into the house, and Kitty asked: "Could that man of yours take me into Penmaen?"

I had forgotten that I was alone. "There's no man and no car, and there are no Saras," I said, and explained what had happened.

We stood within the open door, looking out at the rain-lances smashing themselves on the stone of the terrace. From the first the storm was severe. Our ears were filled with the noise of water: hissing there before our eyes, gurgling in over-full gutters, dripping from trees and shrubs.

"Well," Kitty said, "I certainly can't go back through this. Perhaps you'll be kind enough to give me your company until it's over."

We went into the house, and I put Kitty into a chair in

the drawing-room, and brought wine and biscuits. It was nine o'clock, and at ten the thunder was roaring and the rain falling as heavily as ever. By eleven the thunder and lightning had ceased, but not the rain. Kitty was restless. "I shall never forgive myself," she said, "if anything *does* happen. It would be the first time in my life that I'd let Tom down."

I comforted her. Penmaen, as she had said, was disgustingly healthy. Why shouldn't she take a few hours off if she wanted to?

We talked till midnight, and still the weather was not fit for a dog to be out in.

"You'd better go to bed," Kitty said. "I shall sleep here where I am and walk back when it's light."

I urged her to use the visitor's bedroom that I was proud of. Heaven knows what visitors I had ever expected to use it. I knew no one.

Kitty said she had no night-clothes and would be perfectly comfortable where she was. "Now get to bed," she commanded me. "It's much too late now to start wandering about the countryside, even if the weather takes up. And it doesn't look as if it will."

So I brought her some rugs and left her there and went up to my room. I did not undress, but lay on the bed, listening to the rain, thanking the rain for being beneficent. It had brought Kitty under my roof! Kitty was at Rosemullion, sleeping at Rosemullion! For myself, I would stay awake till I heard her setting off; then I would get up and walk with her into Penmaen.

I was awakened by the sun shining into my eyes. The sky was bright, the earth glistening and refreshed. I leapt off the bed and ran down to the drawing-room. Kitty was gone. I looked at my watch, and found that it was eight o'clock. The telephone bell was ringing, and there was Billy Polwheel, asking if he and the Saras could be absent

or another day. For all I cared, I told him, they could be
absent for another week. I made some coffee, and went
into the garden, whistling.

II

That day I made a lunch of sorts and began to hope
that the Saras would *not* be absent for a week. I was a
helpless sort of creature. I had never learned to use my
hands as my father could. Since he had had a car to play
with, Billy had neglected the garden. The lawns needed
cutting, but I had no idea how to start the motor-mower
or, if I accidentally started it, how to stop it. So there was
nothing to do but moon about in a restless happiness, a
pleasing disturbance of spirit.

In the early afternoon the heat became intense. I
retreated to the hall, which was the coolest place in the
house, paved with large terra-cotta tiles. There was an
oak chest against one wall, with my favourite Cotman
hung above it. I stood looking at the picture, and then
noticed that Kitty had left her parasol behind. It was
lying on the chest. It was so characteristic a part of her,
this old-fashioned silken thing, that I looked at it with
affection. She was so rarely separated from it in the summer months that I could hardly believe she had forgotten
it. I wondered if she had left it behind as a token.

Anyhow, it gave me comfort, and I sat down in an easy
chair, thinking of Kitty, and with the two wings of the
door thrown wide, so that I was looking out of a cool
cavern upon a picture drenched in heat and light. I fell
asleep.

I was awakened by voices, opened my eyes drowsily,
and came fully to consciousness with a shock as I saw
Annie Hocking and Bella standing outside the door.
They did not stand long. Annie was peering in, and

seeing me rise from the chair, she came forward bringing Bella with her. There was not so much as a by you leave. My serenity was dispersed by a shock of anger.

"Oh," Annie said. "So this is where you are? May we come in?"

She stood with her hands on her fat hips, looking greedily about her, taking in the place that was hers "by all good rights."

"Never been in here before," she said.

She was in no hurry. She looked at everything: the carpet on the tiles, the lights hanging from the ceiling, the lovely curve of the stairway. She looked at the oak chest, and I saw her face light with the joy of a spy who has found a clue. She walked to the chest, took up Kitty's parasol, and turned it slowly in her gross hands. Then she raised it to her nose and took a deep smell of it.

I don't know why that should particularly have horrified me, but it did. It threw my mind back in panic to the moment, that now seemed long ago, when I had seen her take up the photograph of the Lady Sylvia, spit on it, and wipe the spit with her sack-cloth. I felt as if she were smelling round for Kitty herself.

She put the parasol back on the chest and said nothing, but looked at me with a smile I shall never forget. It stripped me to the marrow.

Presently she said: "I brought Bella for a little walk. She's never seen your place, Mr. Menheniot. I must say you're pretty comfortable here, and I think she's entitled to a look round." She gave me one of her stripping glances, and added: "All things considered."

Bella seemed exhausted by the heat. She had sat down on the chair from which I had risen, and was looking at the pair of us with unaccustomed listlessness. She was wearing linen slacks and a blue shirt flaring open at the neck.

"Well," Annie said, "I don't want to butt in. I just brought Bella along. Show her round."

She gave her orders like a general addressing a private. "See you this evening, midear," she said to Bella. I saw her pause for a moment on the terrace, surveying her domain, then off she went.

I did not smoke, but there were cigarettes on the table and I offered one to Bella. She shook her head. "Could you give me a cup of tea?" she asked.

When I came back with tea for two and some biscuits she was still sitting there, pale and jaded. But she had undone two more buttons of her shirt, and she was wearing nothing beneath it. Unwell though she obviously was, she could not help making such a gesture. It had become automatic.

She drank a cup of tea greedily, but ate nothing. I poured her another. As she sipped it, some colour came back into her face and she reached across me for a cigarette, letting her shirt fall open. Poor Bella! I thought. I held a light for her, and she caressed my fingers as she had done that first night in the pub. Poor, poor Bella!

She blew out smoke. "Well," she said, "how did you enjoy it?"

"What?"

"Why, Miss Littledale."

Her tone was so cool and scientifically interested that I looked at her aghast.

She laughed in my face. "She's a bit tough, I should imagine, for that sort of thing."

Oh, there was no poor Bella now. All my pity burned up in a flame that shot through me. I could have killed her.

"It's a great compliment to me," she said. "The training I gave you must have been superb if it allowed you to tackle *her*."

239

I could not trust myself to speak, and Bella poured herself a third cup of tea.

"Well," she said, "it'll be in the open once Fat Annie gets back to Penmaen." She looked with meaning at the parasol. "You don't seem to know what happened down there last night."

She told me, and I felt sick with dismay. The taxi had come to take Ray Swithinbank to the station. In a field on the outskirts of the village a sheep-worrying mongrel, that had now been shot, was up to his tricks, and at a weak spot in a hedge a couple of chivvied sheep broke through in panic with the dog at their heels. These three creatures shot almost under the wheels of the cab, and the driver swerved and mounted the bank on his right. Then the cab fell back into the road, upside down.

There were passers-by who quickly helped, and not much damage was done. The driver was unhurt. Swithinbank had a gash in the right leg from broken glass. He was taken back to the Menheniot Arms, and Jim Brokenshire, seeing Annie Hocking in the street, shouted: "Dr. Littledale's away. Go and tell Miss Kitty there's been an accident. She'll know who to ring up."

There was no Kitty, and at last Jim rang up Dr. Renner from a call-box. It was necessary to put half a dozen stitches into Ray's leg; and, so far as he was concerned, it had simply meant that he caught the morning train today instead of the night train yesterday.

"But was the fat one excited!" Bella demanded. "She kept a watch on the Littledales' house till midnight, and was on the look out first thing this morning. She was able to wish Miss Littledale a blithe good day when she came back. And now that parasol. . . . Well, well, Mr. Menheniot, wonders never cease."

In the few months that had passed since I first saw Mr. Savage sitting on the terrace and walked with him to the vicarage, I had discovered many things about myself that had surprised me. So many, indeed, that surprise was weakening. I was beginning to see that my whole life had been a flight from the possibility of unearthing the sort of man I really was. I can now look at the most respectable citizen and wonder whether he would not commit murder itself if he thought there was reason for it, and opportunity.

Bella and I were walking in the garden. Seeing that she had come, I thought I might as well show her round. I could take the opportunity to bring this business to an end. There seemed no limit to the swaying of my mind. Watching her manoeuvres with Swithinbank in the pub, I had felt jealousy; and this had remained even after Ray's frank talk with me. Kitty's visit had swung me round again, and the fear of what the consequences might be for Kitty herself now that Annie Hocking had seen the parasol filled me with loathing for Annie, and, by association, for Bella.

She had noticed the ruins of the keep. "Can you climb to the top?" she asked. I said that you could. "Let's do it," she urged me. "Let's go and see the view from up there. I feel rather queer. Perhaps there'll be a breeze on top."

I knew her well enough to be wary. To get to the tower we should have to pass through the wood of scrub oak, and in the tower itself we should be enclosed. I did not want to be in any place of concealment with Bella, even though today there was a depression upon her, an absence of the sense she usually gave me of an animal sniffing for carnal scents. Thus I was already more inclined to go than I would otherwise have been, and suddenly, too, I remembered the precarious rocking stone in the crumbling top of the wall. "All right," I said. "Let's go up."

We began the ascent through the little wood and I looked sideways at her and her flaring shirt. "Why don't you button yourself up?" I asked. I wanted no distractions.

She laughed. "Really, Mr. Menheniot, that's the first time a grown male has made such a proposal to me." But she fastened the buttons.

In the tower a chill struck us, and she shuddered. The jackdaws beat around with their usual clamour before winging up into the blue. The place smelt foul with stagnant air and birds' droppings and the droppings of bats. It was obviously, too, a place for nocturnal killings. The bones of birds and rabbits were white among the fallen stones.

"No. Let's go out again," Bella said. "I loathe it."

She started for the doorway, and I said: "Now you're here, you may as well see what's to be seen. You'll be at the top in no time—out in the air. It's a wonderful view—right out to the sea beyond Penmaen."

She came back slowly. "All right," she said. "Lead the way."

I did so, and at the top turned to give her a hand up the last step or two. She leaned on the parapet, breathing deeply.

"Yes," she said. "It was worth coming."

The country simmered beneath us in the summer heat. The sea was withdrawn into a just-visible tenderness of blue-grey that mingled with the sky. There was not a soul in sight, not a sound to be heard except, from very far away, the clatter of some machine engaged with the hay-harvest.

I rested my hand on the rocking stone and felt it stir. The stone next to it, against which I leaned, was firm and moveless. I pressed it unobtrusively. Nothing would shift it. My fear of heights seemed at that moment not to exist. I clambered on to the stone and stood erect. Bella looked up at me. "How can you dare?" she asked.

"It's easy," I boasted, "and you see much farther. Come up."

She didn't like it. I could feel her mentally resisting me, but I had discovered that she was always one to accept a "dare."

"You can do it," I assured her. "Take my hand, and put your foot in that niche."

She summoned her courage, took my hand, and was about to lift her foot to the rocking stone when the pallor I had observed in her seemed to deepen and a spasm passed through her. She let go my hand, doubled up, and was sick on the steps.

It was only then that I realized where I was standing. For a panic-stricken moment I looked into the abyss and swayed. I leapt and landed clumsily beside Bella. And then—only then—I knew what I had intended to attempt. My knees were like water. I felt as though I, too, were about to vomit.

Bella was standing on the top step, turned inward to the wall. She leaned against it with her head in her hands. I put my arm round her shoulders, and the poor wretch, even in that desperate moment when she must have felt like death, could not resist taking hold of my hand and pressing it to her breast. She held it there, and I could feel shudders passing through her. "Oh, God, Roger," she said, "I do feel terrible."

It was the first time she had used my Christian name. She sat on the step and began to cry.

My mood changed to one of utter compassion. I sat

beside her and kept an arm round her and talked to her comfortingly.

"Are you feeling better, Bella? Do you think you could get down now? Let's try it, shall we? Take it very slowly. I'll make you some tea."

For a time she would not move. "I feel so cold," she said: "cold and weak."

I took off my coat and draped it over her shoulders. Presently she got up. "This place stinks," she said. "Get me out of it."

Indeed, all the stinks of the centuries seemed to be oozing up out of the stony tube, as if it were a tube filled with noxious matter that some mighty hand was compressing. It was high time she was out of it. I kept to the outside edge of the steps and helped her slowly down: over the rubble, over the fallen stones at the bottom and the skeletons of the small creatures that had shrieked and died there.

"Thank God," I said when pure air was on our faces. I led her some distance away from the door-gap, and she sat down among the little trees. It was hot and still. She rested her head in her hands and said: "I wish the wind was blowing."

Those were the last words Bella spoke to me. After a while I urged her to get up, and we made our way slowly to the house. She did not come in, but sat on the seat where Mr. Savage had sat on that day of our first meeting. It was a long seat. I put her legs up, stuffed my folded coat under her head, and went in to telephone. I called a garage and ordered a car, and then rang up Dr. Renner. He was already waiting at Annie Hocking's cottage when I arrived with Bella. He had had time to tell Annie of Bella's illness, and they were discussing it when I came into the room. "A lot of silly fuss," Annie was saying. "What's a bit of spewing? It's not the first time. She's been sick before. So have I. It's the water, I put down. All these wells. On the public supply we oughter've been, years ago, by all good rights."

Dr. Renner was a new-come youngster. He had Bella put to bed; and while he and Annie Hocking were in the bedroom I sat waiting in the parlour, perplexed by something that worried my mind, that was trying to come into the open. I pondered the talk: "Sick before. . . . So have . . . ." And, by God! so have I, I suddenly thought. I remembered the night when I had spewed my heart through Mr. Savage's window. I remembered the filthy sink in the vicarage kitchen, the weed-killers among the cooking-pots, and Annie trundling the evil assortment in a wheel-barrow down the hill after Mr. Savage had been taken away.

I got up, highly excited, and went into Annie's kitchen. I had not been there before, but it was what I had expected. It was the vicarage kitchen all over again, except that that was immense and this was a cubicle. There were the tins and bottles, the pots and pans, thick with the grease of many cookings, cheek by jowl in filthy confusion. I picked up a frying-pan and a pot or two, walked out with them, and dumped them in the back of Dr. Renner's spick-and-span new car. I waited there for him to come out.

He seemed a prideful young man. He asked me a few questions about what had happened at Rosemullion and nodded his head sapiently. "She's had a bad turn," he said; "but I think she'll be all right. Probably eaten something out of a tin that disagreed with her. I've given Miss Hocking a prescription. Miss Littledale will make it up."

Annie, indeed, as we stood talking there by the car, went scuttling towards the Littledales' house, a slip of paper in her hand. She didn't look alarmed, only self-important.

"I suppose you have no reason to fear arsenical poisoning, Doctor?" I asked.

"No," he said, and added with a smile, climbing into the driving-seat, "have you?"

The car door banged, and I thrust my head in through the window. "Yes," I said. "I know something about it. I've had a touch of it myself. I advise you to look at those pots behind you, and have the content analysed."

He screwed his head round, and for the first time saw the defilement of his car. "Well, of all the . . ." he began angrily, when I cut in: "I've just removed that lot from Annie Hocking's kitchen. Have a look at them."

I had hurt his professional pride badly. "Your anxiety about the young lady is naturally acute," he said. And when he had allowed me sufficiently to realize that even a newcomer had heard all about my vagaries, he added: "However, I don't think we need entertain extreme notions at this stage."

He did me the honour of raising his bowler hat as he drove away.

IV

The idea of returning to Rosemullion was repugnant. I crossed the road and asked Jim Brokenshire if he could put me up for the night. I thought he seemed reluctant but he consented. "All right," he said. "I suppose it can be managed now Mr. Swithinbank's gone. What's happening over there?" He looked across at the lane leading to Annie's cottage.

I gave it to him briefly. "Miss Thoroughgood's feeling a bit queer. She had called on me to have a look at Rosemullion and didn't feel at all herself. So I thought the doctor'd better have a look at her."

"Like her to call up there when you were all alone—the Saras and Billy Polwheel away. My God! She is a one."

It was extraordinary how you couldn't sneeze a mile away without Penmaen immediately discussing your pneumonia. I turned aside wearily.

"All right," Jim said. "The room's all in order."

The little room was like an oven. I threw up the window, pulled a chair over to it, and sat down. Annie Hocking came out of the doctor's house, carrying a bottle. She had waited for the prescription to be made up.

This, I suppose, was at about five o'clock or half-past. I wondered what Kitty was doing over there, and I was tortured by desire to go and comfort her. That she needed comfort I did not doubt, for Annie was not the woman to have wasted her opportunity. In the brief interview that chance had thrown her way she would have mentioned the parasol and said that Bella and I had spent the afternoon together. But I had the sense to keep away. This was no moment for me to intervene. I felt that things were now moving of their own momentum to whatever the end was to be. Worn out, I lay on the bed and fell asleep.

It was eight o'clock when I woke. I went down and asked Jim to cut me a few sandwiches, and I ate them in the bar, drinking a glass of lager beer. Whatever was happening in the sinister little lane across the road was not causing any stir in the pub. Someone asked how that girl at Annie Hocking's was getting on, but there seemed no idea that she was, as I guessed her to be, at death's door. A wit said: "'Er timin' be all wrong—mornin' sickness in the afternoon." A general laugh suggested that this probably hit the nail on the head. Poor Bella! To the very end there was only one thing men would

247

associate with her name. And I suppose that was not to be wondered at.

Far more exciting, and occupying most of the attention of the bar, was the news that Mr. Savage had died that morning. There was an ancient who had been a boy in his teens when Mr. Savage first came to Penmaen, and who little dreamed then that this fortunate circumstance would earn him so much beer three-quarters of a century later. It was his night, and he used it to the full. He babbled of the "quality" they had seen at Penmaen in those days, and of the Lady Sylvia and her imperious ways. "Praaper li'l terror, she were."

I hardly heard him. I was so deeply immersed in my own meditations that I did not see Annie Hocking come in. But I heard the shout she gave and that silenced everyone.

"She's gone!"

They didn't need to be told of whom she was talking. I looked up, and there Annie was, a fat greasy Maenad, with grey hair flying. She hadn't all that feeling for Bella: I was sure of that. She was dramatizing the moment and her part in it. She ranted for a time before I took in what she was saying: "Just a bit sick, she was. There was nothing in that. It wasn't the first time. The doctor thought nothing of it. But the moment I gave her the medicine she was sick again. What was in it? That's what I want to know. You know who makes the medicine up."

Jim broke in roughly. "'Ere! Cheese that, Annie! You better watch what you're sayin'."

"I know what I'm sayin'. She must've hated Bella. She was after Mr. Menheniot herself. Spent the night with 'im last night. That's something you didn't know. But I know it. Wouldn't she want to get rid of Bella, who was the light of Mr. Menheniot's eyes?"

248

I didn't feel angry—not even annoyed. Everybody was looking at me as coldly as if I had murdered Bella with my own hands. Well, I thought, that is what you have been asking for, and that is what you have got.

But, so far as Kitty was concerned, I felt a hatred of Annie Hocking, and this gave me a cold logical impulse to stop her slanders in the most effective way. Saying nothing, I got up and left the pub. I guessed that Annie, with a story and an audience, would be there for some time. The door of her cottage was open and I went in. The shoulder of the cliff never allowed much light to enter that damp little house, and now, with the sun below the horizon, the bedroom was webbed with grey shadow. I was, for a moment, afraid to look at Bella. I had only once in my life looked at a dead face—my father's long ago, and I remembered reflecting how death's refinement accentuated the likeness to the Menheniot in the print I treasured.

Menheniots! Well, at least I had grown out of that nonsense.

There was nothing to be afraid of. She looked merely pitiful, grey, extinguished.

I had come for the medicine bottle, and picked it up from the bamboo table at the bedside. I put it into my pocket, went out of the cottage, out of the lane, certain that no one knew I had entered the place. Kitty was coming down the steps from her house.

V

Kitty said: "I'm going for a walk. Would you like to come?"

"Bella's dead," I told her.

"Dead?" she looked at me, incredulous; then added:

"I knew she was unwell. Dr. Renner sent in a prescription to be made up for her. The formula didn't suggest anything much worse than a stomach-ache."

"Let's go inside for a moment," I said. "There's something I must tell you at once."

She turned reluctantly into the house, and we sat in the drawing-room. "I was across the road in the bar," I said, "when Annie Hocking came bursting in with the news that Bella was dead. She started saying the wildest things—the medicine had killed her."

Kitty laughed.

"Kitty," I said, "it's no laughing matter. You know what that woman is. She'd blacken the reputation of an angel."

"Let her go ahead."

"You can take it calmly if you like," I said. "But I'm determined to kill her slanders once for all. I went to her cottage and I took the bottle of medicine. I shall have it analysed. That'll shut her mouth."

It was almost dark in the room, but there was light enough for me to see Kitty's sudden gravity. At last she said: "Oh, Roger!" I could not understand the look of deep distress that came upon her face.

"What is it, Kitty?"

"Do you think *I* need defending from Annie Hocking? When she came for the medicine she left me in no doubt that she knew where I had spent the night, or how she imagined I had spent it. And she left me in no doubt that Bella was spending the day with you. I didn't mind. I have nothing to say to Annie Hocking on that or any other subject. I thought the time had come when all doubt was ended between us."

"Of course it is. But . . ."

"But . . . There must never be a but, Roger. To think that *you* should find it necessary to have a scientific

250

demonstration that Annie Hocking is a liar and that I am not a murderer! Oh, Roger!"

"I don't want a demonstration for myself. It's other people's tongues I'm thinking about."

"Other people's tongues! That you should even think of them in connection with me!"

"Oh, this is hair-splitting."

"Where is the medicine?"

I put the bottle on the table and she took it up and went out into the hall. I followed her, utterly miserable, into the little dispensing cubicle into which a door opened. She switched on the light, uncorked the bottle, and poured the contents down the sink. Then she rinsed the bottle and turned to me. "Now," she said, "there is no evidence that I murdered Bella, so my reputation is safe. Are you happy about it?"

Happy? I was so unhappy that I walked all the way to Rosemullion through the darkness, saying nothing to Jim Brokenshire of my change of plan. The Saras had returned. "Why, Mr. Menheniot, you look like a ghost! What have you been up to?" Mr. Sara asked.

I certainly felt like a ghost, and, like a ghost, I was restlessly astir till cock-crow. Then I fell asleep.

VI

This bottle of medicine, which had seemed so important to me, was not even called for at the inquest. There were four witnesses: Kitty, Dr. Renner, Annie Hocking and myself. I told of all that had happened at Rosemullion after Annie had left me and Bella alone there: all that had outwardly happened. There was no call to say anything of the dark moment when I had a horrifying glimpse of my own heart's wickedness. I told

251

of Bella's sickness, of taking her to Penmaen, and of leaving her in Dr. Renner's hands.

Renner was called then, and I liked him more than I had done when I talked to him in his car. He proved a very honest young man. I had been asked nothing which gave me an opening to mention Annie Hocking's pots and pans, but Renner conscientiously dragged them in.

The coroner asked him: "Did nothing in your patient's symptoms suggest what we now know to be the fact: that she was suffering from arsenical poisoning?"

"No, sir," Renner answered, "I am afraid not. I admit I was at fault, especially as Mr. Menheniot suggested to me that he feared arsenical poisoning. I dismissed the idea as a layman's unfounded guess, but after the patient's death I analysed the contents of some pots and pans that he had put into my car."

"And what was the result of that examination?"

"I found small but definite evidence of arsenic."

Kitty was asked nothing but to produce the prescription Dr. Renner had written and to testify that that was the medicine Annie Hocking had taken to her house.

Then I was recalled. "Mr. Menheniot, you told Dr. Renner that you feared arsenical poisoning. You went so far as to suggest to him the means by which you thought the poison had been administered. Please tell us why you had these ideas in your head. Take your time now, and tell us everything you know."

Egged on by the coroner's intelligent questions, it took me an hour to tell of all I had seen since my arrival at the vicarage.

"And you have seen Miss Hocking pouring weed-killer into the kitchen sink?"

"Pouring it violently, sir. Splashing it would be a better word."

"Thank you. That is an important amendment. And

hese splashes of a poisonous substance—you think it
possible that some of them landed in the frying-pans or
saucepans?"

"They could hardly help it. The cooking things were
littered all round the sink, and I never saw them washed."

"You have told us of your own bout of sickness. You
think that was caused by the poisonous splashes?"

"I can only say, sir, that I *assumed* it to have been."

"You assumed it so strongly that you never ate in that
house again?"

"That is so."

"And when you took Miss Thoroughgood to Miss
Hocking's house on the night she died, you heard Miss
Hocking say that she herself had been sick?"

Annie answered this for me. "So I 'ave, many a time.
It's the dirty water in the wells. By all good rights . . ."

"Miss Hocking," the coroner advised her, "please hold
your tongue till you are asked to give evidence. I have a
well in my own garden, and wouldn't change it for all the
piped water in Cornwall."

The coroner came back to me. "Mr. Menheniot, you
have been in Miss Hocking's kitchen at Penmaen."

"Yes, sir. I went there to get the pans for Dr. Renner."

"Did you have time to observe its condition?"

"I observed tins of weed-killer cluttered round the
kitchen sink, and I have seen Miss Hocking using weed-
killer recently among the cobbles outside her front door."
I was glad when it was over.

Annie's evidence was little more than a series of out-
crys about "a bit of honest dirt," and "finicky nonsense,"
and "more likely the medicine killed 'er." The coroner
was short and sharp with her.

He surveyed the case very fairly. In his own mind, he
said, he had no doubt that this unfortunate young woman
had died as a result of arsenical poisoning, the poison

253

having been administered in minute doses over a long period. The evidence suggested the possibility that, on the fatal day, food was cooked in a vessel which had been infected by just that small extra amount which would make the difference between a harmful and a lethal dose.

The jury must carefully consider whether these doses, and especially the fatal dose, had been administered accidentally or by intent. It would be useful for them to bear in mind a case which had occurred thirty or so years ago, where a woman was charged with the murder of more than one person by the administration of arsenic. That case and this one seemed to have remarkable points of similarity. It was the duty of one of the dead persons to keep paths free of weeds, and an arsenical weed-killer was used for the purpose. It was the duty of the accused woman to provide the food of the dead men. She also mixed the weed-killer. The evidence in that case was of filthy kitchen conditions, of infected pots and pans, of recurrent sickness by several people, including the accused woman. "I recall this case," the coroner said, "in order to point out to you that the woman was found not guilty, and was discharged. Whatever we may think of deplorably filthy habits that lead to death, we must bear in mind that murder involves intention."

No names were mentioned. The verdict was that poor Bella had died from arsenical poisoning, and that the arsenic had been accidentally administered.

254

CHAPTER FIFTEEN

I

SINCE the night of Bella's death, I had not seen Kitty till we met at the inquest in the schoolroom of the Methodist chapel. In the meantime, Tom Littledale had returned from London, and he was there, too. Neither of them did more than wish me good day. When the business was over, they went home together.

The brief interval between Bella's death and the inquest had seethed with gossip. I don't think one fact came out before the coroner that had not already been unearthed and discussed. The only surprised person was Annie Hocking. She had been, I am sure, genuinely unaware that she had caused the girl to die, and she had been having a gala time, telling everyone what she would say in court. This included a recital of what she had discovered when she brought Bella to Rosemullion. She had gone so far as to hide in my garden, see me leave the house, and then call to tell Mrs. Sara that Miss Littledale had sent her to collect the parasol. With this piece of evidence, she had visited the Menheniot Arms, and God knows what she had had to say there. What is certain is that Penmaen was buzzing with a three-cornered scandal that embraced me and Bella and Kitty. It could hardly have failed to reach Tom Littledale's ears, and his chilly looks had not surprised me.

I was not surprised either by an agitation in Mrs. Sara's manner when she brought my tea, upon my return from the inquest. I knew what she was going to say: the only question was how she would say it. No diplomat could have chosen a point farther from the real matter in hand.

She told me that Rosemullion was a long way from "th
pictures," and it was not for me to answer that, during al
the time I had known them, she and Sara had visited th
cinema about once a year. I was sunk in so deep a dreari
ness that I could not argue. I drank my tea and listened
apathetically to her story of how depressing country lif
was after the years they had spent in London. The recen
visit to Truro had shown them how much they had beer
missing the pleasures of having people about them, anc
they had heard of a job there that Sara could have for the
asking. She gave only one tweak to my tail. "And there'
so much gossip in the country, Mr. Menheniot. It make
a person uncomfortable."

So that was that. In a week's time I should have Rose
mullion to myself. "Well, you fool," I said, "you pined for
it long enough, and now you've got it."

II

I don't know whether I should have gone down to the
Menheniot Arms that night if Billy Polwheel had no
turned up with the car, expecting me to do so. I felt
wanted to have done with the whole place—Rosemullion
Penmaen, and all they had stood for. My mind was in a
state of utter bafflement over Kitty. What on earth had
done wrong? Would not anyone who felt for Kitty as
did have wanted to take that bottle of medicine and kil
Annie Hocking's slanders for ever? Wasn't it a shee
perversion—an utter insanity of egotism—to suggest tha
this normal desire betrayed distrust? At one moment
was flaming with anger at what I thought Kitty's abom
inable treatment of me, and the next wallowing in
abasement, searching my conduct for wrong steps I had
taken. Seeing Billy there, I got into the car. To hell with
the whole business, I thought. If I can't do anything else

I can go and get drunk. It was the first time in my life such a notion had visited me.

I met Ray Swithinbank coming out of the pub. He stood in the doorway holding a pewter tankard and took a swig as I stepped from the car. His overpowering virility oppressed me. The shaggy blue jersey, the black beard from which he was wiping ale with the back of his hand, his stance—legs wide apart—all had a daunting effect on me, and so did the laugh with which he greeted me. He filled the doorway. "Well, well!" he cried. "The very man! I step outside to avoid you, and I walk right into you!"

I answered with a precise pedantry that would have annoyed a less good-humoured man: "You could hardly have wished to avoid me, seeing that I wasn't there."

"Not there! You pop in for a moment and see! You'll be there for weeks, being chewed over like gum in a G.I.'s mouth. I've had a bellyful of you, Mr. Menheniot, during the last hour." He reached behind him and put his tankard down on a table in the passageway. "Let's go for a drive," he said.

There was nothing for it but to obey. He had that effect on me. I got back into the car and he climbed in after me. "Where to?" Billy asked, and Swithinbank said: "Anywhere you like."

Billy seemed to understand his man, for, after a long drive, it was at a pub that he drew up. "This do?" he asked, and was told, "Admirably."

It didn't seem admirable to me. If anything had been needed to complete the depression of my mood, here we had it. This was a part of Cornwall I had never seen, though I had understood it to exist. The pub was a mean, isolated building standing on a secondary road. A few wind-blown sycamores rose behind it, and even in this midsummer moment their leaves were dry and weary.

A wall of rough unmortared stones shut in a bit of kitchen garden from the waste. The waste extended as far as the eye could see: heather and bracken, with here and there a flame of gorse or a small twisted tree. Cottages as mean as the pub stood at wide intervals on the road. More of them seemed to be ruins than habitations, and against the sun, which was now going down, turning the western sky into a smoulder of red and mauve and violet, there stood up a major ruin: a vast crumble of ivy-grown wall with a tall shaft growing out of it, tufted at the broken top by twigs and grasses. Look where you would, the prospect had a desolate grandeur that suddenly made my Georgian hideout, snuggling amid camellias, smooth with lawns, decorated with ponds, seem very odd indeed. There was a pond here: an irregular stretch of water lying on the waste, with no trees to mitigate its primeval shape, no breeze to stir it: nothing but a savage blood-red blotch flat upon the darkening landscape.

Swithinbank seemed to have forgotten me. He said to Billy, who had left the engine running, "Stop that damned noise!" and then in the darkness he walked up and down the road, pulling hard on his pipe as if some internal energy and excitement were stirring in him. Presently he came back to us and said: "Well, well!" Then he stood still, looking about him, before saying at last: "Now, let's have a drink."

We left Billy Polwheel in the pub and took our drinks outside. Across the road was a tumbled wall. We climbed over it, and sat in the heather with our backs to it, facing into the west. The ruin blocked against the sky was darkening swiftly. It seemed to people the landscape with reminiscence: the tin and copper workers, the little dark men, back and back and back. The setting sun gave us a last display. It was as though a fire of nearly consumed logs had suddenly caved in at the centre. The colours shot about and intermixed in one astounding moment before changing to pearl and then slowly to ashen grey. But in that one moment I was back again before those pictures of Swithinbank's that had drawn me with puzzled admiration. I said nothing to him: but, as if his own mind was on pictures, he said: "Well, all's fixed for Paris. The show is to be in the autumn. I flew back and came into Cornwall on the night train. I was sorry to find the Littledales gone."

You may believe that that put pictures out of my mind! "Gone! Where on earth are they gone to?"

"Why, to London. Didn't you know? Tom Littledale heard of a practice going in Islington. He's certainly reeling from one extreme to another. That's why he went up to London—to see how the land lay. Well, apparently it was all right, and he came back to fetch his sister, though he hadn't told her what he was after when he went. And now he's whisked her off."

That news stunned me. For a moment I could say nothing, and then nothing much to the point. "Pretty precipitate!"

"Well, perhaps it wouldn't have been," Swithinbank said soothingly, "if he hadn't come back to find things as they were. Sorry, Menheniot, but the place is buzzing with it. They made me sick tonight. As you know, I've been coming to Penmaen off and on for a few years. I've seen something of Kitty Littledale. I admire her, and I didn't like hearing her discussed as if she were a public whore. That's why you found me outside, taking the air. I needed it. And that's why, I imagine, Tom Littledale has whisked her out of the place."

I felt as though I were involved in universal ruin. Every life I had closely touched since coming into Cornwall had worsened. Old Savage had met a grim end and his son had disappeared, heaven knows whither. Bella

259

was dead. Even Annie Hocking, who had seemed impregnable in complacent evil, had broken down. That she was an unintentional poisoner had made no difference. She was a poisoner. People drew away from her. Such whispers as she had loved to blow upon the reputations of others had now gathered from all quarters and hung in a threatening cloud over her head. She had scuttled to earth like a beetle that knows it is in danger of being trodden on. She would be the next to disappear, I did not doubt. And Kitty was being talked about "as if she were a public whore." I felt like a monster, like something life-destroying.

I said to Swithinbank: "What's the matter with me? Even my old housekeeper, whom I've known for years, seems to think me a plague-spot and is about to leave me."

Swithinbank didn't seem to want the job of father-confessor. He got up and walked over to the pub. When he came back with his tankard refilled, he said: "Why ask me?"

"You're a man of the world," I said feebly.

"What world?"

I had no answer to that, and after a long silence Swithinbank said: "That expression always makes me sick. You hear smart-aleck barristers hand it to witnesses in court. 'Now, Mr. Smith, this is a very personal question, but you mustn't be afraid to answer. We're all men of the world here.' And it's always about some bit of dirty stuff, as though being a man of the world involved nothing but knowing of the world's sins and crooked tricks."

He paused for a grave moment, and then went on: "I'm acquainted with that sort of thing as much as the next man. But a leery bloke who knows all the bar-room stories and can tell you whose wife is sleeping with whom —that's not my idea of a man of the world. The world is an onion, Mr. Menheniot, skin within skin, and anyone who thinks it's nothing but the outside one that lies in the dung can have it if he wants it. A real man of the world knows them all, down to the heart's core of the thing."

He stopped to fill his pipe, and when it was going he said: "Look, why the devil did you get me on to this? It's not a thing one talks about. It's just something one tries to work out as one goes along."

"Go on with it," I said.

"Now you," he said, "when you came down here, you were not what anyone would call a man of the world. You'd spent your whole life building up dams against every sort of knowledge and experience. You were an innocent—or an ignorant—that no lawyer would have appealed to as a man of the world; and seeing the way they use that expression, that should have meant that you were a desirable sort of chap. But, by heck, you weren't! You were a damned nuisance, a public danger."

I had asked for it, but I didn't like it. "What can you know of me?" I asked stiffly.

"Oh, plenty," he said. "I've heard it in the pub, I've heard it from Bella, and I heard a lot from old Savage."

"What did you know of Mr. Savage."

"Probably more than you. This isn't my first visit to Penmaen. Last summer I spent a lot of time with the old boy. We used to walk about every afternoon and drink brandy every night. Now there was a man of the world for you! He knew it all—from his Sylvia down to Annie Hocking—from God to the Devil—from his ancestral mansion to the cottage we used to call at where his old gardener was living and dying."

"Maybe," I said. "But he can't have known anything of me then. I didn't arrive here till a few months ago."

"Believe me, Menheniot, Mr. Savage didn't need to see you with mortal eyes. He knew it all from Phil Menheniot. He knew, don't ask me how, that Phil was dead and that you would be arriving. He knew the oddest things about you. For example, how you trembled one night when Phil was putting you into a taxi after an hotel dinner, because you knew that Phil was going back to pick up a girl."

It was dark now, and I was feeling cold. I was feeling stripped.

"Oh, yes," Swithinbank said, "you were already a major interest in old Savage's life. He was an entomologist of the spirit. He delighted in watching people react to crises, and he knew that to have someone make a dream come true for you would be a crisis all right. It might have been another thing if you had worked to make it come true for yourself. I remember that he quoted *Bishop Blougram's Confession*. D'you ever read Browning?"

"No."

"I should have thought not. Not all on the surface, is it, like a nice David Cox water-colour. Well, the old man gave me that bit beginning *When we are safest there's a sunset-touch*, and 'That's the time the apple-cart is apt to go over,' he said, 'when we're safest, or think we are. We shall see this Mr. Menheniot down here, my boy, feeling in a very safe mood. I promise myself some interesting observations.' "

"You're being damned metaphysical," I said, "and you seem a long way from the point."

"Well, have the point then," he said. "Have it right in the guts if that's how you want it. You've spent your life dodging everything, building dams around your precious niminy-piminy existence. Well, at the first touch your dams have bloody well bust, that's all, and you're in the flood up to the neck. I wouldn't care a hoot about that if other people weren't in with you." He paused, then added savagely: "Why did you have to do this to Kitty, you blundering fool?"

I was taken aback by the passion of those last few words. I felt at once that I was on the edge of something I had not expected when this discussion began. It was now as dark as it would be on this summer night. The pool of blood had become a pool of tarnished lead.

"Kitty's not the only one," I said.

"To me she is. I could wring your blasted neck." He got up, towering over me, and for a moment I feared violence.

"Do you think," he demanded, "I should have been going round with that little bitch Bella if Kitty would have had me? Everybody knows that Kitty spent a night with you, and though you're such a bloodless worm I don't suppose it was a night of innocence. That she should take *you* when she'd refused *me*! You—a piddling connoisseur, and me a maker!"

He looked insane in his pride and wrath. "That night I took you sailing," he said, "I gave you some advice. I didn't cross the t's. I thought you'd have enough sense to see what I was getting at. Tom Littledale had quietly warned me off. He'd given me a plain hint about what Kitty felt for you. Yes, even though she saw the fool you were publicly making of yourself, she went on waiting for you to come to your senses. A woman like that waiting for you, and you make a muck of things even after you've had her in bed!"

"Do the people in Penmaen really believe that?" I asked. "Do *you* believe it?"

"Of course they do."

"But you," I insisted. "Do *you* believe it?"

"What else can I believe?"

"What indeed," I goaded him. "As a man of the world you must believe every lie that comes to your ears."

He looked at me incredulously. "Do you mean it's not true?"

"You've been talking as though you knew Kitty well. I see now that you don't know her as well as I do."

To my surprise, his face lit up. It was as though a worshipper whose faith had been shocked had re-established his belief. He said, quite humbly: "Thank you, Menheniot. How could I have doubted it?"

I told him about the medicine bottle. "Was I in fault?" I asked miserably. "I was thinking of nothing but disproving a slander. She was utterly unreasonable."

He sat down again beside me. "Reason!" The word came out of him like a groan. "Here is a man," he said, addressing the night, "who has been playing the goat with a little whore till he is the scandal and laughing-stock of everybody in sight. Despite that, a woman he isn't fit to touch with a barge-pole still wants him. And he asks for reason! Why, you fool, if reason had had a hand in the matter, Kitty'd have tied a brick round your neck and drowned you like a mangy dog. It was feeling she wanted, not reason. You'd gone so far from her that how could she ever take you back unless she felt an absolute trust flowing out of you?"

He got up again and looked down at me with disgust. "Why do I talk to you?" he asked. "Why do I try to drive a glimmer into your wooden block? But there's humour in it, Mr. Menheniot. *You*—my successful rival!" He walked towards the pub.

I sat there for a long time, thinking of many things. I thought how shamefully I had treated Kitty and how, after all that, she had come back to me on the night before Bella died. Would she ever come back to me again? I doubted it.

Presently, I went across to the Streamers, as the pub was called. Billy Polwheel and Swithinbank were standing outside, and Swithinbank was giving orders to Billy. "So ask Jim to put all my stuff together and bring it over here as soon as you can tomorrow. I shall be staying here for some time." He turned to me. "You don't mind, Menheniot?"

Let him do as he likes, I thought. Let him order my servants about. Let him go and take over Rosemullion if he feels like it. I was sick and tired of everything to do with Menheniots and Cornwall.

"I don't mind," I said.

I wished I were capable of a devotion, a dedication, like his. He seemed already to have forgotten what we had talked about and his contempt for me. "What a place!" he said. "I shall be happy here."

I looked at the mangy crumbling pub, cowering in front of the smitten but hardy sycamores, at the darkness about it, the stars blazing over it. Nothing lit it but a few oil lamps. It was a hovel in a wilderness. But I had no doubt Swithinbank was right. He would be happy there. He was, as he had boasted, a maker. What was I but a man relieved from the need to make even his daily bread— relieved by the death of a livelier spirit than I had ever been? What had I ever made but a desolation? Swithinbank could make a home in a wilderness. I seemed doomed to make a wilderness out of my plenty.

Swithinbank didn't even say good night. He went into the pub, shouting "George!" Already someone was George to him. How on earth did he do these things?

PART THREE

By Kitty Littledale

CHAPTER SIXTEEN

I

THE YEARS my brother Tom and I spent in Cornwall seemed endless. I never liked the place. It would not be too much to say that I was afraid of it. Here and there, of course, busy men have clotted themselves into towns and built cinemas and dog-tracks and hotels and boarding-houses. Racing yachts are in the harbours; there are surf-boards on the billows; and in the summer months children innocently shout and play on the yellow sands that border the seas flashing with the colours of a kingfisher's flight. Motor-coaches by hundreds, cars by thousands, tea-shops with fancy names, corrugated-iron shacks where bits of carved granite and serpentine are sold: all that sort of thing. I was not afraid of these dabs of stucco: they have nothing to do with Cornwall: I was afraid of what lay underneath. One was aware of it when summer was over. Especially one was aware of it in a village like Penmaen whose face was never distorted by an artificial smile. The place seemed haunted. To be out on the moors, amid the ancient standing stones, in a winter's dusk, was to feel as though one were in front of a thin veil; and more than once I have hurried home to Tom and a cheerful fire for fear that I should learn too much.

This feeling, which deepened with the years, did not touch me at first. The knowledge that I was helping Tom sustained me, and there was all the busyness of settling into a practice. Tom and I had always been close together. He was mundane and down-to-earth as I never was, and the consequence was that each of us felt a need to help the other. I wanted to help Tom because, from the first,

I suppose, I had an instinctive feeling that the things of the world, which alone seemed to matter to him, could hurt him if they went wrong; and on his part was the odd erroneous notion that any sort of artist was weak and susceptible. The truth is that such people have inexhaustible resources.

Anyway, we sustained one another; and the death of Tom's wife, so soon after marriage, threw him upon me with almost frantic need. I did everything possible to learn the practical things that would make me useful to him. There are those who say that I sacrificed myself to him; but that is nonsense; and, even if I had done so, what would be wrong with that, especially in a world clamorous with self and its greedy satisfactions?

The pang of Eve's death abated. There are men to whom a marriage is eternal and who are crippled for ever when it ends, largely, I think, because of the passion and completeness of their own contribution to it. They embark their all in one frail craft, and, if that goes, the wreck is total. That was the tragedy of Mr. Savage, the greatest man I have known, though his greatness was unfulfilled. But Tom was not of this quality. The war was over; little of the stress of events reached us at Penmaen; we were able to persuade ourselves, as so many did, that the war had indeed been to end war, the memory of Eve faded, and he became a competent contented G.P. with a sister helping him. It was a small unexciting practice, but enough to live on. Tom would not have taken it if the need to forget Eve had not pushed him as far as possible from all the associations he had shared with her. Once she was, if not forgotten, at any rate no longer a burning pain in memory, Tom had become fixed, accustomed to a rather lazy life, and he just stayed where he was. The only thing that would stir him was any affront, even if an imagined one, to me. This became more noticeable after

I had begun to write. My first three books were the most successful, and Tom insisted on treating me as a precious porcelain creature. He even suggested my devoting all my time to writing. He could employ someone else, he said, to do what I was doing. He began to speak of himself as a man standing in my light. He said this once to Mr. Savage, who laughed and asked: "Where do you think light comes from, Littledale?" Tom looked blank at that, and Mr. Savage said: "No one creates, my dear boy, except by grace of the Creator. It would need a bigger man than you to stand in His light. So don't worry, and don't bluff yourself with big notions."

This was putting it rather too high; but I was disturbed by the knowledge that Tom *was* bluffing himself. He didn't really want any change in the comfortable and convenient routine that we had established. Neither did I. So far as writing went, I was never prolific, and there was plenty of time for what I wanted to do.

However, the oppression of Cornwall was beginning to settle on my spirits. The books themselves showed that. They were my escape from the place. They were always set in the country scenes I had known as a girl, far from cliffs and cormorants and the heartbreaking pipe of curlews. If they had an affinity with anything in painting, it was with the meadow sweetness of Constable. I was fond of London, too; and I began the practice of going up occasionally, making the excuse that I wanted to spend my royalties on things that could not be got elsewhere.

It was when I proposed the first of these visits that I became aware how dangerously Tom had come to depend on my presence, and how much, whatever he might say to himself, he resented my absence. At first, he said he would come with me; and it needed tact to make him see, without hurting him, that that was the last thing I wanted. I had my way, not at the expense of a quarrel but

271

of something almost as bad: that glum reproachful look of the wounded male asking without words, but for days on end: How can you do this to one who would lay down his life for you?

I was determined that Tom should lay down, at any rate, a couple of weeks. I disliked the deadlock of our life together. It would be better for him as well as me that we should know some separateness.

I am sure that it was. I made these trips as often as my means allowed. I didn't mind if I spent every penny I had earned. I stayed in good hotels; I visited galleries, sale-rooms and theatres; I dined with my agents and publisher; and I brought back some souvenir of my holiday.

Tom became reconciled to these aberrations; he even at last pretended to welcome them for my sake; but I knew that he would gladly have seen them end. And so they did at last, because I ceased writing and had no money to spend.

The unbroken humdrum returned, tolerable but unpalatable, like hygienic unimaginative food, though I hoped Tom did not realize that. I did my best to permit him not to; and his consideration for me, so long as I was at his side, was so great that I began to feel that my restlessness was, somehow, a fault. "When are you going to write again?" he would ask. I couldn't. I was being smothered.

Everyone knows that during the Second World War publishers struck a bonanza. There seemed no end to the demand for books to read. So it came about that my publisher re-issued cheap editions of my three best-known books, and even these were bought. Between them, they didn't make much money, but there was enough for me to renew my acquaintance with London in the year when the war ended. So I came to know Ray Swithinbank. He had been demobilised from the navy and had spent his gratuity in hiring a London gallery for his first exhibition of pictures. I chanced to look in there on the opening day. Save for a man sitting at a desk, from whom I bought a catalogue, the room was empty. There were about thirty pictures, and now that Ray is famous I need not try to describe what they were like. They moved me deeply. I had been used to liking and buying pictures so different from these that I was surprised by my own wish to possess one. I decided which I wanted: they weren't dear in those days: and I approached the young man at the desk. The transaction was completed and he stuck the usual red disc on the frame. Then I walked back and stood looking at my picture, wondering how on earth I should explain to Tom this singular preference. The room was deeply carpeted; there was no sound save the scratching of the young man's pen at the desk. The lighting was devotional. Suddenly, into all this a bomb exploded. It was a young, bearded, bareheaded man wearing grey slacks and a blue sweater. "Good God!" he shouted. "A port light!" His face was grinning with delight, and an extraordinary animal animation flowed noisily out of him. "Charley," he shouted. "Who has done this? Who among London's millions has at last shown a glimmer of sensibility?"

The young man, looking shocked at the tumult, said quietly: "The lady standing by the picture, Mr. Swithin-bank."

Ray rolled like a bear towards me, stood looking at me for a moment, then burst into laughter. I have always looked a demure creature. "Well, I'm damned!" he said. "I'd as soon have expected Charlotte Brontë to buy a Paul Klee."

I didn't know what to make of him, but pardoned everything because of his manifest joy. "One minute," he said. "Don't go away." He rushed out of the room. He was back ten minutes later, bearing an enormous bunch of

273

flowers. In Bond Street they must have cost him a prett
penny. He presented them to me. "My first patron," h
said. "I can do no less."

I felt rather sheepish, standing there holding th
flowers. He said: "You've picked the best. Let us dir
together tonight at the Ivy."

I was by now blushing and embarrassed, but I saw tha
beneath his noise he was moved, that he really did wa
me to dine with him. Perhaps he was a stranger in tow
like myself. And after all, I thought, to sell one's fir
picture must be rather a moment in an artist's lif
"Thank you," I said. "I'd like that." And I gave him th
name of my hotel.

"I'll call for you at half-past seven," he said.

II

That London visit was altogether different from any
the others. I was not important enough for my publish
or my agents to have reason to waste much time on m
Between them, they were good for two rather form
meals; apart from that, I spent my time alone. I ate alon
I went alone to the theatres; I went to bed alone. Now
found that I need not do any of these things. Ray Swithi
bank called on me every day, took me out either to lun
or to dinner, and offered to solace the loneliness of m
nights. I decided to endure them as I had always don
but I found myself, somewhat to my own surprise, neith
shocked nor annoyed by his proposal. It did not at a
embarrass my relations with him, which were very happ
For the first time in my life I was receiving the attentio
of a man, and one who looked as if he were going to l
famous. After a halting start, his exhibition had becon
successful. Before I returned to Cornwall he had so
every picture. And thus the young man who was showe

ing attentions on me—meals, flowers every day, theatres
—was on top of his own world. He was in that heaven of
indubitable success at his own chosen job which gives,
I imagine, the most exalted joy the young can know. That
at such a moment he should find so much time to spend
on me, a woman so far beyond him in years, a woman
whose own success had never known this completeness
and was now, anyway, only a memory: in short, that he
should spend his time on an ageing nobody surprised me
and filled me with humility and joy. It was such a week as
I had never known, and, I suppose, shall never know
again.

I recall how, one night, we were dining at the hotel
where he was staying. He had just moved in there. He was
an impetuous spendthrift, and as soon as his pictures
began to sell he left the lodgings he had been in and came
to this imperial palace. A note was delivered to him: an
invitation to take dinner the next night with one of those
lion-hunting hostesses who infest the town. She said, as an
inducement, that a dramatist and a sculptor, both world-
famous, would be among those present. He handed the
note to me, and I gave a little cry of disappointment.
"Then for once I dine alone."

"Do you think so?" he said, and his look was of such
devotion that, for the first time, I knew beyond doubt,
and despite the absurdity of it, that he was in love with
me.

"But of course I shall," I cried. "You must go to this
dinner. It's important to you to meet people like this."

"Is it?" he asked, with an arrogance that he often
showed. "I don't think so."

He tore up the note and didn't bother even to answer it.

He had by now read all my books and professed the
deepest admiration for them. "But mind you, Miss
Brontë," he said, using the name with which he liked to

275

tease me, "when I first met you I had no idea that you were a distinguished writer. It was you I fell for, not your books."

"Don't talk nonsense. I am in no way distinguished."

"Don't *you* talk nonsense," he reprimanded me, rather heatedly. "Don't belittle or undervalue yourself." With a boyish grin, he added: "It just shows how instinctively unerring my taste is. I could never fall in love with any woman who was common or garden."

III

When I was back in Penmaen the week began to fall into perspective. I suffered none of the pangs that afflict parted lovers. I had enjoyed my week enormously; I missed Ray for a time; I was fond of him and would gladly have seen more of him; but I felt nothing deeper than that. As for him, I could well understand how, fresh from years of war, he had found pleasure in a woman's company. It was not unusual for a boy to fall in love with someone motherly, especially at a moment of release from dangers. Forced into maturity, he would be glad to relapse into dependent sonship.

But I wanted to keep it to myself. I said nothing to Tom of what had happened, and when my picture was delivered from the gallery I was relieved that he was out. Tom would have been perplexed by such a picture. To talk about it would inevitably lead to talk of Ray, and that was something I could not face. I took the canvas out of the frame, rolled it up, and left it in a drawer in my room. Psychologically, this was a bad thing to do. It created a forbidden territory between me and Tom; it made me think often of such questions as: What on earth would Tom say if he knew that a vigorous young man had proposed himself to me as a bedmate? Especially what would he think if he knew that I had been able to regard such a situation without horror, and go on meeting and greatly liking the young man?

Inevitably, seeing that I never loved Ray Swithinbank, the matter gradually faded from my mind, save as an agreeable memory. I was back in the Penmaen routine, back as Tom's assistant and indispensable companion. Ray did not write, though he knew where I lived, and knew a lot about our village. He had liked to hear me speak of Cornwall, and it didn't take long to give anyone the complete geography of Penmaen. So it happened that one day early in the next summer Jim Brokenshire, the landlord of the Menheniot Arms, said to me: "Got a visitor coming down from London tomorrow, Miss Kitty. Bit unusual for these parts. Most of 'em want Newquay or St. Ives, or at any rate, somewhere with a better pub than my little rat-'ole. This is a chap name of Swithin-bank."

If I had wanted to be convinced that Ray had never been more than a delightful companion, I was convinced then. My heart gave no bound of joy but rather of apprehension. He could have kept from me if he had wanted to. That he had deliberately chosen to come and seek me out suggested that his feelings were still engaged, and I feared what I went so far as to call his annoyance.

I did Ray an injustice. Despite his overpowering exterior, he had great sensibility. He did not seek me out; he waited for chance to bring about a meeting, which took place on the beach, and when I made clear, as I felt I now at all costs must, that I had no feeling for him but of friendship, he forlornly acquiesced, but warned me that to him the world was free, Penmaen with the rest, and that when he wanted to come there he would do so. It was easy to see no more than a little of him. What with painting, sailing, making friendships in the pub and with Mr.

Savage, he was occupied. Everybody liked him, even Tom, who met him in the Menheniot Arms and never knew that Ray and I had met before. But when Ray went back at the end of that holiday Tom said: "You've made a conquest, Kit! At your age! That chap Swithinbank's half in love with you!"

Tom never knew how passionately I wished to answer: "Ah! If only I loved *him*!" For, if it had done nothing else, that week in London and this return of the lover had shown me how ready I was for love. But I answered: "It takes two to make a match, Tom."

"Ah well," he said placidly. "I don't suppose you'll ever be one of the pair. Seen my slippers?"

IV

The next summer Ray came down to Penmaen again. Roger had arrived a few months before. I recall so well how he came in to tea, invited by Tom. Tom went out to bring in the tea-things and left me and Roger alone.

As a novelist, I had written about love-affairs; I had written about love at first sight; and as a woman I had experienced love at first sight—Ray's, not mine. But I had never known that it could be such a trembling timid thing. I had imagined two flames rushing hotly together and so it would have been if I had loved Ray as he loved me. Nor do I know why, as soon as we were alone together, I felt as I did about Roger Menheniot. No one would call him a distinguished-looking man, and his quietness was unbelievable. He seemed afraid of me, and that was indeed something new, for though I have never myself been afraid of anybody, except Mr. Savage, whose dormant greatness used to overpower me, I have all the same as my protective skin that demureness that used to cause

278

Ray to call me Miss Brontë. I could sit for hours in company without uttering a word, fiercely despising everybody.

I think it was Roger's extraordinary timidity that excited my compassion. Seeing that he appeared to be genuinely interested in the pictures on the walls, I did all I could to put him at ease by talking about them. He had a few words to say, and I know now that, by his standards, he even achieved garrulity; but when he was gone, I had no feeling of two rushing flames but rather of two candles, lit indeed and aware of one another, but burning with a terribly precarious light.

That was in March. Tom was called out that night and was away for hours. Usually, when that took place, I went up to my own room and read there; but that night I made up the fire in the drawing-room. I wanted to stay in the room where I had been with Roger and think over what had happened. I realised how important the undramatic can be. The contrast between Ray's rushing into my life with his terrible energy, his flowers, his dinners, his endless exhilarating talk, and this arrival of Roger was almost comic; but, all the same, I knew that something had happened to me that Ray had never caused to happen. I am sure that Ray was never, as they say, putting on an act, but there was a histrionic quality about him that amused and even excited me but that did not survive as a permanent deposit of his character in mine when we were apart. I was never longing for a renewal of what he could give. I could do without it. I thought him a tonic, not a food. But at that first meeting with Roger I was pierced by the feeling that, for me, he was wholesome and permanent. That was how I first began to think of it; but I had learned enough about myself to know that there must be more than this if I was to be satisfied. I was an ageing woman, but I had recently been sharply reminded of what I had missed by diverting my torrents into the safe pool in which Tom and I had for so long existed.

I am writing this as an *addendum* to what Roger has written. I have read it, and I need not go over all that. He could give me much, but his pathological fear of women caused me to abandon him, and so, as chance had it, to throw him into other, more ruthless, hands. What I want to make clear now is that attitude of my brother Tom. It surprised me. Before I met Ray Swithinbank men had occasionally loitered about me. In particular, there was a curate whom Mr. Savage engaged soon after we came to Penmaen. He was the product of some intensive parson-training scheme that had been set up after the First World War. Mr. Savage sacked him with the remark: "I would prefer my parishioners to go to the devil in their own way rather than with your illiterate assistance," and that was that. No more curates. But while Mr. Schofield lasted he was a nuisance to me and anathema to Tom. Tom would literally chase him out of the house if he found him there; and with others he was profoundly discouraging. Not that I had wanted any of them: I could have dealt with them in my own way: but, all the same, I became aware of Tom's deep subconscious dislike of the idea of my getting married. He thought he was protecting me. I knew he was protecting himself.

Well, it had been a long time since there was any need for him to worry; and when I met Roger I could not help wondering how Tom would take it. Not that that would have affected me. I would have married Roger, Tom or no Tom, if Roger had understood marriage as I did. To my surprise, Tom seemed to throw me into his arms, and when Bella Thoroughgood appeared in Penmaen and took Roger away, Tom's wrath was terrible. "What is going to happen to you?" he would demand. "I'm practically penniless. What will become of you?"

He never seemed to think of the agony I was suffering, for indeed it was that. The candle-flame, on my side, at any rate, had grown to something that burned me horribly; but Tom, I am sure, was unaware of this; and I was too witless to realise what was behind his constant cry: "What is going to happen to you?"

When Bella Thoroughgood died he was in London. He said he had heard of a practice in Islington and wanted to have a look round. I was amazed that he should do that after the long years in Penmaen, for frankly he had become old-fashioned and out of touch. He never in his life took a refresher course. He came back the night before the inquest. He ate little at our evening meal, and when it was over he said: "Let's take a walk on the beach, Kit."

We went as far as the cliffs on the other side and sat down there. It was a warm beautiful evening. I had told him of what had happened in his absence, and after a long silence he said: "The inquest shouldn't take long to-morrow. You'll have to be there to give evidence, but there should be time to get in to Plymouth and take the evening train to London. Could you be ready for that?"

I was dumbfounded. I had left Roger in anger. His childish attitude over Annie Hocking and the medicine had thrown me into a mood that I regretted as soon as I had come out of it. We had come together again, and I knew that he had come as a different man from the one whom Bella Thoroughgood had taken away. I could forgive—I did forgive—that poor wretch everything. And then all that I had suffered from him and her had blown up into my ridiculous self-righteousness with the medicine bottle. I was longing for the inquest to be over, the whole appalling episode to end. Then, whatever Tom might do with himself, Roger and I would find what we both wanted.

"But, Tom," I said. "Is there such a hurry?"

"Yes. This is Wednesday. The inquest is on Thursday. My operation is on Saturday, and I shall need the Friday to prepare. I should like you to be near."

I sprang to my feet. All those years with Tom, that long close life together, produced their automatic reflex. Instantly, he was my first thought. I looked down at him sitting there, and he looked incredibly forlorn. I gave a cry of dismay, and he reached up, took my hand, drew me down on to the rock beside him, and kissed me. "Darling Kit," he said. "I didn't want to hurt you."

"Hurt me!" I cried. "Do anything if I can help you. What can I do to help?"

"Just be with me," he said. "As you have always been."

He said that the Islington practice was a bluff. For some months he had suspected what was wrong, but obstinately persuaded himself that things were not so bad as he feared. Then he could hold out no longer. He invented his tale and went to London for an examination. "If all had been well," he said, "I could have come back and said that the Islington idea didn't look good enough on the spot. However, all was not well. As I feared, cancer of the right lung."

We walked back, with me weeping unrestrainedly, Tom silent, maintaining with difficulty an air of calm. In the house he said: "You must forgive me, Kit."

"Oh, for what? For what?"

"For everything. For all the years."

He plunged upstairs to his bedroom.

He came with me to the inquest, and how either of us got through it I don't know. When it was over, Roger was hovering about outside the schoolroom where it had been held, and I longed to go to him, to explain to him, but Tom took my arm brusquely and said: "Come, Kit. We shan't be ready by the time the car comes." And then there was this and that to do, and I had just taken up a pen to write Roger a note when Tom shouted: "The car's here. Come! We'll miss the train." So that had to be left.

The operation took place on the Saturday, and on the Sunday Tom died.

v

No one in Penmaen knew why Tom and I had gone to London, and the death of an obscure general practitioner was not a thing to be reported in the press. An announcement in the advertisement columns would not have interested me, even if I had been in the mood to think of such matters. I wasn't. Nor did I write at once to Roger. Sir Robert Falconer, who had performed the operation, was kindness itself. He and Tom had been medical students together, and together they had served in the R.A.M.C. during the First World War. Thereafter, their careers had been very different. They had not kept in touch, either personally or by letter, and it would have been odd if Sir Robert had not forgotten Tom completely. But it was to him that Tom had gone in his trouble; and it was to him that I owed a quiet time when Tom was dead. He was another of those who had read and liked my books, but he had not associated my name with that of his old friend. He was surprised to find that I was virtually destitute. Like many another, he had the notion that writers did well financially. Not many do, and certainly not those, like me, who write little and whose readers are few. The truth was that I was at a desperate pinch, and but for Sir Robert's help would not have known which way to turn. He was a bachelor, with a flat in Kensington and a country cottage in Hertfordshire. He insisted that I should go down to the cottage for a fortnight to recuperate under the care of his housekeeper.

Tom, who must have known that his chances were small, had left a letter with Sir Robert in which he explained his situation, of which the chief fact, financially, was that there would be a thousand pounds of insurance money to come to me. Sir Robert saw me off at the station and handed me a note as the train moved out. It contained a cheque for £250 which, he said, I was not to repay till the insurance affairs were settled. He was indeed a friend.

At the cottage I regained some composure. The events of the year in which Roger, Bella Thoroughgood and I had been involved, followed by this new blow of Tom's death, had completely disrupted me. I had, before settling down at the cottage, found it impossible to write to Roger; and now that I was able at last to look things more calmly in the face I did not want to. We had parted not in anger, but with a cloud of misunderstanding between us. I recognized it as something of my own creation, something arising out of a worthless vanity, and which must have hurt him deeply, seeing that he had been concerned in his fumbling way with my good name. I longed to tell him that I understood, that I was at fault; but now I was prevented by my pride again. I could hardly write without telling him that Tom was dead, and this, whether I intended it or not, would be an appeal to his pity that I could not make. I decided to stay out my fortnight in Hertfordshire and then to go back to Penmaen where no one knew of Tom's death.

VI

I went to the Menheniot Arms and asked Jim Brokenshire if he could put me up for a few days. "I don't want to start housekeeping again," I said. "I'm just spending a few days to clear up my brother's affairs here"—not exactly a lie, but an evasion.

"Bless you, Miss Kitty," Jim said, "us'll be glad to 'ave 'e. You'll make up, if only for a day or two, for all that's missin' from Penmaen. Old Savage gone. He'll write no more epitaphs. A dab 'and 'e were at that, and d'you know, Miss Kitty, 'e'd written 'is own. They found it among 'is papers, an' it's to go on a plaque in the church. No kick in this one, either—proper 'umble. Just this: 'Henry Savage, unfaithful servant, trusting his Redeemer's mercy to say "Inasmuch as it was in thine heart." ' Just that."

Jim paused a moment, then went on: "An' Annie Hocking gone Lord knows where. The place won't seem the same without ole Annie stickin' 'er nose in wherever it's not wanted. The doctor gone, an' you off to join 'im. Mr. Swithinbank packed up an' left me. Paintin' somewhere among them God-awful ruins of the mines, they tell me. He was another caution, if you like. Proper lad. An' then, to crown all, Rosemullion's goin' into the market again."

"Rosemullion?"

"Aye. That old place seem bewitched. No one don't stay there nowadays. 'Aven't done for many a year."

"Then where's Mr. Menheniot?"

"Don't know. He cleared off a week or so after you an' the doctor went upalong. Not that that surprises me. Oo'd 'ave thought it of 'im? That girl! I've read about that sort in the Sunday papers, Miss Kitty, but to 'ave one livin' an' breathin' in Penmaen! That don't seem natural."

I wasn't listening to him any more. I went up to the bedroom—the room Ray and Roger had both used— and lay down on the bed, exhausted and frightened. Frightened is the only word I can use. I was terrified by what I had done to Roger. Knowing nothing of the real reason that had taken Tom and me away, seeing me go with apparent coldness and unconcern, he had waited a week, and no letter had come, and he had decided—

reasonably, I had to admit—that I had ended all that
had been between us, and had ended it on that hideous
note of mere irritated pride. I could imagine his desperation. The shocking initiation that his make-up and the
circumstances of his life had made inevitable in one form
or another; and the coming through it to the happiness
I could have given him; and then the feeling that I had
withheld it, gone coolly away. . . . . His desperation would
be terrible. I knew that in my bones, as I knew him. He
had always feared women. Now he would hate them.

I had not been wrong in telling Jim Brokenshire that
I had come to clear up Tom's affairs, and during the next
few days I addressed myself to the depressing job. There
was no one I wanted to see except Roger, whom I should
see no more, and I lived in a dull activity, eating and
sleeping at Jim's, going through the things in the house,
the accumulation of so many years, tearing up, burning,
not knowing what to do about this and that, baffled by the
thought of my own future.

It was the evening of the third day. I had eaten at Jim's
and crossed the road for what I hoped would be the last
hour or two of this heartrending business. I was working
by lamplight, clearing out the last pigeon-holes of Tom's
desk. There was a bundle tied in red tape and labelled
"Letters from Kit." I opened them without spirit, having
no intention to read them, merely to throw them upon
the already choked fireplace, smouldering with years of
ink and paper. As a bundle, they would not burn, so I
untied the tape. They must be very old. It was so long
since I had needed to write to Tom. I casually opened
the top one and began to read. It was the letter I had
written when Eve died. "My darling, darling brother."
I couldn't go on with it. As if I had written it this morning, I recalled how I sat down to it, how I had faltered
over the condolence and become stronger as I promised

286

him my life. Yes—there it was. "And so, dear Tom, as long as I live and God gives me strength I will do what I can to take Eve's place as a comfort to you, as your helper. Count on me, Tom, tell me what to do. I will do it. Your loving Kit."

Well, for what it was worth, I had done it, sometimes bitterly, rebelliously, but he had never known that. "I don't suppose you'll ever be one of the pair. Seen my slippers?"

It was in this very room that Tom had said that. Life seemed to me so sad and hopeless that I allowed the letters to fall to the floor, and I sat there and wept.

I had left the front door open, and I heard footsteps in the hall and Jim shouting: "Miss Kitty! Miss Kitty! A visitor for you."

It was not Jim who opened the door but Roger. I had not bothered to wipe my eyes. Tear-stained, dusty, bedraggled amid the ruins of a life, I stood up and faced him. He was too nervous even to speak of my condition. He said: "Please pardon me. I had no idea you were here. I am at Rosemullion. I'm leaving, you know. I had a few affairs to settle, so I slipped back from London."

"I had heard you were going," I said dully.

"I wonder," he said, "whether you'll accept this? It's a little picture. I knew that you or Tom would have to come back to clear things up here, so I brought it over, hoping Jim would give it to you. I thought the place would be empty." He laid the parcel on the table. "It's a little house-warming present for Islington," he said. "It would help us, I thought, to—to—part without ill-feeling."

He seemed unaware of the shambles about him, and I knew this was because he was seeing nothing but me, as I was seeing nothing but him. I took up the scissors with which I had snipped open the bundle of letters and cut the string of his parcel. It was a small picture by Gwen John: a woman standing at a window with the earliest light falling on her, light from a sun that is about to rise but has not yet risen. In the pearly greys the artist had caught, as she always does, the sad austere beauty of human existence.

I looked at the little nun-like picture, so full of what I had always tried to do in my writing. It was so beautiful and so sad that my tears continued to flow.

Roger said: "Well, there it is. I'm grateful to you, and to Tom. I think he will like the picture."

"There is no Islington practice," I said. "Tom is dead."

There was a long silence, out of which Roger cried: "Oh, my darling, my darling!"

He too began to weep. The flood must have been near the surface and it burst through. We looked at one another, he on one side of the room and I on the other, our faces hideous with tears. Then with one instinct we moved to one another, and our arms went round one another, and our bodies touched till we were one vibration of happy weeping.